Wind kicked up, blowing frigid air into her face. It was enough to get her feet moving faster to the quilt's inviting warmth.

"Sheen?"

"Yes?"

"Don't ever try to run away from me."

She pulled the quilt over her nose so that only her eyes showed. "What if I do?"

"Trust me, you won't like the consequences."

There was a hint of mockery in his voice that accompanied the threat, and Sheen didn't quite know what to make of him.

"You are a puzzle, Mr. Tanner. First you say you won't harm me, then you threaten me."

Praise for Loretta C. Rogers

"You will hold your breath during this emotional, action packed adventure."

~Flossie Benton Rogers, author

~*~

"*THE WITCHING MOON* drew me in from page one. The book's clever plot twists and unique combination of paranormal and western elements kept me turning the pages!"

~Dylan Newton, author of Despite the Ghosts

The Witching Moon

by

Loretta C. Rogers

The Witching Moon

Cover Art by *Debbie Taylor*

The Wild Rose Press, Inc.
PO Box 708
Adams Basin, NY 14410-0708
Visit us at www.thewildrosepress.com

Publishing History
First Cactus Rose Edition, 2013
Print ISBN 978-1-61217-899-8
Digital ISBN 978-1-61217-900-1

Published in the United States of America

Dedication

The Witching Moon is dedicated to my friend
Margy,
whose personal connections with the paranormal
inspired this story.

The Beginning

Ireland, 1848

Keelin O'Reilly tried to shut out the voices inside her head. "No...no...please, I'm sorry, so sorry." The cry ripped from her throat. She struggled to shut out the vision. Her stomach lurched in revolt, and her terror grew so strong it left a metallic taste in her mouth.

She shivered, and in spite of the chill inside the thatch-roofed hut her body broke into a sweat. She slapped away the hand that nudged her shoulder.

"Keelin, wake up." Colm O'Reilly folded his young wife into his arms and held her trembling body against his chest.

Too grief-stricken to utter a sound, she struggled to hold back a sob. She pulled from her husband's arms and tumbled from the bed. Barefoot and oblivious to the dank straw matting, she lifted her sleeping daughter from the cot. "The fire has gone cold, Husband."

Colm hastened to do his wife's bidding. He knelt before the fireplace and, with gentle breaths, blew until embers sparked red. Then, banking a new bed of kindling, he encouraged life into the timid fire.

Keelin stared at the flames caressing the stacked wood and watched how the smoke spiraled up the chimney. Her voice sounded hollow. "That is my destiny."

"What do you mean—your destiny?" Then, as if understanding, he said, "Ye've had one of your visions, haven't you, Wife?"

For the sake of the child nestled against her chest, Keelin fought the panic in her voice, the fear threatening to consume her. "Aye. They come, Colm, and the vicar leads them."

"In the dead of the night? Why?"

"They burn witches at night, don't they?"

"You are no *cailleach*. You perform no divinations, you—"

She sensed it even stronger now—the movement. "Ignorance begets ignorance, Husband. 'Tis what happens when we fear those who are different from ourselves. Do not blame the villagers."

Colm O'Reilly stroked the white streak of hair that shone stark against his wife's shiny black mane.

"Then who should I blame?" He bunched his fist and smacked the palm of his hand.

"Whatever happens, Husband, promise you won't let them take our beautiful daughter." Keelin absently smoothed ringlets that reminded her of a newly plowed field. "Though her hair is not as mine, she carries the same curse as I."

"No, you canna be certain of such a thing." He grabbed the scythe that lay against the wall and held it as a weapon. "I'll die before one hair on your head or our daughter's is harmed."

"Remember our plan, Colm. Remember how much I love you."

"Then let us go, now, before 'tis too late."

The sound of tramping feet and angry voices filled the night. It was a sound Keelin had heard dozens and dozens of times inside her mind. She'd seen their hatred. Only now it was more terrible because it was no longer a vision, and she was powerless to stop the fates.

The vicar's voice rent the night. "Colm O'Reilly, bring the witch outside to stand before God and man."

When Sheen whimpered, Keelin soothed her daughter with a soft word and a tender kiss on top of the head. "You must do as we planned, Husband. Leave Ireland. Take Sheen to America, where no one will know she is cursed. For surely she is the same as I and my grandmother before me."

She watched the denial in her husband's eyes. "'Tis no denying what ye've always known, Colm, and yet you loved me without judgment."

"Mommy, I 'fraid."

"Hush, Sheen. Let us play our game of hide-and-seek." Keelin set the child on her bare feet, bent low, and tugged at the door she had fashioned behind the bed. "Gather your nightshirt and run hide inside the scarecrow. Stay there until either your papa or I come for you."

The fear in Sheen's eyes mirrored that of her mother, and Keelin knew for certain her daughter possessed the gift of inner sight.

"Bad people come, Mommy. I see here." The child pointed to her head.

Whispering a quick prayer and making the sign of the cross over her breasts, Keelin O'Reilly asked God's protection over her child. "I love you, my wee *baïbín*." She removed the necklace and hung the chain with the gold crucifix around the toddler's neck. "Do not be afraid...never be afraid."

Before she crawled under the bed and out the

escape hatch, Sheen wrapped her arms around her mother's neck and held tight.

"Scoot! Be off with you to the scarecrow." Keelin was more afraid than she'd ever been in her life. She placed a finger to her lip and reminded the child, "Remember, quiet as a church mouse."

****

Though barely in her third year, Sheen O'Reilly felt her mother's fear. Huddled under the bed, she watched dozens of dirty, boot-clad feet push through the door to drag her mother and father into a curtain of darkness.

She remembered how mother had said that one day bad people would come, and, when it was time to hide in the scarecrow, that she mustn't disobey. Sheen did just as her mother had shown her many times when they played their game of hide-and-seek.

She gathered the nightshirt in a tiny fist and, on hands and knees, she crawled through the hole barely big enough for a large rabbit. On bare feet, she ran to the pumpkin patch as fast as her baby legs would carry her. She lifted a tiny foot to the wooden peg her father had driven into the post. With the clumsy efforts of a toddler balancing herself, she wriggled inside the straw man, not realizing her father had built it as a special hiding place to protect his wee child.

She seated herself on the small keg that formed the scarecrow's body, and, hidden from sight, she did what she always did when she and her mother played the game. Sheen used her tiny fingers to part the straw enough to peer through a buttonhole.

****

"Burn the witch. Burn her." Voices rang out in

unison.

Desperate to save his wife, Colm O'Reilly fought the men who bound her hands and feet. Blood dribbled down his face from the deep gash over his eye. He raged against the strength of the men who held him, raged against the vicar. "You dare condemn my wife because the women of the village come seeking her knowledge of herbs and healing potions. You dare condemn her for all the good she has brought—"

The vicar raised his staff. His voice bellowed loud and pious. "Keelin O'Reilly did the devil's work when she took the knife to Alroy Geralt's wife and cut the babe from her belly."

Geralt held the torch high. "Aye, and me blessed wife were murdered by the hands of this 'ere *witch*."

Colm yelled above the din. "*My* wife saved the son *your* wife was too weak to birth." His eyes were accusing and his voice dripped with contempt when he spoke to the man clad in white robes. "We both know the truth, do we not, priest? It isn't my wife's healing powers or her knowledge of herbs and potions that has brought about her condemnation. 'Tis her numerous rejections of *you* and your sinful lusts." Colm hawked and spat. He watched spittle slide down a pallid cheek and puddle on the collar of the crisp white robe.

"Nay, I renounce your untruths. Keelin O'Reilly is a practitioner of evil." The priest raised his voice as he pointed a bony finger toward Colm. "I forgive you, Colm O'Reilly, for your vile accusations." And then, with a barely perceptible smile, he commanded, "Light the fires."

Colm struggled against his captors until it felt as if the veins in his neck would burst. His gaze locked with his wife's panic-filled eyes. It took no special gifts for him to understand her horror.

****

Keelin looked toward the scarecrow. She knew her daughter watched. In her spirit she willed Sheen to look away, and when the child didn't, she attempted a reassuring smile.

I 'fraid, Mommy.

Guard the crucifix, Sheen. Wear it always.

Dada help Mommy, peez.

Oh, my baby, your father is not like you and I. He canna hear your words.

Flames sampled the hem of Keelin's gown and hungrily licked their way up her body until her eyes dilated with searing pain.

My baby, I will always hold you in my heart.

Keelin choked on a scream, and then there was only the snapping and crackling of the fire, and white smoke that spiraled toward the heavens.

****

Even stillness could be terrifying. In all her three young years, Sheen O'Reilly had learned the lesson well. She stayed huddled inside the straw man, the silence of her surroundings vibrating in her ears.

Chapter One

Montana Territory, 1868

The land lay empty around him, lonely and still. On his right, a ridge of mountains with scattered cedars rose up black and stark against a bleak sky. On his left, an open plain swept to a far horizon where a blanket of white met with a gray haze that threatened to dump more snow on an already burdened land. In all that vastness there was nothing but the creak of the saddle and the labored breathing of the horse beneath Guthrie Tanner.

He hunched his shoulders against the cold. "Only a couple of miles, now." He spoke to the gelding whose black mane was crusted with ice. The buckskin plodded, its head bobbing with weariness. Then as if to reassure himself, Guthrie said, "Two more miles, ol' son, to a warm stall with extra oats for you, and a double shot of whiskey for me."

Frigid weather had forced Guthrie down from the mountains. It'd been almost a year since he'd last visited a town. In all that distance, he'd not seen a ranch, or a miner's shack. Nor had he carried on an intelligent conversation with a civilized human being.

The gelding stumbled, nearly toppling Guthrie from its back. He spoke softly, encouraging the animal. "I know you're tired. Hell, we're both near our end."

Two miles.

Guthrie hoped he'd correctly calculated the distance. The horse plodded on, each step a struggle, the pace so slow that the cold leaching through his buffalo-hide coat caused Guthrie's bones to ache. Pellets of ice settled heavy on the brim of his hat, crusted his eyebrows and thick black beard.

His chin wobbled against his chest. Exhaustion wrapped around him like a warm cocoon. He jerked his eyes open. Going to sleep in weather like this guaranteed a death sentence for both man and beast. For a distraction, he tried to whistle, though his wind-parched lips emitted no sound. He fought the heaviness in his eyelids.

There was a reason why he needed to stay alive. He searched around the fuzziness of his mind, trying to remember why living was important when dying was so easy.

By sundown, Fort Smith loomed like a solitary ghost, square and bare, without shrubs, without trees, and one hundred miles from the nearest town.

Guthrie urged the gelding to pick up its pace. The horse reared as it tried to lunge through chest-deep snow. Losing its footing, the buckskin fell backward, then rolled over. Guthrie's boot caught in the stirrup, and when the horse rolled, the pommel came down hard on Guthrie's shoulder. His first thought was how warm the blood weeping against his cold flesh felt.

There was no pain, no shock, only a kind of surprise. Death, he knew from experience, was dramatic and often filled with suffering. He needed to cheat death—if only he could remember why.

The horse thrashed and struggled to rise, then fell

back. But Guthrie was free of the horse's weight, even though his boot remained trapped beneath the animal's heaving body. Somehow Guthrie rolled to an elbow. He felt faint and sick.

Then he looked at the horse.

One leg was broken. An ugly compound fracture with the naked bone exposed. He knew nothing could be done for the faithful animal that had carried him hundreds of miles through Indian Territory as he looked for a band of Sioux renegades led by Otaktay, better known by white settlers and soldiers as Kills Many.

Guthrie inched his hand down and pulled his pistol free from its holster. A string of oaths erupted from his throat. "Sorry, ol' son." He fired. His throat tightened, and a heavy feeling of remorse filled his chest.

A moment longer he remained on his elbow. The pistol stayed in his hand. He tried to pull his leg free from the dead animal's weight, thinking perhaps he could drag himself the few hundred yards to the fort's massive log-hewn gates.

He hoped the wind hadn't carried away the Colt .45's blast. He prayed a sentry had heard the shot. Guthrie Tanner knew all too well that if the snow buried his body, the remains would rest frozen until spring thaw.

He was tired, more tired than he'd ever been in his life. Now there was pain, a poker-hot pain that seared through his shoulder.

Rolling to his back, he gazed up at the sky. He thought he saw a face staring down at him from a gray cloud. A face with large blue eyes, surrounded by spirals of golden ringlets. Snow stung his wind-burned cheeks like pellets of ice and drove against him.

Through lips made blue from the cold, he whispered, "I'll find you, Rachel. I'll find you, baby girl."

With the last of his ebbing strength, he lifted the pistol and, as he pulled the trigger again, remembered why it was important for him to live.

****

White light woke Guthrie. Hearing a voice, he tried to sit up. Pain ripped through every inch of his body.

"Better lie back down, mister. Unless, of course, you wish to open up those broke ribs and aggravate your collarbone."

Guthrie winced against the searing agony tearing through his body. He forced the words, "Who are you? Where am I? How long have I been here?"

Guthrie flinched when the cold stethoscope touched his chest. The white-haired man leaning over him said, "Better draw a breath, young fellow, before you suffocate yourself. As to where, you're at Fort Smith, and I'm the sawbones, better known as Doc Patterson, and you've slept most of forty-eight hours."

"Horse fell on me. Broke his leg and had to shoot him." Expelling a painful breath, Guthrie added, "He carried me far and without complaint."

"Good thing the sentries heard your shots." The doctor straightened and rubbed the small of his back. "Although freezing to death isn't so bad...just go to sleep and never wake up."

Guthrie attempted to sit up. He ground his teeth against the throbbing. "How bad am I hurt?"

"Oh, not so bad you'll die. Broken collarbone ripped through your skin. Few more inches and it would've pierced your jugular; a few stitches and a couple of broken ribs. Far as I can tell, you didn't suffer any internal injuries."

"How long before I can ride?"

"It's December... Say, what's your name?"

He spoke between painful breaths. "Guthrie...Tanner."

"As I was saying, Mr. Tanner, it's December. There's nearly five feet of snow on the ground, and you won't get far without a horse. Besides, you'd freeze to death before you got a hundred yards from the fort." The doctor uncorked a vial and poured a creamy liquid into a spoon. He held out his hand. "Here, take this."

"What is it?"

"Laudanum. From the grimace on your face and the way you're grinding your jaw, I'd say the pain is setting in something fierce."

Guthrie's whole body quaked with agony. He welcomed the bitter liquid's relief.

"To help yourself relax, take a deep breath and let it out slowly. Think good thoughts, Mr. Tanner. It won't take long for the effects of the laudanum to take hold."

Guthrie obeyed. The edges of his lips tingled, then numbed. Darkness slid beneath his eyelids, and the buzzing inside his ears turned to music. A brilliant light exploded behind his eyes and he was dancing with his wife. It was their wedding day. And as the laudanum continued to work its mercurial magic, the fair-haired beauty gowned in white took flight and disappeared into a hazy mist. *Abigail...*

****

December passed into February, leaving a tapestry of white across all of Montana. After spending two months in the post hospital, Guthrie Tanner shared a friendly game of poker inside the enlisted men's barracks, his back toward the potbellied stove, garnering its stingy heat, his broken collarbone and ribs still mending. Somebody poured coffee into his cup and he muttered his thanks without looking up from the cards in his hand.

"You headin' out soon, Guthrie?" Private O'Hanlon wanted to know. A quick-tempered, heavy-fisted Irishman, Paddy O'Hanlon had been busted back to private as many times as he'd been promoted to sergeant.

"Shoulder's healed, got the use of my gun hand back, only thing I'm waiting on is spring thaw, and a horse."

"How 'bout I trail along when you leave?"

"Last I heard, Private O'Hanlon, the Army shoots deserters."

The private scowled over the top of his pasteboards. "Aw, had to go and remind me, didn't you?"

The soldiers seated around the table concentrated on the game of poker until a man growled, "You gonna jaw us to death or bet?"

Private O'Hanlon laid his cards face down on the table. "Fold. Too rich for me blood."

Guthrie eyed the lone man in the game. "Queens and eights."

The hostler slapped his cards down. "Reckon you just won enough to buy yourself a sorry hay burner."

"Aw, hell, Smitty. Just 'cause yer arse is all swoll up 'bout losing don't mean you shouldn't sell the lad a decent saddle mount. Ain't like the Army's shy of good horses." Private O'Hanlon rose to Guthrie's defense.

"What'll fifty dollars buy me?" Guthrie cut an eye toward the slack-jawed man who sat across from him.

The hostler pushed from his chair and walked toward the door. "I'm sure I've got a bag o' bones that'll tote you a ways. Won't be no Army mount, though. 'Ginst post regulation."

Private O'Hanlon shrugged. "Reckon you'll take up trailing Otaktay again? He's slicker'n them pesky leprechauns in me dear ol' Ireland. Otaktay don't want you to find 'im—you won't."

Guthrie wrapped his hands around the coffee cup. "Spring's coming. Sioux are no different from the rest of us. I imagine their winter cache is 'bout empty. They've got women and children to feed too. And Otaktay is a bastard with an ego that's gonna make him slip up. When he does, I'll be there to put a bullet in him."

"His name don't mean Kills Many for nothing. What about yer wee lassie? You kill Otaktay and you might never find 'er...might never, no how."

Guthrie turned a mean eye toward the private. O'Hanlon held up his hands as if in surrender. "I'm just sayin' 'tis a vast country out there."

The big Irishman crooked a smile at Guthrie. The mischievous twinkle in his brown eyes was unmistakable when he leaned forward and whispered, "'Course, there always be the witch."

"Witch?" Guthrie harrumphed. "Talk sense, O'Hanlon."

"I ain't actually seen her. Only heard 'bout her from a peddler who comes to the post to trade goods ever so often. From the way he tells it, she lives alone on the prairie...her and a few wild animals."

Guthrie felt rough and mean, with a steady itch for the spring's first thaw. It was time he moved on. "All right, you've got my attention. I can see you're busting to tell me."

The clock on the wall chimed twelve. O'Hanlon slapped his hands together. "Hot damn. 'Tis noon and legal drinkin' time. First round's on me."

Hefting into his buffalo-hide coat, Guthrie grasped the brim of his hat as the wind threatened to steal it from his head when O'Hanlon opened the barracks door.

Bracing against the cold, Guthrie raised his eyes to the southwest to look at the foaming clouds and mountains rising to the heavens. His heart felt as cold as the snow on the ground. He tamped down the seed of guilt growing inside him. What if he never found the Sioux warriors who'd raped his wife and left her body broken and stained scarlet? They'd stolen his child. What if his little girl was dead?

His thoughts were unwelcomed interlopers. Who was he trying to fool? It was his fault he'd lost his family.

A delicate flower, his wife had never shared his dream of leaving Charleston and coming west to start a new life after the war. Afraid of snakes and wolves and Indians, she'd pleaded with him to send her back to South Carolina. Even after the death of their son, and the birth of a daughter, he'd stubbornly refused to admit that she would never adjust to being a rancher's wife.

He damned the snow, damned the weather that kept him from tracking his enemy, but most of all he damned himself.

Lost in thought, Guthrie barely remembered

hustling across the yard until Private O'Hanlon bellowed, "Rot gut, Pete. Make it a double. Me innards need warming."

Guthrie stamped snow from his boots before entering the sutler's store. He embraced the building's warmth. The small establishment was alive with voices of off-duty troopers, and he scanned the room to find an empty table in the corner. He shrugged out of the heavy coat and draped it over a chair. "Bring the bottle, Pete."

O'Hanlon slapped his hands together. "I'd give a year's wages for a bottle of Kilbeggan. Best blended whiskey in all of Ireland, aye 'tis, for sure. Makes a man's puddin' stick stiff as a poker and achin' for, well, puddin'."

Guthrie mustered a wan smile. "Reckon it's been a while since you've visited town."

"'Tain't like Bozeman's a spit 'n the wind. More 'n a week's ride."

Filling each shot glass to the brim, Guthrie offered a silent salute to the private before slogging back the amber liquid. He sucked in a breath, allowed the whiskey to sear the back of his throat, then poured another round.

As if talking to no one in particular, Guthrie said, "*Wanageeska*—white spirit."

Offering a pensive glance toward the big Irishman, he kept his voice low. "Mind you, O'Hanlon, I don't hold with superstitious nonsense, but you were saying about a witch?"

The private leaned forward and winked. "Oh, aye, laddie. Though I don't think she be a true *cailleach*, more like a *fairy doctor*."

Guthrie rubbed the ache in his shoulder.

"Witch...fairy doctor. It's all hocus-pocus, isn't it?"

"Well, me boy, I'll be tellin' you. A witch casts spells. 'Tis said a true *cailleach* can change a human into a mouse, but t'other has the gift of inner sight, knows 'bout herbs and healing, and has an unnatural way with animals."

Guthrie chuckled, a harsh sound devoid of humor. "And does such a woman have a wart on her nose and fly about on a broom?"

O'Hanlon quietly poured himself another drink. "Poke your fun, laddie. Before leaving Ireland, I seen things. Things that defy reasonable explanation."

"You say this witch lives by herself. No lone woman is safe on the prairie. I don't buy it, O'Hanlon. Powers or no powers, we both know what Indians do to unprotected women."

O'Hanlon scratched the scruff on his chin. "Aye, to be sure, I do." He leaned forward, his voice hushed. "Indians revere witches. Holds 'em sacred."

Guthrie flipped a coin on the table. "Like I said, it's all hocus-pocus. I don't put stock in ghosts and goblins." He lifted his coat off the chair.

O'Hanlon ran a beefy finger around the rim of his glass. He squinted up at Guthrie. "I hear tell in Africa there be witch doctors who practice powerful med'cine. The Sioux, Pawnee, Apache—they all put a lot o' store in their shamans."

"Make your point, O'Hanlon." Guthrie's gaze shifted to the Irishman's heavy-jowled face.

O'Hanlon tossed back a drink, then poured another. He seemed to mull over his answer. "You came to Fort Smith a broken man, in body and spirit. Doc said ye ranted with the fever 'bout what was done to yer dear

16

wife. You've likened how ye've spent a year of your life searching for Indians you called *ghosts*.

"Spring thaw comes and you'll take up the hunt again. Ye'll wander from hell and back trying to find yer wee girl...'til you take an arrow in the back, or your harse steps in a gopher hole and rolls atop you, leaving you all busted up and waitin' for the buzzards to pick yer sorry hide clean.

"All I'm sayin' is what can it hurt to visit the lassie, be she a *fairy doctor* or a mortal woman?" Private O'Hanlon tipped the glass and gulped. When Guthrie didn't answer, he slammed the glass on the table. "Me dear sweet mum, bless her soul, used to say, 'Paddy, don't give cherries to pigs or advice to fools.' "

A defiant snarl died on Guthrie's lips. "You shoulda listened."

Only when he walked outside did Guthrie realize his hands were bunched into fists.

The sky was dark and the wind whipped cold. Gray slush lay on the parade ground from a late snow. Guthrie shivered as he turned his collar up and snugged the coat more closely about him.

It was late February and supposed to be near spring, but the grim clouds hurrying across the leaden sky gave no suggestion that warmer weather lay in the near future. Rather, the clouds had the air of going out to battle, as if they were rushing to obey a sharp imperative command.

Guthrie found nothing encouraging in the afternoon scene to improve his mood.

He stepped off the boardwalk and sank boot deep into the snow. Stringing a line of curses, he squinted up at the shy sun. By his calculation it was almost two o'clock, another long day at Fort Smith.

Battening his hat against the wind, he trudged toward the stables, his mind first and foremost on selecting a sturdy mount. He was a man with a purpose and enough hate to fulfill it.

Chapter Two

Da-ddy. I want my da-ddy.

The child's screams disturbed Sheen O'Reilly's sleep. The cries echoed in her ears. She clenched her jaw until her teeth ached. She pulled the pillow over her head and groaned, telling herself it was a mere dream and nothing more.

Cailleach!

Swimming through a murky haze of disembodied faces, she struggled to fully awaken, fighting back the dark fear that threatened to surface. With a burst of adrenalin, she bolted upright. "No. I am no witch."

Her scream still echoing in her ears, it took a moment for her to realize she was alone in the cabin. She sat until her eyes adjusted to the darkness. A chill had invaded the two-room house. Tossing the quilt from her shivering body, she hastened barefoot across the cold floor to check the slide-bolt on the cabin's door. She pressed her back against the wooden barrier and tried to shut out the thundering sounds of horses' hooves. Her breath came in uneven gasps as she released the bolted lock and gripped the knob. She hated the darkness, had feared it for as long as she could remember. Feeling her heartbeat all the way to the pit of her stomach, she drew a deep breath and eased the door to a mere crack.

Darkness.

There were no horses, no riders, no fierce faces—only the wind that seemed to whisper, *Hang the witch!*

Sheen slammed the door, secured the lock, and, terrified, threw her full weight against it. Then on quivering limbs she rushed to the fireplace and added a log to the dying embers.

Every muscle in her body taut, she hugged her flannel nightgown tighter as she walked to the table and lifted the ladle from the bucket. She drank deep, allowing the icy water to slake her parched throat.

The room's cold air quickly enveloped her shivering body, and she hurried to the bed and snuggled deep beneath the quilt. Hot tears welled up on her eyelashes. Fingering the crucifix that hung on a chain around her neck, she prayed, "Please, God. Like my mother before me, I did not ask for this curse."

Expelling a dispirited sigh, Sheen pressed her arms across her breasts and closed her eyes.

****

The rooster's crowing disturbed the morning silence. Sheen squinted against the light piercing between the blue gingham curtains. She rubbed her eyes and rolled to her side.

Again the rooster's shrill cacophony jarred Sheen's eyes open. She shivered beneath the heavy quilt. With a sigh and a groan, she stumbled barefoot to the fireplace. Laying two logs inside the hearth, she knelt on the cold floor and blew with gentle breaths until the sleeping embers glowed red.

This morning she felt every minute of her twenty-two years, and then some. More than hot tea she wanted a bucket of warm water for a bath and to wash her hair.

An hour later, she unlocked the front door.

Songbirds greeted her, along with sunshine and a mild morning that promised an early spring. As welcome as all of that was, she couldn't help but remember the frightened cries of a child's voice, mingled with blood-curdling whoops and yells, and the sounds of many riders. Voices that still haunted her.

A lowing from the barn served as a reminder that the cow needed milking. Sheen grabbed an apron from a wall hook. After tying a neat bow at her waist, she gathered the woolen cape around her shoulders, then lifted the lid of a wooden keg and filled a tin cup with chicken scratch.

Stepping down the porch steps, she called, "A good morning to you, Agata and Penny, and to you, Mr. Cluck." Sheen spoke to the chickens, and the geese, to a doe and fawn, a three-legged fox, and to the crows lining the fence, while she scattered feed over the ground. As she made her way to the barn, she checked the yard and circled the cabin. It disconcerted her to find no hoof prints. She listened...not that she expected to hear anything.

She trudged to the barn, grabbed the pitchfork, and filled the cattle crib with fresh hay. Then, lifting the milking stool from a nail, Sheen settled next to the cow. "Well, now, Colleen, 'tis a fine morning for milking." Sheen laughed as the heifer answered with a swish of its tail.

She leaned her forehead against the Jersey's warm, tawny haunch and concentrated on the sound of milk pinging against the bottom of the bucket. She closed her eyes, her hands working with a memory of their own.

He's coming.

Experiencing a moment of unease, she scolded

herself. *Stop this, now. No one is coming.* Her heart thudding, she yielded to the urge and looked over her shoulder toward the yard.

The cow mooed, and then there was only the soft munching of hay. Closing her eyes and concentrating on the movement of her hands, Sheen saw the anguish on the rider's face and felt his determination. He was coming, and she was powerless to stop him. Choking on a sob, she knew her most dreaded fear was about to begin—again.

That night, mentally and physically exhausted, Sheen bathed before the fireplace, then dressed in a gray flannel nightgown. Nestled comfortably under warm blankets, she was drifting between sleep and wakefulness when she thought she heard the anger in his voice.

Witch...fairy doctor. O'Hanlon and his damned Irish blarney.

Opening her eyes, her body tensed as she listened. How odd, she thought, gazing up at the rafters. Perhaps she'd been more asleep than she believed. Perhaps she'd already begun to dream and was replaying thoughts about the rider inside her head.

Then she heard his voice again, and knew she'd guessed wrong.

"Leave me alone," she whispered.

He was thinking about her. No, not about *her*...about the witch.

She clasped the crucifix nestled between her breasts. Visions of a little girl huddled inside a scarecrow and watching flames licking her mother like a lover's tongue left Sheen feeling exposed, vulnerable, and deeply raw.

She'd remembered this, felt this. She remembered the stench of burning flesh, and smelled it even now.

Glad she was lying down, for a moment she felt jarred, dizzy, as though the air had been sucked out of the room. She'd not known of her telepathic capability until the night of her mother's death. But more than that, she'd learned how dangerous it was to allow others the knowledge of her propensity to hear voices and see visions.

Recovering somewhat, Sheen sighed and rolled to her stomach. The man would come. This she knew for certain. The question remained, why did he seek her? Did he mean her harm? The scar that marred the soft flesh around her throat ticked. Sheen fingered the rough puckered disfigurement that she kept hidden beneath high-collared dresses. An icy shudder washed over her as she clutched the edges of the quilt. Life had taught her humans were heartless and brutal.

She wondered if it were time to pack up and move on, to seek another solitary place where she might live out her days nurturing her garden and tending injured animals. Yet there were times when she missed interacting with other people.

For three months she'd had no contact with another human being. She was ready and eager for old Mr. Tatum's visit to help take her mind off the recent occurrences of her second sight.

For nearly two years she'd lived at peace, allowing her mind and body to heal. Now fear, something so rarely tasted in those two short years, slicked hot and burning in her throat.

She found herself yawning, a huge, hollow yawn that stretched her diaphragm up against her heart.

As the hours of darkness wore on, her eyes drooped and she allowed the sounds of the night to lull her.

Images, thoughts, voices washed over her in waves of shapes and sounds. Go away, she demanded. Just...leave me...alone.

****

At midmorning on Saturday, the braying of a mule and the clanging of pots and pans against the peddler's wagon created a mild uproar among Sheen's animals. Though his visits were infrequent as he made his rounds throughout the territory selling his wares, she'd grown fond of the old peddler.

What a day, she thought. What a beautiful spring, for that matter. She stood in the weathered barn, in a patch of sunlight, stood watching the brown, long-legged mule resist the driver's commands to "Step on up, Daisy. Any slower and I'll have to trade you in for a younger Daisy."

Sheen had laughed when Mr. Tatum had explained that he'd named all his mules Daisy. Said naming them all the same didn't tax the remembering part of his brain.

She stepped from the barn and lifted a hand to shield her eyes from the glare. A smile brightened her face when the old man reined the mule to a halt. "'Tis a fine spring day, and 'tis even finer to see you, Mr. Tatum."

"And a good, good morning to you, Miss Sheen O'Reilly. You're as pretty as a prairie flower in full bloom."

"I see the winter hasn't dulled the silver in your tongue." Sheen laughed. "Step down. I'm eager to hear what's happening beyond the mountains."

"Oh, it's a bit of gossip you desire instead of looking at my wares, is it? Cain't make a profit telling gossip."

"Then we'll trade, Mr. Tatum."

It was a game they played, and Sheen knew the old man enjoyed it as much as she.

"What is it you have to trade?" He thumbed the sun-faded suspenders forward and puffed out his chest as if ready to do some serious dickering.

She placed her hands on her hips. "I've fresh-baked bread, wild honey, and hot water for tea. And for something a wee more hearty, a creamy wild onion soup simmering over the coals. What say you to that, Mr. Tatum? Are you ready to do business?"

The old man slapped his hands together, giving them a vigorous rub. "Lead the way, young lass. My head is brimming with news, and my belly's grumbling for lack of your good cookin'."

She led the way up the steps and into the cabin and hummed as she bustled about laying the table with food. She poured the tea, then sat across from the peddler. It did her heart good to see the way he filled his mouth with soup-soddened bread.

She refilled his cup and watched him sweeten the tea with honey. She folded her hands on her lap, and, eager as she was to ask him her question, she waited.

When he pushed back his bowl, she smiled. "'Tis time to trade for news."

"I cain't argue over that fact." He scratched his bald head. "Let me see, hmm. Miz Crawley had herself twin baby boys. Born on Christmas Eve. Ugly little critters, all red with prunified faces." He gave a mock shudder.

Sheen scolded. "Shame on you, Mr. Tatum. Though I don't know Mrs. Crawley, I'm certain she'd be highly incensed to know you called her babies ugly critters. Do you recall their names?"

"Who?"

"Mr. Tatum!" she chided.

"Oh, the young'uns. Good Christian names straight from the Bible—Ezra and Ezekiel."

Sheen clapped her hands like a happy child. "What else? Surely 'tis not all you have to tell?"

"No, 'tain't. Carl Simmons took himself a bride. Had supper with 'em. The new Miz Simmons cain't hold a candle to your cookin'." He crossed his heart and said, "Hope to die if I'm lying."

He rambled on about newborn calves and then about Miz Magnolia dying of consumption. "As hoores come and go, she was a good hoore." Then as if he'd breached etiquette by speaking about such things to an innocent young woman, he added, "Beg pardon, Miss Sheen. My tongue tends to wag onct it gets started."

"No offense taken, Mr. Tatum. It's all very interesting. Surely you've more?"

He tore a slice of bread in half and dipped it into the pot of honey and butter Sheen had warmed. "Hope this isn't too delicate for your ears, but the bank in Bozeman was robbed. Mr. Jenks, the teller, was plugged right 'tween the eyes. Damn shame. Jenks was a kindly old gent."

Sheen placed her hands to her cheeks. "That's terrible. Did they catch the bank robber?"

"Man named Curly Jim. Yep, he was caught and hanged the same day."

"Oh...dear. Still, I suppose he deserved the punishment."

Tatum pushed from the table. "Gettin' late. I have some pretty green gingham, gray wool, lace, thread and needles, flour, taters, sugar, coffee, tea, seeds fer plantin', and trinkets, too."

Sheen also stood. She smoothed her hands down the sides of her apron. She forced a brittle smile. "Mr. Tatum, have you, um, have you told anyone about me?"

The old man stopped at the door, his back to Sheen. "What do you mean, told anyone about you?"

She knew he was hedging. "I mean, have you told anyone about me living alone out here on the prairie?"

When he didn't answer, she said, "Mr. Tatum, did you break your promise not to tell anyone about me?"

He turned as if to study her, and then smiled foolishly. "I don't hold with such beliefs, Miss Sheen, and hope you'll take no offense, but sometimes I purely believe you can read my mind."

He shifted a rheumy eye toward her. "Answer me one question. Why is it a pretty young girl like you has hidden away from civilization?"

Sheen stayed absolutely still. She didn't trust herself to speak. "My father paid with his life at the hands of so-called *civilized* people. I've no desire to live among such cruel ignorance." Then fearing she'd said too much, she added, "It'd please me, Mr. Tatum, to know you've not spoken to *anyone* about me."

"Well, Miss Sheen, I did stop by Fort Smith, and I did wet my whistle a time or two with strong spirits, and I might have told about seein' you treatin' a grizzly like a pet bear."

She didn't like the feeling that threatened to

overcome her. "What else, Mr. Tatum?"

"I could have, now I ain't swearin' an oath, but maybe I told how you cured a half-dead Injun boy of snake bite, and how the chief gave you that spotted pony out there in your corral fer saving his son when the med'cine doctor couldn't do nothing."

The wind blew off the mountains, bringing a faint smell of damp earth and prairie flowers. You never know where a road will end, Sheen thought, as the breeze curled around her ears, you just knew roads ended. She'd hoped hers had ended here, on this abandoned settler's place. Unwanted and neglected, and a hundred miles from civilization, the homestead was perfect. Out here, she could hide. She'd spent two years turning it into a home with a kitchen garden, bee hives, and hope for a future without fear.

The scar, beneath the collar of her blue plaid dress, seemed to tighten around her neck. She resisted the urge to touch the throbbing blemish that served as a reminder of the night she was nearly hanged. And all because she was different.

All she'd ever wanted was to live happily ever after. But not Sheen O'Reilly, she thought. That wasn't the way things went for her and her father—ever. She wasn't about to let that get her down. She couldn't let it get her down. She wouldn't die like her mother had.

Tatum's voice broke through her reverie. "Now don't you go frettin' yourself. Fort Smith is a good hunnerd miles from here, and the only time them soldier boys leave is when they go off to chase Injuns. 'Sides, folks at the fort know me for my tall tales. 'Specially when I get liquored up. 'Tain't nothing to worry your noggin about."

Even as he was speaking she heard the words inside his head: *I tell you, Private O'Hanlon, it ain't natural, the things I seen this girl do.*

Yeah, like what?

I seen her pull a thorn out'n a grizzly's paw.

Go on with yerself, Tatum. You musta been pullin' hard on the cork.

No, sirree, I weren't drunk. I seen it with my own eyes, and she's got a three-legged fox that follows her 'round like a tame pup.

You mean she be a fairy witch?

Don't know nothing 'bout no witches, but she's got some kinda special powers. Ain't never in my whole life seen a grizzly bear act all friendly-like to a human.

And then Sheen heard him lower his voice and saw the ale dribble from the sides of his mouth as he spoke again to the Irishman named Private O'Hanlon. Tatum said, *She ain't got no black cats, but she's got a crow what sits on her shoulder.*

What be this 'ere witch's name, Tatum?

Now thash my shecret. Tatum hiccupped and then slurred his words. *I pro-promisched I w-wouldn't tell, but she's I-Irish, like you.*

Big troubles, Sheen knew, had little beginnings, just like little troubles. At least Tatum hadn't spoken her name. Yet there were still things to worry about.

Her chin went up. She tried to stop the frown that threatened to take over her face. Keeping her mouth still, she had a feeling her eyes were giving her away. She steadied her voice. "I'll trade you three crocks of honey, five loaves of fresh-baked bread, and two jars of gooseberry jam for ten pounds of flour and two pounds of salt. I'll also need ten potatoes—only the ones with sprouted eyes—and ten pumpkin seeds."

"What 'bout a pretty trinket to wear 'round your neck?"

"Who would I wear such a thing for—my animals?"

Tatum shook his head over her response. "I've never understood why a pretty young woman like yourself de-sires to live like one of them nuns I read about in a book onct."

"We all have our secrets, Mr. Tatum. Even you." Sheen tried not to sound angry.

Tatum reached up and scratched his head. As if knowing he'd been dismissed, he walked to the rear of the wagon and hefted himself inside. Once he'd unloaded the goods he was trading, set them on the porch, and loaded what she gave him, he gathered the tethers from the hitchpost and climbed up to the wagon seat. "I'm offering my 'pology for upsettin' you, Miss Sheen. I know how the liquor loosens my tongue when it's been a spell since I talked to someone 'sides Daisy. I don't want you to fret none. Whatever your reason for living out here all alone is your business. I truly don't think anybody at the fort would believe an old man who talks to his mule."

Sheen smiled up at him. "Next time you visit, I'll need a bag of sulfur, a bottle of castor oil, a jug of blackstrap molasses, corn mash for my chickens, two sacks of oats for my horses, and several bales of hay for the cow. Safe journeys to you, Mr. Tatum."

Sheen was glad to see the peddler drive his wagon from the yard. She needed some quiet time to think.

Chapter Three

The sun was now full in the sky. Scattered patches of snow littered the ground, with shades of green peeking through.

Guthrie smelled spring coming in the chilly air. He also smelled his own anticipation. He was saddle weary, after his many weeks of idling, and his shoulder hurt like hell. He'd spent the better part of three months healing, and now he prepared to meet the woman Private O'Hanlon proclaimed was a fairy witch.

Even as he rode down the trail from the fort to the small farm he sought, he thought of the woman and his conscience bothered him with the plan he had in mind if she refused to help him.

With that settled, he looked ahead toward the cabin he'd been told was just fifty or so miles from Fort Smith. He adjusted his weight in the saddle to ease the jarring of his shoulder and ribs, cursing the hostler for a sorry selection of horses—an ill-tempered, green-broke mount or a nag that should have been put out to pasture a long time ago. He'd settled on the half-trained sorrel gelding, knowing the skittish animal was unreliable.

Guthrie cursed the Irish soldier. The gelding's ears flicked back and forth as if listening to the man's voice. "Fifty miles, my aching backside. The only distance that Irishman can judge is how far it is from his elbow to his mouth or how long it takes to guzzle a pint."

By his recollection, he'd already ridden near a hundred miles. He spoke only to himself, the horse, and the pines. "Blast you, O'Hanlon. I'd like to rid you of your boots and make you walk barefoot over a patch of cactus."

Urging the plodding horse to a faster gait, Guthrie thought about the woman. He would be gentle with her, for she was no doubt a woman of years who kept to herself and lived quietly. A grandmotherly sort, he imagined, a woman set in her ways. Not a woman to tempt him from his celibate lifestyle with her charms. *Charms.* He chuckled over the word. She was a witch. What if she used charms and potions to cast a spell over him?

He'd topped a rise when he spotted the spiraling wisp of smoke. Guthrie rode into view of the house, reined the sorrel to a halt, dismounted, and tethered the horse to a patch of chokeberry bushes.

He pulled a field-glass from the saddlebag and scanned every detail—the yard, the house, and the barn. He allowed the thrill of meeting the witch to seep into his awareness. While he didn't buy into O'Hanlon's Irish nonsense, a year of chasing the elusive renegades who'd murdered his wife and abducted his daughter gnawed at him like a canker. He was a man obsessed with exacting the cruelest form of revenge on the warriors who'd destroyed the only happiness in his life. If this woman had magical powers, he intended to take advantage of them.

Scrutinizing the house once more for good measure, he turned his focus to the barn, noting the pinto mare and foal in the corral. It appeared there were no men to cause him concern. O'Hanlon had said the woman lived alone. Still, life had taught Guthrie to err on the side of caution.

He dropped to one knee and continued to inspect the lay of the yard. Then a woman walked out of the barn. One long, russet braid draped over her shoulder. Guthrie adjusted the magnification on the field glass. She didn't fit the image he'd built in his mind. Rather than wrinkled and stooped as he'd imagined, she was a tall, lush, willowy redhead with a complexion that reminded him of peaches and cream. He thought tension rode hard on the girl's face.

And then, with her chin high, she looked in his direction almost as if she knew he was there. The nerves in his gut twisted, leaving him edgy. He didn't like the feeling, but there it was.

A powerful shudder roiled through his body. He allowed himself a vinegary little smile. "Damn."

He moved silently into the shadows of the bushes where the sorrel waited. Guthrie snapped the binocular shut and tucked it away inside the saddlebag.

He had an almost visceral feeling of a plan about to go very wrong. He let the feeling spread through him.

Setting his toe in the stirrup, he swung into the saddle. He drew a deep, silent breath and faced the crucial decision—take up a cold trail and hope to find Otaktay's band, or seek help from a witch?

****

A snake of fear curled in Sheen's stomach. Her eyes scanned the distant slope. He watched her. His eyes, she knew, were the same color of storm clouds, and he watched her with a kind of edgy patience.

The man had come.

Beneath his buffalo-hide coat, this man's build was

33

rangy, she envisioned, his forearms with tough muscles. A man not afraid of hard work or long hours in the saddle.

What should she do? Her alternatives were limited. Except for the pitchfork in the barn, she had no weapons. A loathing for violence had kept her from accepting the rifle Mr. Tatum had tried to give her when she'd refused his offer to trade for the foal.

He'd called her a fool, then apologized. But she'd been so sure her only enemy was the vigilantes who'd tried to hang her, and they were thousands of miles away.

Sheen commiserated with her dread. The pulsating silence wore on. It amazed her that for years she'd actually embraced what was in her, had explored it, used it, even celebrated it. A legacy, her father had told her. A gift from her mother's blood and her mother's mother. Now those flashes of memory hurt her heart. And it frightened her.

She flashed on the image of him riding down the slope littered with yellow pine. A dark, unrelentingly handsome man, a stranger. She knew before she saw him there was nothing soft in the sharp bones and high planes of his face. Weather had left its mark there, as well, with lines etched into the corners of his eyes.

She sensed a feral meanness in him, and smelled her own fear. Fresh, hot gushes of it.

****

Guthrie rode down the narrow cut toward her holdings, admiring the neatly kept yard of the ramshackle homestead. His skittish mount was in a nasty temper. Guthrie understood. He was in one himself. The pain that raked his body made him want to puke.

In the middle of the yard, he reined the sorrel to a halt. "'Morning, ma'am. Name's Guthrie Tanner. I've ridden a long way. Mind if I light a spell?"

Luminous hazel-blue eyes looked up at him. She was lovely and definitely not what he'd expected when he'd heard of the woman living alone on the prairie. He caught the faintest drift of her scent and thought of the night-blooming jasmine in his wife's yard before they'd left South Carolina.

Guthrie felt heaviness in his groin as he watched the young woman staring up at him, and he fought it with a sense of scorn. He wasn't here to take advantage of the woman, only to seek her help.

When she didn't answer, he shifted in the saddle.

And though he hadn't touched her, she edged away in a small but deliberate motion.

"You're most welcome to water your horse, Mr. Tanner. The well is there." She pointed the direction.

In a subtle way, she hadn't invited him to step down.

"Your husband away, is he?"

Her breath made little puffs in the cold air. "My companions are my animals."

"So you live a hundred miles from nowhere, alone."

"Not completely alone. Sometimes I trade with the people from the Crow tribe, and then there is Mr. Tatum, the peddler who comes every few months."

She reminded him of a delicate flower, yet there was wariness to her, like a frightened rabbit searching for a place to hide.

Ignoring her lack of invitation to light and sit a

spell, in one fluid motion he dismounted. Knowing the horse wasn't trained to ground tie, Guthrie held tight to the reins.

She seemed to hesitate. "If you have no business other than to water your horse, I suggest you do so and then be on your way."

The sensual grit in the accent of her cultured voice plucked strings Guthrie had forgotten he possessed. It made him weak-kneed.

He didn't cotton to the sensation at all, which immediately put him out of the mood to be friendly. "I have business with the witch."

She fingered the silky braid of hair that reminded him of rich, red South Carolina clay. For an instant, he thought he saw panic in her eyes. Her chin went up. "No witch lives here."

"A peddler named Tatum spends time at Fort Smith. He bragged about a witch to one Private O'Hanlon. Would you deny this is the same Tatum who trades wares with you?"

She stared at him, unblinking. "Nay, I would not. He has admitted to getting into his cups with the drink and speaking of things he only imagines."

A raven darted behind Guthrie, a quick black flash that swept by and found a perch on Sheen's shoulder. Sheen turned as if dismissing Guthrie.

A weight descended on his chest, like hands pushing. In no mood to explain himself, he reached out and grabbed her arm. "Private O'Hanlon is from Ireland. He believed Tatum's story about watching you remove a thorn from a grizzly's paw. O'Hanlon said women with powers to control animals are called fairy witches. Though more refined, you have the same Irish brogue as him."

Guthrie watched her fingers curl into a fist before jerking her arm away and placing her hands behind her back. Her eyes remained serious and watchful. "Aye, 'tis true Ireland is my motherland. I was but a wee child when my father brought me to America. I canna help the way I speak, and I canna help that your Private O'Hanlon believes the blarney spoken by a drunken fool."

Her voice was vocal honey, so sugary sweet the mere sound sparked cravings in Guthrie any randy bear would appreciate. He raked her curves with a hungry glance, then reminded himself why he was here.

A low growl caught Guthrie's attention. His survival instincts kicked into high gear as a three-legged fox, ears flattened against its head and lips drawn over vicious teeth, lumbered snapping and snarling toward him. Guthrie whipped the revolver from its holster. "Rabid fox."

His aim faltered as Sheen grabbed his arm and shoved it upward. The shot caused the raven to fly away. Sheen's eyes narrowed. She scolded, "What kind of man are you to shoot a poor crippled vixen?" She bent and cradled the animal into her arms.

Guthrie wasn't sure what to believe about this woman. He said nothing for a moment. "I hesitate to call a lady a liar, but with you holding a wild animal in your arms like it was a pet dog, that's exactly what I'd have to do."

She didn't smile, and this time took a step closer while hugging the fox to her chest. "Call me what you will, Mr. Tanner. Liar or witch, I have a right to my privacy." She lifted one arm and pointed. "Get off my land, or—"

"Or you'll what? Put a curse on me?"

"Were I a witch, yes."

Then silence settled again. Heavy. Awkward.

He turned from her and, gathering the reins over the sorrel's head, stepped into the stirrup. The fractious gelding side-stepped. Guthrie spewed a string of oaths. He gripped the saddle horn and swung heavily into the saddle.

And then a strange thing happened. Three crows flew at the sorrel's head. The birds cawed and pecked. Guthrie struggled to keep his seat as the frightened gelding reared and bucked. "Damn you, horse, straighten up." He took five precious minutes to steady the animal.

He gigged the spooked gelding with a spur and rode from the yard. He wanted something from this girl. He wanted clues. Clues to where he'd find his daughter.

Guthrie's heart raged against his chest. Planting his feet firmly in the stirrups, he gripped the reins in a clenched fist, and allowed a plan to formulate inside his head.

****

Sheen stumbled inside the cabin and slammed the door. She didn't bother pouring water into a basin. Instead she dipped her hands into the wooden pail and splashed the cold liquid over her face. Her throat tightened, impeding her ability to swallow or move her tongue. *Witch.* The word could still undo her, even after all these years.

Ever so slowly she lowered her hands to grip the edges of the table. To balance herself. To feel.

Was Guthrie Tanner still lurking close by? She

listened. His thoughts were quiet. Yes, she decided, she was alone.

She could sense it now...and see the effects through the window. The chickens were returning to the yard, the crows lined the corral fence, and the vixen lay quietly on the cabin steps. Her animals remained cautious, but they were back.

Her nerves had yet to recover from the violent confrontation with a stranger who'd accused her of more than she was.

She lay on the bed. The child in her wanted to curl up, to cover her face with her hands, to will herself invisible. She was alone. Defenseless.

The heifer's lowing stirred Sheen. She'd slept without realizing it. The cow needed milking, the horses fed, and the afternoon eggs needed collecting.

Reluctant to leave the house, Sheen opened the door, walked down the steps and glanced up at the sky. No stars glittered. Shivers prickled up her spine. This year, the full moon fell on her birthday. The witching moon, her father had called it, and her sixth sense grew stronger. An odd confusion, half eagerness and half reluctance, tossed Sheen's spirits to and fro.

With quick steps and only the faint light from the moon and stars to guide her, she allowed long strides to carry her to the barn, knowing the cow would be miserable if she were not relieved of her milk.

The cow lowed impatiently from the stall, and Sheen pushed the door aside, entering the dark musty barn, able to find her way by touch, so familiar was she with the contents of the building.

Her milking pail hung from a nail, just inside the door, the three-legged stool on the ground next to it.

She retrieved them, then entered the stall where the Jersey cow waited. In seconds she was seated near the animal's flank, holding the bucket between her knees as she emptied the heifer's strutted bag of its burden. The Jersey lowed once more, as if thanking Sheen for soothing her unease.

Fifteen minutes later Sheen completed her chores and had given the animals their feed for the night.

And then she saw it, the faint shifting of light as someone stepped into the path of the moon. She lifted her skirt and raced to the house.

Someone was watching, waiting. She sensed it even through the fear. She struggled to blank her mind, to bring the face, the form, the name into it. All she conjured was a sheer wall of terror.

Not all the terror was hers.

He was afraid, too, she realized. Why?

Her hand trembled as she turned the rope latch, shoved through the opened cabin door, then slammed it. She grabbed the broom. She would defend herself. She would take charge. Holding the broom handle like a weapon, she aimed it at the door.

And then there was nothing except the darkness and the sound of her panting breath.

She groped her way to the table. Her fingers knew where the matches lay. A small flash flared when she struck the sulfur head against the table's rough surface. Her hands trembled as she lit the lamp. The beam flickered as she hurried to lock the door, a habit she'd developed when she and her father had lived in the town limits of Connecticut. Yet she was well aware how useless such a precaution was here. One hard kick would knock the hinges off the door jamb.

She willed herself to regulate her breathing, until it began to come slow and quiet. She couldn't see if her thoughts were tumbling, couldn't concentrate if her nerves were screaming.

For the first time in over two years she prepared to open herself to the gift she'd been cursed with at birth.

She sat rigid, her back against the bed's headboard, her eyes on the door until the dark softened. She didn't know how long she slept.

She woke in the body of a dead woman. Benevolent contempt filled Sheen as she rose from the bed to stand in front of the antique mirror. Sheen saw the pale oval of the woman's face, so pretty, with thoughtful brown eyes and skin the color of fresh cream, a smile that lit up a room. She was young, fragile of bone, delicate of feature. Her hair, the color of honey, slid prettily down her narrow back. She smelled of honeysuckle.

Her name was Abigail.

Running now, running through a cornfield. Terror so sharp in the throat that it slices the screams before they escape. She must get to the house. Why hadn't she brought the rifle with her? She'd been warned to never leave the house without the rifle.

Horses' hooves pounding behind her. Fast, too fast, and too close.

Something hits her from behind. Bright pain between her shoulders that vibrates down to the soles of her feet.

The jolt of bone and breath as she falls hard to the ground. Air rushes from her lungs in a sob as a half dozen brown hands snatch at her dress, her petticoat.

Tearing. Ripping.

Odors of sweat and rancid animal grease mingle with her own fear. Her breakfast, the contents of her stomach, soils the ground.

She screams now, one long cry of desperation, and calls out for her daughter.

Run Rachel. Run, hide.

She hears their laughter, harsh, and knows the panting, fetid breath against her face.

She screams again.

Guthrie! Guthrie, help me!

And Sheen, trapped inside the dead woman, wept.

Chapter Four

When Sheen came back to herself she was lying on the floor of her cabin. Her face was wet, and she tasted the salt of her own tears.

Screams echoed inside her head. She didn't know if they were her own or those of the woman she couldn't forget.

Shivering, she pushed from the floor and on rubbery legs walked to the water bucket to cool her cheeks and wash the tears away.

The spell left her weak and queasy. For two years she had held the spells at bay, and now the second sight had returned.

****

Outside, the moon hung high in the sky, illuminating the rough path to Sheen's cabin. Guthrie stepped from the barn, a saddle in one hand, a rope in the other. He shifted his gaze toward the darkened house and thought how ridiculously simple to break in.

A soft whicker drew his attention to the task at hand. In his experience, most Indian ponies weren't saddle broke. He wondered if the girl rode bareback or if she simply considered the horse a pet and didn't ride at all. Settling the saddle over the fence rail, Guthrie lifted the leather latch from the gate and entered the corral.

He spoke to the mare as she stepped between him

and her foal. "Easy, mama, I'm not gonna hurt your baby. Just want to see if you cotton to the saddle."

Satiny flesh quivered beneath his touch. He crooned reassuring words to the mare while he ran his hands over her body. Guthrie knew horses. Before the War Between the States, his daddy had raised the finest thoroughbreds in all of South Carolina.

A flash of bitterness momentarily drew Guthrie from his task. He remembered the raid on the family farm, the burning of the barns, the torching of the plantation house that had belonged to the family since his great-grandfather had left England and settled in Charleston.

Guthrie used the rope to fashion a hackamore around the mare's head, and then led her to a fence post and tied a strong knot in the rope.

He lifted the saddle blanket and eased it to the pinto's back. He waited for a reaction. It didn't come.

The horse's ears flicked back and forth as if listening to the man. "Well, now, that was easy. Let's see how you react to something a little heavier."

With the greatest of ease, he lowered the saddle in place. He reached under her belly for the girth strap, all the while speaking to the mare.

"Truth's in the doin'. If you're gonna buck, now's the time."

With that, he laced the latigo through the cinch ring. His hands worked quickly to pull the strap tight, snugging the saddle to the mare's back.

In response, the mare grunted and stamped her foot.

Relief sighed through Guthrie. "I hope your mistress is as willing as you. And don't worry, we'll take your baby with us." He placed a gentle slap on the mare's white rump.

He opened the gate and led the pinto from the enclosure and toward the hitch rail in front of the house. The foal followed.

Guthrie tensed. Keenly aware of his earlier encounter with the fox, he searched through the darkness for signs of the critter.

Satisfied the vixen wasn't about, Guthrie crouched low and scuttled across the yard to stand next to the bedroom window. In one smooth motion, he lifted the casement. With the agility of a puma, he slipped through the opening and for a moment crouched in the darkness. The glow of moonlight illuminated the girl's face and Guthrie inhaled sharply.

She was lovely. He figured her no more than twenty years at the most. Her green woolen dress clung to her shape, and the dusky-red hair she'd earlier flung over her shoulder formed a dark cape around her shoulders. Lying there, like that, she reminded him of a china doll he'd once seen in a store window—all porcelain and perfect. He wanted to reach out and touch her.

Though his footsteps were nearly silent as he crossed the room, the heel drops of his boots seemed magnified in the stillness of the night.

****

Without warning, a rough hand covered Sheen's mouth, jarring her awake. The bed dipped, and a tall figure shadowed her. She remained silent, his hand not allowing her mouth to open. Deciding to fight soundlessly, her hands reached up, fingers curved and aimed at his face.

Her fingernails dug deeply into flesh, and elicited an indrawn breath and a hiss from the intruder who held her. With a quick move and using his free hand, he captured both her wrists and imprisoned them above her head.

"Hellfire, woman. Hold still. I'm not going to hurt you."

His voice was graveled and deep. She stiffened in his grip, as she forced her bruised lips to open. Dipping her chin, she clamped down on the soft part of his palm until she tasted the salty tang of his blood.

He yowled, and the sound resonated in the small bedroom, bringing delight to Sheen.

"Get off me, you oaf, or I'll scream."

"Who'd hear you? The chickens, your pet fox, the crows?" His voice mocked while he looked down at her with dark eyes that were barely visible in the moonlit room. "For whatever reason, you've chosen to live alone, miles from civilization, and let me tell you, that isn't a smart choice for a woman without a man to protect her."

She willed the red wash of fury to dull inside her. For a split second, he'd opened himself and Sheen had heard his regrets.

Where was I when Abigail needed protecting? My fault...my fault she's dead.

"I have no intention of calling for help, you wretch." Her voice rose an octave. "What do you want with me?" A vision of violence filled her mind, with herself as the victim, and she shivered against the wintry chill that slithered up her spine.

"I've already told you I won't hurt you, if that's what you're worried about. Besides, I hope you've got a potion to keep me from getting blood poison." A touch of humor colored his voice. "You didn't have to bite me."

She pulled away from the fingers he allowed to trace the lines of her cheek.

The bed's rope cords groaned when Guthrie lifted himself from the mattress. "You certainly aren't what I expected to find when I rode into the yard this morning," he said quietly. "Why, you're only a girl."

She laughed scornfully. "I'm a fully grown woman, with more than twenty years of living. And, yes, I do have a remedy for your hand and the scratches on your face."

Guthrie's face twisted with surprise. "Good God, woman, you really are a witch."

Sheen lifted her chin. "Nothing quite so drastic, Mr. Tanner. You did say your name is Tanner, didn't you? As I was saying, nothing that ordinary lye soap and water won't cure."

He only laughed beneath his breath.

She swung her legs to the floor. "I'll light the lamp," she said, walking to the living area of the house.

"No," he said quickly.

"There's no one around to see the light," she told him, aggravated at being a prisoner in her own home. Whatever his plans, it boded no good for her.

He chose not to argue with her, apparently, for he simply waited until she lit the lamp.

Spent and confused, Sheen pressed fingers against her eyes. She listened. Nothing. His mind was closed. She turned on her heel and walked to the pail, ladled water into a basin, grabbed the bar of soap, then set the contents on the table. "While you wash, Mr. Tanner, perhaps you'll explain what it is you want from me?"

Guthrie rolled up his sleeves and dipped his hands into the icy water. He slowly lathered his palms, wincing visibly from the lye soap's sting. The scratches on his face smarted from the cleanser's bite.

"You neglected to tell me your name, this morning."

She looked straight into his storm-blue eyes. Her heart sank within her. Probably no more than thirty, but well-worn, she decided. He was hard, his features forming a harsh visage, dark hair badly in need of a barber's scissors, and eyes that hid behind lowered lids and lashes. "You called me *witch*."

"I'll only ask once more—your name?"

She sighed in frustration. "Sheen O'Reilly. I'm nobody important. All I wish is to live alone, and in peace."

His voice low and authoritative, he spoke as he toweled his hands. "Put together enough food to last for several months. Clothes and blankets for traveling, and whatever female necessities you'll need."

Her arms crossed over her breast, Sheen backed against the table. "No."

He reached out and grabbed her by both arms, hauling her against his chest. "With or without food or suitable clothing, you're coming with me. Make it easier on yourself and do as I say. Game might be scarce along the trail, and nights in the mountains get mighty cold without proper dress."

He released her abruptly and she stumbled backward. Her thoughts were her own. *You will rue the day you met me, Mr. Tanner. This I promise.*

With quick steps, Sheen carried items from the

small pantry, filling two gunny sacks with bacon, beans, several loaves of bread, coffee, a tin of sugar, a small sack of flour, potatoes, onions, and a jar of wild strawberry preserves.

She walked to the bedroom, stepped inside, and turned to close the door.

His foot jammed it opened and he laughed. "I'm not taking a chance on you slipping out the window, *witch*."

Stricken and trembling, Sheen entered the bedroom and gathered her only good petticoat, a clean pair of bloomers, a flannel nightgown, a gray woolen dress, an extra pair of shoes, heavy stockings, a hairbrush, several tins of dried herbs. She placed the contents in the center of the quilt on her bed and drew the four corners together to form a knot.

"We'll go now." Guthrie's voice was low, his touch firm against her arm. He gathered the two sacks of food as he steered her toward the front door. She walked ahead of him. Without speaking, he followed her to where the pinto mare stood tied to the hitch post.

"Where are you taking me?" She saw the flash of his white teeth in the moonlight.

"Right now, all you need to do is haul your bohunkus into the saddle, little lady. The rest will come in due time."

She did as he said, knowing that, for now, she was under his control, and heaven forbid she make him angry with her.

Her mind was spinning like a child's top. All she'd ever asked for was a peaceful life, alone here on this property. She'd done well, raising chickens. Then there was the cow she cared for, and the three-legged vixen, the mare and colt.

A kitchen garden thrived behind the house and her nearest neighbor lived too far away to visit. It was a good life. One she'd thought held a measure of safety and peace to last into her old age.

Sheen's only knowledge of him was her encounter with the dead woman whose body she'd entered. Was this Guthrie Tanner the same Guthrie the woman had called out to?

Her mind whirled with thoughts. The dark-haired man beside her probably outweighed her by a hundred pounds. A big man, whose piercing eyes had frightened Sheen with their lack of emotion, as though he felt nothing, as if his feelings were locked up somewhere inside, he gave no hint of softness, no apology for his rough treatment of her.

Physically she was no match for him, leaving only her wits to depend upon.

The mystery was too much for her tonight, she decided. Just getting through the hours 'til morning was what concerned her most right now.

"It won't do you any good to give me a hard time, *witch*."

"Don't call me that," she said sharply. And even as she spoke she heard her mother's voice, soothing her, encouraging her and speaking the words in a gentle voice. *Don't worry, my precious child. Your mamai is here.*

Sheen inhaled sharply as a tear slid down her cheek. *Oh, Mother, if only it were so.*

"Don't stand there like a wooden post. Mount up."

Sheen fisted her hands against her hips. She looked at her enemy with eyes as steely as his. "Where are you taking me?"

"You'll find out soon enough."

"Then what is it you want of me?"

When he didn't answer, she clenched her jaw and turned to walk away.

Guthrie growled low in his throat. His strong hands caught her around the waist and he lifted her into the saddle. He thrust the bundled quilt into her hands. "Tie this around the saddle horn."

He untied the mare and, without looking at Sheen, said, "Don't talk, and don't cry. Anything I can't abide, it's a yammering female who blubbers."

She felt her anger rise at his implied warning. She was stubbornly silent while Guthrie walked the mare to where he'd left the sorrel tied behind the barn.

Sheen flung her leg over the saddle horn. "This is outrageous. I'm not going anywhere, and especially not with you."

"Damn it." Guthrie's loud oath startled the sorrel gelding, causing it to tug against its tether. "Lady, I don't have time for your foolishness. Haul your butt back in the saddle."

She slapped at his hands. "Why are you kidnapping me?"

"Don't make me tie your feet to the stirrups."

For an instant, Sheen knew a moment of panic. Was this all a ruse? Why was this dark-haired, whiskered giant of a man kidnapping her?

She drew a calming breath into her lungs, squeezed her eyes shut, and tried to conjure a vision. When the attempt failed, she stalled. "What about my cow? She'll need milking."

"I already turned the heifer loose. She'll make her

way to a stray bull. Nature will take care of the rest, and it won't be long before she'll have a calf tugging on her."

"You are a man with a mean spirit, Mr. Tanner."

Dark clouds passed over the moon. The wind was cold, so cold Sheen fought the shivers threatening to chatter her teeth.

Without the heart or the energy to build up her wall again, she heard the voice inside her head.

No...no...please don't hurt me. Guthrie, where are you? Oh, God, Guthrie, where are you?

Sheen wanted to ask Guthrie about Abigail but feared his reaction. She swayed in the saddle and worried she'd fall to the ground.

Hands reached up to steady Sheen. "What's wrong with you, girl? You're as pale as a ghost."

She had trouble breathing. Her heart pounded against her chest. Looking down at him, she stared into his eyes. "Is this the way you treat all women, Mr. Tanner?"

They stared at each other, neither willing to break the gaze. For a timeless moment nothing seemed to exist but the two of them connecting, feeling drawn to each other.

His eyes measured her, and he smiled

Confused by the emotions slithering inside her stomach like tiny snakes, it was Sheen who broke the connection. She tossed him a look of scorn. "You really are a bastard."

Guthrie blinked several times as if forcing himself to concentrate. Holding the pinto's reins, Guthrie tied the sacks of food to the saddle horn of his horse. He stepped into the stirrup and mounted in one easy movement.

"No more talking, *witch.*"

"Please call me Sheen. I prefer my given name to...the other."

"I will when you've proven otherwise. Let's move out."

In silence, they rode out of the yard and up the cut toward the mountains.

Sheen's mouth felt as parched as bones dried by the sun, and she licked her lips as she aimed her glare at the broad back of the man who rode ahead of her. She couldn't be attracted to him.

Could not.

Chapter Five

Sheen hunched low in the saddle. She shivered from the cold's bitter bite. The pinto mare galloped along unmindful of the inclement weather. Flakes of snow drifted from the leaden sky, and she heard Guthrie curse. She glanced to the right, making sure the foal hadn't lagged behind.

She looked at the road ahead. The dismal night grayed her disposition. "Mr. Tanner, what do you want of me?"

Silence greeted her.

Thoughts of her warm bed, thick quilts, and a fire burning in the hearth filtered in. She refused them any credence. She planned her escape—not so much from Guthrie but from everything else in life. It seemed, in one sense or another, that she'd been on the run her entire existence.

She called out again. This time louder. "Where are we going?"

The wind whipped his words away. She thought he said, "Up to the powder."

Within minutes, exhaustion sapped the last of her energy. Gripping the saddle horn, she slumped forward. Her chin bobbled against her chest. Soon, her eyes drifted shut.

****

Sheen woke slowly, cocooned in a blanket of

warmth. She looked up, still hazy from sleep, and for a moment she forgot where she was and with whom. The man named Guthrie Tanner cradled her in his arms, carrying her through the darkness.

The snow had stopped. The night was eerily still. Carefully, Guthrie set her down, her clothes damp, her hair clinging to her face. She wobbled on her feet, and then righted herself, taking in the small clearing surrounded by brush and trees.

Guthrie left her. He removed hobbles from his saddlebag and set to tending the horses. Then he unsaddled the bone-weary mounts and rubbed the animals down with a ratty blanket he'd found in Sheen's barn.

She watched him gather sticks and twigs, finding enough to make a fire. Without the comfort of his arms, she felt chilled to the bone. She hugged herself to quell the shivers.

"We'll have a small fire. Not enough to attract attention, but enough to keep warm."

"Is someone after us?"

Crouched down, setting small branches and brush ablaze, he nodded. "This is Crow land. When game is scarce, the Sioux, even the Cheyenne, get brave enough to invade the Crow's territory. 'Course all three tribes are enemies. Sometimes they just want to count coup."

Another tremble shook her. "I've traded with the Kootenai. They'd do us no harm."

"I guess the Kootenai are what you'd call tame Indians. Now, you take the Crow, Sioux, Cheyenne—they're all warriors from the first slap on their bare bottoms."

"You don't like the Indians very much, do you, Mr.

Tanner."

Guthrie rose and eyed her carefully. As he approached, there was menace in his gaze. "Do you...like them?"

"I-I, well, yes. The ones I know call me *wakuntanka.* We trade and then they leave me in peace. Unlike *civilized* people."

His gray-blue eyes lit with curiosity, making them appear almost silver in the moonlight. "*Wakuntanka...*I suppose you know what that means?"

"I haven't learned their language. We communicate mostly in gestures."

"And you've never had any problems with the Crow or the Sioux?"

"None." Her voice was quiet. "I suppose you have a theory about that?"

"Indians, doesn't matter which tribe, wouldn't dare cause problems for a *wakuntanka*. In fact, they would treat her with great respect for fear of provoking her wrath."

She folded her arms and walked closer to the fire. A small heat wafted up, barely enough to penetrate her thick coat. "Why would they fear me?" she whispered. In the depths of her soul she guessed the answer, but she wanted to hear him say the words.

Guthrie stood by her side, watching the flames. "Because *wakuntanka* means *witch woman.*"

He kept his gaze fastened on the burning embers, squinting away smoke that billowed up from the slight wind shift. "Private O'Hanlon said you were a witch; he heard it from your peddler friend, Tatum. And now you've confessed Indians call you 'witch woman.' "

"I've confessed no such thing. How was I to know

what they were calling me?"

He didn't answer, and she felt the withdrawal of his energy. He blinked several times as if forcing himself to concentrate.

From his profile, she watched the tight clench of his jaw. "Is that why you kidnapped me? Because you believe I am a witch?"

He nodded.

"And you think I have some kind of mystical powers?"

He nodded again.

She wondered if she should ask—wondered what his reaction might be if she asked about Abigail. Hesitating, her words were soft. "Who is Abigail?"

Guthrie turned to face her, his blue eyes narrowing to silvery slits. "How do you know her name?"

Sheen bit down hard on her lip. She debated sharing anything about her personal life with him. She didn't trust this man knowing about her past, and her dubious future. "Sometimes, I hear voices, inside my head. Sometimes, these voices tell me their names. D-did you know Abigail?"

Guthrie seemed startled for a moment before he turned away from her and peered again into the flickering flames.

Sheen knew the tears in his soul, and the murderous rage in his heart. Guthrie Tanner was a man living in his own personal hell. The sound of it repeated in her mind, making her hate the ability of second sight that was both a gift and a curse.

"Can't talk about her just yet." Guthrie crouched once again and added a few more small branches onto the fire. "That'll do for the night."

Sheen watched the firelight. Guthrie laid out his woolen blanket. "Only a few hours before daybreak. Might as well get some sleep."

Sheen untied the knot in her quilt and removed the clothing she'd brought along. She stuffed them inside one of the gunny sacks Guthrie had set atop a rock, and then laid the quilt on the opposite side of the fire. She waited, uncertain of being alone with this man.

He jerked the coverlet from the ground and laid it next to his blanket. She watched him pat the area where she was to lie, next to him. "Nights get cold. You'll freeze," he warned, as if guessing at her thought to sleep away from him on the cold hard ground.

He stretched out and covered himself with half the blanket. "Come to bed. You need rest. I don't need you falling out of the saddle for lack of sleep."

Sheen moved slowly, watching him.

Judging by the quirk of his lips, he seemed amused at her discomfort. "Sleep, Miss O'Reilly. Don't worry. I'll stay on my side of the blanket."

She drew in a deep breath, wondering if she could trust him. At least this time he hadn't called her *witch*.

"I prefer you call me Sheen."

Wind kicked up, blowing frigid air into her face. It was enough to get her feet moving faster to the quilt's inviting warmth.

"Sheen?"

"Yes?"

"Don't ever try to run away from me."

She pulled the quilt over her nose so that only her eyes showed. "What if I do?"

"Trust me, you won't like the consequences."

There was a hint of mockery in his voice that

58

accompanied the threat, and Sheen didn't quite know what to make of him.

"You are a puzzle, Mr. Tanner. First you say you won't harm me, then you threaten me."

Guthrie closed his eyes before settling the hat over his face and scrunching deeper inside the blanket.

She lay awake for long minutes. The soft sounds of Guthrie's breathing comforted her somehow. Still damp from the snow, and wrapped in her woolen coat and quilt, she told herself she should be terrified. Oddly, she didn't feel frightened at the moment.

Guthrie rolled to his side, his arm draped over her body, resting loosely against her waist. She wondered if it was instinct that caused him to draw her against his chest. His size alone should worry her. With her diminutive frame she was no match for him if he decided to take liberties with her.

She didn't know exactly why, but she trusted him. She'd been duped by people all her life and now had little use for placing faith in humans anymore. But with him, this man who'd kidnapped her, she felt protected and safe.

She questioned the way of it and decided perhaps it was because no other options were available to her.

A cold wind bit the air, and Sheen snuggled down farther into the quilt, taking what comfort she could, accidently bumping Guthrie with her backside. Realizing she'd touched his male parts, she let out a horrified little gasp.

Her body stiffened. She listened to the soft grunt from the depths of his slumber, thankful she hadn't fully disturbed him. After long moments, her rigid position and the damp cold from the ground caused her limbs to ache.

Trying not to squirm, yet seeking a more comfortable position, Sheen wriggled her body.

"Keep still, Miss O'Reilly," he warned, his voice a deep rasp of a whisper. "Don't move like that."

"Oh," she whispered back, realizing she had awakened him, if he'd been sleeping at all. She rolled over to face him, an apology on her lips.

Moving was a mistake, to turn, to look into Guthrie's narrowed, sleep-hazed eyes. To witness the shadows of his face, sharp, sculptured and strong. Sheen's heart raced from looking at him so close up.

Her only intimacy with a man had happened at the age of thirteen when she'd been trapped in the woods by a preacher's eighteen-year-old son. He'd pinned her against a tree, pinched her breasts until they hurt, and slobbered against her mouth. That kiss had sparked no desire, no yearning, and no sensations except revulsion.

He'd run his hand up her dress, tugging at the waist of her pantaloons, and she'd lashed out, leaving deep, bloody tracks along his cheek where she'd gouged the flesh with her fingernails.

And then she and her father had fled to another town.

"I'm sorry, Mr. Tanner. I didn't mean to wake—"

A low rumble erupted from his throat. "Don't talk. Go to sleep."

His eyes wide open now, Sheen looked her fill, and in the darkness she saw that spark of silvery blue again. Her throat caught, a hitch of meaningless sound. "The ground is hard, and I'm cold," she explained.

His gaze slid to her mouth. The tip of her tongue dampened her lips. He touched his finger to the line of her jaw and murmured, "You want comfort? I can manage that, heat up both our bodies real good. Just keep wiggling against me like you're doing and I'll make you hotter than a misfired pistol."

Sheen stared into his eyes, and then bowed her head just a little, trying to get hold of her emotions, to make what was happening between them an aberration to be dismissed, a futile thing, like a butterfly trying to stuff itself back inside its cocoon.

Her voice reduced to an emphatic whisper. "You wouldn't dare."

"Don't ever dare me, Miss O'Reilly. You'll be sorry you did. Then again," he added, his voice deepened to a husky purr, "maybe you'd like a little warming up."

She wriggled away, and rolled to her side, far from the comfort of his arms, relying solely on the thickness of the quilt to see her through the night. "Don't flatter yourself, Mr. Tanner."

She was foolish to pretend she hadn't just imagined what it would be like to kiss him. She was human, after all.

****

Guthrie slept for a time, his slumber light, halfway between restful and alert. Over the past year he'd learned to sleep with one eye nearly open; a matter of survival.

Deep inside, he ached as he'd never ached before. Something about Sheen, something so rare he couldn't define, a spirit that refused to be quashed or seduced, made him want her more. A year without bedding a woman threatened to spin his urges out of control.

A nostalgic smile curved his lips as he tried to

conjure up images of his dear Abigail. He wanted to remember the way her hair smelled, the way her hips swayed when she walked, the way she tasted when he caressed her lips.

Time was taking its toll—eroding the pictures he'd thought were permanently tattooed in his mind. A slice of guilt knifed through him.

Folding his hands behind his head and crossing his boots at the ankles, he gazed morosely at the shy moon peeking through the murky sky.

A fist of sorrow squeezed at his gut. Abigail was gone. Deep in his heart where love had once bloomed, now emptiness ruled.

Chapter Six

Sheen woke with a start. Something was amiss. She felt the gnawing truth of it deep down in her bones even before she realized Guthrie was no longer sleeping beside her.

She pushed from her warm nest and rose to a cloudy dawn, the bite in the air slightly lessened from yesterday's reluctant sun. Surveying their little campsite, she was relieved to find the horses still hobbled and standing nearby. Yet, as she walked the slight perimeter, there was no sign of Guthrie anywhere.

"Mr. Tanner?" She moved past the pinto mare and away from the thicket of shrubs surrounding her. "Guthrie Tanner," she called again, her attention darting around full circle, hoping to find him.

Then she heard the sounds. Scuffling sounds, voices low and menacing, one of them sounding distinctly like Guthrie's. She headed toward the ruckus, hugging her coat to her chest, fearful of what she might find as the clouded light helped guide her; and not fifty yards from where she slept, she found Guthrie, fending off two bronzed men, their bodies of near equal breadth and strength.

Sheen held back her alarm with a hand to her mouth. Guthrie fought both men, his fists bloodied, his face enraged as the taller man came at him with a knife, while the broader one with beefy hands grabbed Guthrie from behind. Guthrie managed to slip from the man's grip, punched him in the gut, and sidestepped the brave with the blade.

Fists flew fast and furious. The Indian grunted and growled at Guthrie, but dogged him like a predator stalking prey. Sheen's heart raced with dread. The taller brave lurched forward, the knife angled toward his enemy's heart, but Guthrie jumped to one side in the nick of time.

Sheen knew Guthrie was in trouble. Without a knife of his own, the two warriors would surely wear him down until they killed him.

Guthrie danced to one side. The blade flashed past his cheek in a vicious arc.

A weapon, she needed a weapon. A glance showed an empty holster hung from Guthrie's waist. She did a quick scan of the brush, hoping to spot his revolver. It must have been knocked from his hand somehow, because Sheen believed he'd never have relinquished his weapon otherwise.

She knew she had to do something—anything. It was better to die fighting than grovel before the enemy. There was no backing down. Guthrie was losing ground, the scar-faced man with the knife seeming to have the better advantage. She'd already seen him swipe at Guthrie's arm, slicing through the thick buffalo-hide coat. She prayed the slash hadn't broken the flesh. Without wasting another second, she intuitively called upon the spirits of her mother and grandmother. *You've always said you were near if I needed you. I need you—now!*

Ten seconds passed, or perhaps twenty. And then

the wooded glen echoed with screams. Brief, terrible, and unmistakable, the sound cut through the bright early morning like the most awful of nightmares.

Sheen clapped her hands over her ears, her memory shooting into overdrive. Images flashed in her eyes, pictures of other times, darker places, and cruel deaths.

Instinctively, she lifted her arms high, and the surge of power that passed over her made her feel almost weightless.

"Oh, by all that is holy!" She gasped at the sight that met her eyes. A gush of blood rolled from the back of one warrior's head, felling him to the ground. An unerring sense of power washed over her. The mare had done her bidding as if she'd heard Sheen's thoughts.

The pinto whinnied, then planted all four feet in the warrior's back, while the scar-faced brave stared in horror. He dropped the knife and turned to run as if he'd willed his feet to take flight.

Fearful for a moment, Sheen lowered her eyes, but silently commanded the horse to stand. She sucked in a breath; she did not understand what she'd just discovered about her gift but gave thanks to the spirits of her mother and grandmother.

Guthrie staggered back for a moment. He held the knife in his right hand, and drew back and pushed all his weight into the throw. Sheen watched the weapon find its mark as it sank deep between the man's shoulder blades, crumpling him like a wet rag.

And then there was silence.

****

Guthrie imitated granite. He did not breathe. He did not twitch. The seconds became a minute. The minute became two, until he drew several shallow breaths. In spite of the cool air, perspiration beaded his face and trickled into his eyes.

He slashed a sleeved arm across his face to wipe away the sweat. Stalking forward, he pointed at Sheen, the tip of his finger almost touching her nose. "I don't know what the hell just happened, but you have some explaining to do, lady."

She summoned a dry smile for him. "Shouldn't we leave this place, in case those two have friends?"

"Maybe you can conjure up where my shooter landed, *witch*. That one"—he nodded toward the taller of the two dead warriors—"caught me by surprise and knocked it from my hand."

Guthrie sighed, blowing out his breath in a frustrated rush. He turned in a circle, searching the brush for sign of his weapon.

His features clouded when Sheen pointed. "It doesn't take a witch to find what's under your nose."

Other than the screech of a hawk to the east, the forest was quiet. A carpet of pine needles muffled every step. Not a single leaf stirred as Guthrie stepped to where the Colt .45 rested beneath a bush.

He plucked the pistol from the ground, checked the barrel, and, satisfied no dirt clogged it, holstered the firearm.

As Sheen turned to leave the gruesome scene, Guthrie grabbed her arm and jerked her forward. "You try any of your hocus-pocus on me, and I won't hesitate to use this." His free hand lifted the pistol butt from the holster to emphasize the seriousness of his warning.

She pulled from his grip and stood back to look into his face. "You *are* relentless, aren't you?"

"About finding the men who killed my wife and

stole my daughter? Yeah. About you using your magic to help me locate those red devils and bring my daughter home—" His voice faltered.

She stared at him. "Tell me about Abigail."

He bit out the words. "I don't want to talk about her. Not yet."

"Then I'm not budging from this spot until you tell me more clearly what you want from me."

Guthrie laughed, loudly. "You are my prisoner, and you will do as I command. And right now, I command you to get your trappings together so we can ride out of here, pronto."

She didn't answer, though he saw her eyes flicker with uncertainty. An awkward silence fell between them.

In the soft morning light, Sheen looked striking. Guthrie studied her as one would study a complex painting with color and layers he'd never explored. Not even with Abigail. This he didn't understand. He wanted to know more.

The sarcasm in his voice was evident. "The mare was hobbled. How did she get loose?"

Sheen sputtered over her shoulder as she tromped back to camp. "How should I know? Maybe you didn't make the knot tight enough."

He walked the few feet to the camp to find Sheen huddled over the fire, blowing into the embers. In the aftermath of the fracas, Guthrie knew he'd overreacted. "If it's coffee you're thinking to make, there's no time. Those were Crow warriors. Their friends won't take kindly to finding members of their tribe dead. The longer we linger here, the more we put ourselves in danger."

"You committed murder. Aren't you the least bit affected?"

He scowled at her. "A judge and jury would call it self-defense. 'Sides, if those men had scalped me they'd be singing their victory song, not to speak of what they'd do to you."

Without a word, Sheen dusted off the front of her coat.

Guthrie made haste in getting the horses bridled and saddled while Sheen gathered her belongings inside the quilt as she'd done the night before.

As much as he wanted a smoke, Guthrie refrained from rolling a cigarette. Experience had taught him that Indians possessed a keen sense of smell and could trail a white man by the faintest scent of tobacco.

He used the toe of his boot to scatter the ashes from the fire, then a pocket knife to cut brush to sweep away evidence of his and Sheen's boot prints.

It was common knowledge that other tribes often wandered into Crow territory with the expectations of counting coup. But rapping the enemy on the shoulder or the head with a war cudgel wasn't the same as killing. With a little luck, Guthrie hoped to use that to his advantage.

Sheen carried her bundle to where the placid mare stood and, after hitching the loop over the saddle horn, curled her arms behind her mass of ginger-colored hair and stretched. The wool coat pulled tight against her chest. Guthrie swore he could see her breasts strain against the fabric. It caused his dry mouth to go even drier and his mood to grow even darker.

"Time to head out, Miss O'Reilly. Our lives depend on how many miles we can put between ourselves and those dead bodies."

Sheen twisted around as she grabbed the saddle horn. They were face to face. Their noses nearly touching. "Now that you've killed two of their own, they won't give up, will they?"

"If we stand here jawin', they'll catch us sooner than later."

His features clouded. His mood darkened further when he swung into the saddle. As soon as Guthrie settled, the sorrel snorted and stomped and hunched against the man's weight.

Guthrie reached forward and laid a resounding slap against the gelding on the neck. "Settle down, you worthless bag of bones."

The horse flicked its ears and tossed its head as a final token of annoyance and was still.

He cursed the peevish gelding. The jarring ache in his shoulder served as a grim reminder of the injury he'd suffered a few months earlier and now aggravated in a near-death battle with an enemy he hated.

****

Sheen watched the long-legged foal nurse and spoke to it in gentle tones. "'Tis a fine stallion you'll grow into, and make your mama proud, but be a good lad, Skye, and finish your breakfast later. We must go now."

She bit back the smile that threatened to turn into a full-blown grin when Guthrie's sorrel once again tried to unseat him. A less experienced horseman would have landed on his arse. And it would have served him right, she mused.

"A gentleman would give a lady a boost."

When he ignored her, she led the mare to a fallen

log and used it as a stepping stool to climb into the saddle.

"It seems uncivil not to bury the dead."

Annoyed at his lack of response, she huffed, "Mr. Tanner, are you listening?"

"Your words are like bee stings. No time to bury 'em."

She knew his growled response held considerable truth. Besides, their exchanges were stressful enough. This whole situation with Guthrie, and now with the awareness of a power she'd never known she possessed, Sheen felt as if she were being drawn into a surreal world.

She bit her lip and looked to the sky for stability. As much as she hated her gifts, she could not deny them.

She clucked the mare forward. "You said we were going to the powder. What did you mean—the powder?"

"Powder River country." He pointed.

She gazed off in the distance toward the mountains, then at the broad back of the man who'd tied the reins of her pinto to the tail of his horse.

Stark daylight revealed an uncommonly tall man, tall enough to make the gelding he rode appear small. Guthrie Tanner had the legs of a man who'd spent many hours in the saddle, long and lean, with thighs that looked strong enough to crush a man's head between them.

Sheen's breath caught in her chest, and she squared her shoulders.

"I do not mean to nag, Mr. Tanner, but you've kidnapped me, you've endangered my life, and you've made vile accusations against me. I have a right to know what it is you want of me."

"Name's Guthrie. Mr. Tanner died a long time ago. And you're right...about the naggin'."

Guthrie slapped his legs against the sorrel. Instantly the gelding spurted into a gallop, racing across the plain.

Sheen let out a little shriek. The pinto's unexpected burst of speed toppled Sheen sideways. She clutched the saddle horn and righted herself, bouncing up and down with the bone-jarring gallop.

She envied Guthrie. With every surging stride, his supple spine rolled in rhythm with his horse as if the two were one, his arms at his sides, his shoulders square and facing straight ahead as his strong legs hugged the horse's sides. Not a hint of light shone between his buttocks and his mount. His boots swayed to the beat of the gelding's pounding gait as horse and rider raced along, churning up clods of dried grass with grace, agility, and power.

Sheen drew in a deep breath, wanting to hold it inside her chest for a moment. She envied his horsemanship. By all that was holy, if he kept up their current pace, she feared all her teeth would rattle loose and fall from her mouth. Not to speak of the bruises on her backside from the brutal pounding against the saddle.

****

Satisfied that he'd put enough distance between the dead Indians and himself and Sheen, yet risking no chances of their safety, Guthrie rode on without stopping until a blood-red sun balanced on the brink of the world.

Glancing over his shoulder, a pang of guilt ratcheted in his chest. He could only imagine the brutal beating the girl was experiencing. Her arms flapped like a ruffled hen, she bounced up and down in the saddle high enough for daylight to shine through. Her muscles would scream with pain once they settled for the night. He regretted not having a bottle of horse liniment to rub her down.

A languid heat rolled up from his belly, melting what was left of his indifference toward the young woman. A sensation he hadn't experienced in quite a while.

Aggravated at his train of thought, he slapped his legs against the gelding's sides, calling for more speed.

He barely heard the words before the wind whipped them away. "Mr. Tanner...Guthrie...please, you must stop. You are running the horses into the ground. Whatever demons are chasing you, we cannot outrun them this way."

A bitter taste of disgust rose in the back of his throat. Sheen had asked for mercy, not for herself, but for the horses. It was not his normal nature to punish animals. He slowed the pace, and rode for another hour before he clucked the sorrel down into a hollow.

Chapter Seven

Sheen's legs wobbled. She clung to the stirrup to keep from collapsing to the ground. She felt herself turn faint and sick with exhaustion, lack of food, and a day of hard riding. With effort, she forced herself to stand straight.

The day was spent and only a few lost tufts of cottony clouds floated in the wide sky.

The mare whinnied and champed at the bit. Sheen leaned her head against the pinto's sweaty shoulder. "I know, Moon, we're both tired and in need of a good feed."

With deft fingers, she loosened the cinch strap and pulled the saddle from Moon's back. Exhaustion and the weight of the encumbrance sapped the little remaining strength from Sheen's body. Her legs buckled, landing her in a sitting position.

Blue blazes, her sore rump ached even more.

Dusk was falling, with the last rays of sunlight filtering through the canopy of aspens, the air cold and dampened from rotting timber.

She shoved the saddle to one side and lay back on the ground, allowing the tiredness to weep through her bones.

****

The darkness was welcomed. Not even the Crow could track at night. Guthrie lifted the sleeping woman and cradled her against his chest. Shards of moonlight reflected across her face. Witch or not, Sheen O'Reilly was a remarkably attractive woman. High eyebrows accented wide-set eyes and an aquiline nose. Full cheeks framed lips as ripe as cherries.

He carried her to the small fire and gently laid her on top of the quilt. He unbuttoned her coat and eased the lapels apart. Melon-sized breasts rose and fell gently, bulging the faded fabric of her dress.

While she slept, he tended the horses, double-checking the hobbles on the mare. Puzzlement caused him to lift his shoulders and let them fall. He was certain he'd secured the mare their first night of riding. Recalling how Moon had reared and stomped the Indian to death mystified Guthrie. His first thought—how did she get free of the hobbles? The next—how would a horse know to attack in such a way?

Back in South Carolina, on the plantation, he'd heard the whispers about the darkies practicing voodoo. Though still doubtful about witchcraft, Guthrie supposed there was a bit of truth in Private O'Hanlon's fantasy about fairy witches.

His stomach rumbled, a reminder of the last time he'd eaten. He set the bacon to frying, sliced two pieces of bread from the loaf, and added a film of chokeberry preserves. Not knowing how long their food cache would be needed, he figured it best to stretch it as long as possible.

Longing for a shot of smooth bourbon to lace the Arbuckle, he removed a coffeepot and filled it with ground coffee and water, then set the pot on a flat rock he'd placed in the fire.

He ran a hand across his face. Heaven help him,

why did Sheen have to look the way she did? The ache in his loins was more than just the cold. It was lust, pure and simple.

He walked to her and, squatting, nudged her shoulder. Despite that ache, at this point all he wanted was to fill his belly and get a few undisturbed hours of shuteye.

Sheen sat up. Her lips parted and a gasp slipped past. "Oh, I need to see to Moon and the colt."

"They're taken care of." He shoved the plate of fried bacon strips and bread toward her. The meat sizzled on the plate, and its rich smell filled the air.

"Here, eat." He placed a steaming cup of coffee next to her.

An awkward silence fell between them. The fire crackled, burning orange and blue. In the soft light, Sheen looked delicate and highly refined.

"After witnessing the mare strike a man down dead, my gut tells me it was no coincidence. Will you finally admit you are a witch?"

She wrapped her hands around the cup of steaming coffee and sipped. It was as if she were weighing her answer.

Impatient for a response, he tried to gentle his voice. "Sheen, what is it you fear? If you are one, admit it. I won't think less of you."

Her voice shook. She spoke so softly he had to lean close to hear her reply. "I don't know what I am. I've never met a witch. I've no one to ask. I don't know what I...what they can do."

She tossed the remains of the bitter coffee into the fire. Sparks danced skyward and hot embers sizzled. Her hands balled into fists, and her shoulders started to shake.

Guthrie felt her anguish. Damnation. She was scared. Scared to admit she had powers she didn't know what to do with and afraid to admit what she was. Worse, he'd added to her fear.

He rose and offered his hand. "I wasn't always a bastard."

Sheen did not take his hand. She stared into his face, her eyes unreadable.

Guthrie lowered his arm. "I guess we all have our secrets."

"I've done everything I can to break this curse. Restless ghosts and bad memories follow me everywhere I go."

His nod was tacit, as if he understood. The strain and the sorrow seemed to swallow her up.

He looked into Sheen's strange cat-like eyes—eyes that seemed to look deep into his soul. Although she and Abigail looked nothing alike, the memory of his wife pierced his heart. "You're not the only one who lives with ghosts, Sheen. We all have them."

"Tell me about Abigail."

The mention of her name caused a pain in his chest that was hardly bearable. "I've asked you before—how do you know my wife's name?"

Sheen shrugged. "You must have spoken it, else how would I know?"

He looked at her without emotion. He inspected her hair, her coloring, and her face. She flushed as his eyes went over her figure.

She gathered her skirt and with quick strides walked to where the pinto mare stood hobbled.

In one long-legged bound, Guthrie stepped over the

small campfire. He grabbed Sheen and spun her around. "Where the hell do you think you're going?"

She jerked against the iron grip on her arm. "I hate the way you treat me, and your loathsome accusations. I don't want to be here with you."

She whirled in his grasp and left him with a look of surprise on his face as the coat slid over her arms, freeing her from his clutches.

He thrust his hand forward and grabbed the bodice of her dress. "Come back here."

As she turned to flee, the sound of ripping material surprised both of them.

"No, Guthrie, please don't." Her hands tried to hold the ruined collar high enough to cover her neck as she sagged to her knees.

He hesitated as he saw what she attempted to conceal, then gritted his teeth as he hauled her to a standing position and pulled her toward the firelight. He exhaled in anger.

"Who did this to you?" Burning with rage, he shook Sheen by the shoulders. His voice rasped, "Answer me, girl! Who did this?"

A hideous mass of blackened, puckered flesh ringed Sheen's neck. His blood turned cold. Guthrie had witnessed hangings when the Yankees raided his father's plantation in South Carolina. He'd seen the gruesome effects of a noose cutting deep into the flesh.

Fury flared in Guthrie's soul. He lifted the coat from the ground and brushed it free of dirt and leaves, then draped the garment around Sheen's shoulders. He tried to hold her close. She drew back.

His gaze met hers. "My God, Sheen. Tell me."

She gulped back a sob.

****

Sheen, breathing hard sank to the ground. She fingered the top button of her coat, closed now to hide the rope burn around her neck. She admonished herself to tell Guthrie the truth about her gift and be done with it.

Her voice quavered. "Are you in a mind to listen without judging me?"

Guthrie eased down to the ground. He uncorked the canteen and poured water into the coffeepot, setting it on a flat rock next to the fire. "Tell me all of it, from the beginning. I need to understand who you really are and why anyone would want to put a noose around your neck."

She rolled the tension from her shoulders and folded her hands in her lap. Her words rushed out now, popping like hail on a rooftop.

"'Tis true. I was cursed with the gift of second sight. It comes from my mother and her mother, and further beyond. Sometimes I see what has happened to people...horrible things, and I hear their voices.

"When I was but a wee child of three years, my mother was burned as a witch. But nay, my father said she was hated because of her knowledge of herbs and healing.

"My mother's dying wish was for my father to leave Ireland, go where no one would know about me, where I would be free from harm." She had to take a breath to settle herself. "He bought passage on a ship bound for America. One day, while on deck, I pointed to the lookout in the crow's nest and told father the wind would kill the man. Father admonished me, severely. He said I was to never speak of such things, ever, to anyone. He also said people would misunderstand my gift as a thing of evil.

"Da was never cruel, but that day he shook me until my teeth rattled. I knew he feared people would think me possessed of the devil. I was only four years old and didn't realize how afraid my da was for me, not until—"

Her voice trailed off. The image of her father hanging from a tree stilled her. She bit her lip and looked at the sky for stability.

Guthrie poured steaming water over tea leaves, and handed the cup to Sheen. "Did it—did the wind kill the man?"

She had already sensed that though he didn't want to ask the question about the sailor's fate there was a perverse need to know.

Guilt, long tucked away, circled in her belly and threatened to cut off her breath. She nodded. "Within the hour and without warning, the skies darkened and the wind screamed like banshees. That's when a huge water spout settled over the crow's nest. One minute the sailor was there, and the next minute he was sucked away, never to be seen again.

"Passengers panicked, and there were accusations of the ship being cursed."

Realizing she'd begun to raise her voice, she heaved in a deep breath. "When the ship landed in Massachusetts, Father decided Boston was a good place to settle. He plied his trade as a cobbler. For the most part, we were happy. I learned to live with my nightmares, and soon forgot the horrible visions of my mother's murder."

Sheen fell silent, and used the silence to gear up for

the rest. Guthrie said nothing for a moment, just sat there watching her.

He gave her an easy smile, but behind it she saw anger and frustration. Most of all she saw bitter unhappiness.

No maneuver he could have devised, no plan he could have calculated, could have hit her weakness more effectively.

"Thinking about Abigail and Rachel makes you sad. Tell me about them." She didn't touch him. The connection tended to be too close with physical contact

Sheen watched the shield go up. He stood, stalked away from the campfire, then back. He removed his hat and scrubbed a hand through his hair. She felt his agitation. He settled the hat back on his head.

He sucked in a deep breath as he pointed a finger at her. "Is that how it works, you just crack open a mind and take a peek at what's inside?"

She forced herself to relax. "No, that would be rude."

He harrumphed and dropped back to the ground. "Damn, what I wouldn't give for a double shot of whiskey right now." He reached for the coffeepot.

Sheen shouted, "Don't, you'll burn—" The warning came too late. He'd already gripped the hot handle with his bare hand.

Guthrie yowled and cursed. "I don't recall inviting you to read my mind."

"I don't read minds." She gripped her fingers together—taut wires, white at the knuckles. She let out a breath to relieve the pressure in her chest, and stared straight ahead. "It's more like reading feelings. I've learned to block it out, because it's not pleasant.

Whatever you may think, I hate having other people's emotions pounding inside my head, my heart, interrupting my life."

She glanced away, then back at him. "I'm sorry for intruding on your thoughts."

"Forget it. Never had anyone peek inside my mind before. Set me on edge, that's all."

"I've lived with mistrust all my life."

"Is that why you live alone on the prairie?"

"There are always people who want to take advantage of my gifts, use them to their benefit. Then those same people have questions and doubts that lead to resentment and distrust."

She shifted, leaning on her crutch of bitterness to face him. "I am what I am, and I can't change it. I know how to cope and how to manage, alone. I don't want or expect anyone to love me. I don't need anyone, either. As difficult as it's been, I've learned to accept my life just the way it is, and I don't give a tinker's arse if you or anyone else doesn't."

Sheen pushed from the ground and walked to the gunny sack that held their cache of food. She reached inside a cloth bag and withdrew a handful of flour, then returned to the fire. "Give me your hand."

His reluctance annoyed her even more. "I've no magic potion, if that's what you fear. 'Tis plain flour...see?" She opened her palm to reveal the white powdery grain.

"My ma used bacon grease for burns."

"Aye, and it made a large blister that hurt for days, did it not?"

She read the question in his eyes as he nodded. She gently patted the seared skin with the fine powder, then ripped a strip from her petticoat to wrap around his hand. "The flour will draw the moisture from the wound and create a paste. Your hand will be healed by the morrow. You'll see."

"How do you know this stuff?"

Sheen rocked back on her knees. She shrugged her shoulders. "'Tisn't magic, as you're thinking." She offered a thin smile. "Only common sense. Grease is for frying. Flour is for coating."

His eyes were on her fully now, and he beseeched her for honesty. He remained quiet for a time. When he spoke, his voice was filled with sincerity.

"I don't mind making you nervous, but I do mind scaring you."

"If I were afraid of you, I wouldn't be here." The wind flowed over her face, through her hair. "I knew you were coming. Your mind was closed, so I didn't know what it was you wanted of me. Why didn't you ask for my help instead of forcing me to come with you?"

"Man has his pride, Sheen."

She turned her head just a little, studied him with a sidelong glance. Her heart ached at the misery gnawing through his soul.

"Stop blaming yourself, Guthrie. What happened to Abigail and Rachel isn't your fault."

He grabbed her shoulders and squeezed. Sheen felt the vise-like grip bruising her flesh. She knew he couldn't bear her words.

"I've never hit a woman, and I'm not about to start now." She watched as he gathered his composure; heard his long-suffering sigh. "Get the hell out of my mind and stay out."

She knew she should be furious. Instead, she calmly walked to where the horses stood hobbled. With deft fingers she removed the straps from the mare's legs.

Sheen grabbed a handful of mane and readied to swing her leg over the mare's back.

Guthrie bounded across the clearing to Sheen's side. "No, you don't." He scooped her into his arms.

Sheen bucked and fought. "Let me go."

He held on tighter, his arms locked around her. "Settle down, girl. It's pitch black. You want that mare of yours to step in a gopher hole?"

The truth of his words echoed inside her head. She nibbled on her lower lip. Guthrie stood too close for propriety. She breathed in the scent of his hair, his skin, that seemed to mingle with the smell of horse and leather.

"L-let me go."

He pulled her closer.

Sheen opened her mouth to cry out, and Guthrie shocked her by covering it with his own.

Chapter Eight

Sheen lifted her arms to push Guthrie away, but he was too strong for her. His mouth was hot and hard against her lips and she couldn't move, could not breathe. His warmth and the scent of his maleness enveloped her.

Against her will, her lips parted.

He pulled her even closer, wrapping his arms around her. His tongue entered her mouth, wet and warm and tasting of coffee.

Her mind screamed no, yet a part of her body was saying yes. Her mouth slacked. She stopped fighting him. The taste of him and the feel of his body molding to hers overcame her.

She had never tasted, never felt, anything so astonishing. Her skin leaped in reply.

Shocked by her own reaction, Sheen jerked back and Guthrie released her. She struck him hard in the face with her palm. "You ought to be ashamed of yourself," she accused heatedly. "I'll not be treated like a...a trollop."

A smile played on his sensuous lips. "You don't kiss like a trollop, Miss O'Reilly. More like an inexperienced school girl."

Sheen lifted her skirts, turned and huffed back to the campfire. She longed for the sanctity of her small but cozy bedroom.

Her breath came in great gulps. How dare he kiss her? First he'd accused her of being a witch, then kidnapped her, and now poked fun at her lack of kissing skills.

Unconsciously, her fingertips brushed her swollen lips as waves of heat washed through her. She swallowed against the constriction in her throat and tried to pretend that his lingering scent didn't cling to her skin and her coat.

Worse, she was shocked by her own behavior. A part of her had taken pleasure in the exhilaration. A part of her had enjoyed the passion of his kiss.

She was mortified by her response to Guthrie's mouth on hers. She grabbed her quilt, spread it before the fire, and lay on her bed, trembling as she cocooned herself inside the blanket. Her heart plummeted. She feared she'd never be the same after knowing this man.

****

Dawn hovered just below the horizon in a specter of pinks and grays. Pine needles covered the ground, crunching under Guthrie's boots as he walked along the trail. Ponderosa and jack pines lifted to a clouded sky, and from this distance the Powder River looked eerily dark and ominous.

He strode into camp, where red embers glowed low in the fire pit. He found Sheen covered to her chin with the quilt, fast asleep.

She'd exhausted herself, these past days of hard riding. His lips twitched at the sight. Her coppery hair framed her oval face, those soulful eyes rested closed as she made little sounds. She looked like a child right now, but a flash of memory struck and he recalled how she'd opened herself to his kiss.

Guthrie shoved the thought from his mind, bending low to add a few branches to the fire. Sheen stirred from the small noise and lifted her head, grabbing the quilt to her chest. "Guthrie?" she whispered softly.

"Go back to sleep, Sheen."

"The colt?"

"He's fine. Nursing."

With that, she nodded slightly, then lowered her head back onto the saddle that served as her pillow.

Guthrie took one last look at her and then lifted the frying pan to the fire, filling the iron skillet with thick slices of cured bacon.

He blew out a breath and suppressed a groan as the flames of his need quickly fanned through him. Damn, he thought, what he'd give for a shot of whiskey.

His gaze drifted over her face and flickered down her sleeping form. Hot shivers coursed the length of his body. He stabbed the slices of sizzling bacon and turned them over to brown on the other side.

****

Sheen thought her eyes were open. Someone watched the camp. No, not someone—the watcher wasn't human, but it was hungry. Her aura rose from the quilt and glanced down at her sleeping form.

Wake up, Sheen.

She pressed to read the intruder's mind. There was nothing for her to see. Its mind was closed to her, but the vision went on in spite of her distress. She saw herself, and felt the stark terror as she turned to warn Guthrie.

Wake up. Get up, now, Sheen.

Even as she heard the orders, Sheen realized she was lying on the ground and needed to open her eyes.

86

Seconds later the pine forest rocked to blood-curdling screams. Fully awake now, Sheen threw back the quilt and scrambled to her feet.

The horses snorted and plunged, threatening to break free of their hobbles. Another roar sent the animals into a frenzy.

Sheen shouted, "Guthrie."

Another roar reverberated in her ears.

The most enormous mountain lion she had ever seen leaped across the fire. The powerful cat's bulky frame was corded with rippling layers of solid sinew. Its rapier teeth flashed as they sank into Guthrie's shoulder.

Mesmerized, she watched his large hands grip the cat's throat. Guthrie yelled, "Sheen, get the rifle. Shoot, damn it."

Not wanting to risk missing the tawny monster and hitting Guthrie, she grabbed the iron skillet and reared it above her head, tossing sizzling bacon to the ground.

Screeching at the top of her lungs, "No! Get away from him," she brought the heavy pan down, landing a resounding blow on top of the mountain lion's head.

The cat let out a rumbling growl and twisted in midair to face Sheen, its lips drawn back to expose its horrid fangs, its thick tail twitching wildly. Its two front feet planted firmly on Guthrie's chest.

Sheen wielded the frying pan forward in both hands. Acting braver than she felt, she shouted, "Away, you brute!"

The mountain lion simply stared, its fetid breath filling Sheen's nostrils. Attempting to communicate with the animal, her own sea-green eyes met the cat's amber slits.

Be gone from this place. We mean you no harm.

Its head slowly turned, those baleful eyes fixed on Guthrie, and an ominous snarl grumbled from its thick throat.

Sheen never hesitated. The pan arced at the cat's head. Sliding off Guthrie, the beast dodged to the right. The pan missed. Snarling, the cat flattened, then leaped straight at her.

She barely heard Guthrie's cry, "Sheen."

The immense cat rammed into her chest, flinging her rearward. It felt as if she had been slammed into by a runaway freight wagon. The jolt of smashing onto the ground rivaled the impact.

Sheen froze. The cat's claws dug through her coat, and her skin pricked as if by a thousand stinging mosquitoes. She flinched when the blast from Guthrie's Colt .45 punched the air.

The cat squalled terribly before it bounded off and disappeared into the Ponderosa pine forest.

Sheen had dropped the frying pan and, sitting up, pressed a hand to her throat. "You saved my life," she said.

"And you saved mine," Guthrie noted. "I reckon that makes us even." He replaced the spent cartridge and spun the cylinder before snapping it shut.

"Do you think it'll come back?"

Holstering the revolver, he looked at her long and hard. "Not likely."

Her nerves were so frayed she felt she might scream at the slightest provocation. And though she already knew the question he was about to ask, she said, "Why are you looking at me like that?"

"You did it again, didn't you—used your magic."

In the distance a bird twittered, but otherwise the morning remained hauntingly silent.

Her gaze focused on the ground. "I've told you. I have no magic."

"Yeah, sure. I saw what I saw, not once, but twice." He jammed his hands into the pockets of his coat. "I better see to the horses. They're bound to be skittish, what with the gunfire, and the scent of a mountain lion."

To busy her trembling hands, Sheen grabbed the iron skillet and, using the hem of her coat, wiped it clean of dirt. She scoured the ground until she found the slices of bacon. Too dirty to rescue. She tossed them into the fire.

"Sheen, let it be. The coffee's unharmed. We both need a cup. Food can wait until later."

Her eyes met his, and her heart seemed to collide with her ribs. To cover her discomfort, she stabbed a slender finger at a dark stain on his right shoulder.

"Sit. I'll tend your wounds."

"No need." Guthrie moved toward the horses. "It's just a few nicks and scrapes."

"I'll be the judge of how bad off you are," she responded. "Now sit down."

Grinning, Guthrie did as she commanded. Until that moment he hadn't realized that his right shoulder was damp, or that his coat had been torn in a dozen other places.

"Take off your shirt."

"There's really no need for you to make all this fuss."

"Just do it," Sheen said testily, I don't want infection to set in because you're too mule-headed for

89

your own good."

Without further argument, he shucked off his coat and tugged at the torn buckskin shirt. There were three cuts on his shoulder and one at the base of his neck, several inches long. Fortunately, the buffalo-hide coat had prevented the cat's claws from gouging very deep. In all, nine slash marks dotted his chest and arms.

"I got off easy. Not nearly as bad as when I broke my collarbone."

She took his hand and unwrapped the soiled cloth. Then, using water from the canteen, she washed away the caked flour she had applied to his burned palm the night before.

Guthrie harrumphed when he saw no blister, no oozing burn. "Well, I'll be damned."

"You doubted me?"

He answered with a lopsided grin. The depths of his eyes were like a frozen pond and as impossible to fathom, the eyes of a man accustomed to hiding his inner feelings. His nose, broken, set, and allowed to mend between battles, now rested slightly off center from the rest of his features.

The morning's feeble light washed across his thick mane of hair heavily streaked with gleaming silver highlights.

Sheen hiked the hem of her dress to her knee, revealing creamy flesh and a bit of her thigh. She ripped at the hem, tearing off another strip of petticoat. She poured water from the canteen and, wetting the cloth, dabbed at his wounds, cleaning off every last drop of blood.

Guthrie leaned back. The damp cloth eased him, as did her touch. She rubbed gently, first the side of his neck, then his shoulder. A single small cut on his chest came next. She bent low, examining it.

Slabs of muscle rippled over his broad shoulders.

When she spoke, her voice was husky.

"You have so many muscles. I've helped deliver babies, but I've never before seen a man's body. Not even my father's."

"Keep touching like that and you'll see a lot more of me, Miss O'Reilly."

Sheen breathed hard, flushing scarlet and giving a little gasp as he ran hands up and down her arms.

The thought of seeing him naked heated her flesh. He was a powerfully built man, strong and broad. And her traitorous mind thought of other delights. What would it be like to lie with him? To bear his weight, not from horrific injury, but from unmeasured lust?

With the bleeding stopped but for minor seeping, Sheen gazed a moment at the manly hairs on his chest that curled every which way.

To cover her frustration, she rose to her feet. "The gash to your neck is rather deep."

"Where do you think you're going?" His words belied the pain he must have felt.

"To get the jar of honey. Since I have no needle and thread to stitch the wound, I'll swab the area with honey to ward off infection and then wrap your neck with a strip of clean petticoat."

He laughed, a low sound of wonderment, from his belly. *Witch.*

Though her back was to him as she walked toward the gunny sack hanging by a rope from a branch, she heard his thought and then shrugged as if it made no difference to her.

Chapter Nine

Guthrie drifted in and out of sleep, his conscious moments plagued by frightful nightmares. The lifeless face of his wife, mingled with the hangings of father and uncles when the Yankees raided the family's plantation, destroyed hope of a restful slumber. Then Rachel, his daughter with her mop of unruly blond curls, flashed through his mind just as vividly. The dream wrestled away any chance for solace as the child beseeched him, with blue eyes that matched his own, when he'd hugged her before going off to gather strays and herd them back to the ranch.

Don't be late, Daddy. You promised to tell me a story.

Our little Miss has spoken, Guthrie. Fried prairie hen for supper. He'd hugged his wife and then his daughter.

Guthrie had promised. But gathering the stray longhorns had taken longer than he'd imagined. The sun had set and the night creepers were singing their songs by the time he'd pushed the cattle toward the main herd and swung his buckskin gelding toward the small three-room house. He knew Abigail would fuss because supper was cold, and Rachel would already be asleep.

He thrashed in his bedroll, tossing back and forth as the nightmares shook him. "No, no, Abigail. Rachel,

Rachel," he called out wildly.

Someone touched him. He felt the steady coolness of her hands on his forehead. Guthrie heard her tranquil voice, an angel's voice humming gently in his ears, the melodious song with words he didn't understand, flowing soft as a peaceful river.

Guthrie surrendered.

He slept.

****

Sheen lay awake nights tending to Guthrie's bouts of fever, succumbing to sleep in the wee hours of the morning. His fever, she knew, had less to do with the physical wounds caused by the mountain lion and more to do with the emotional injuries to his conscience.

She slept at peace only when Guthrie was at peace, and when he woke, burning up, his skin raging with heat, she cooled him with water she'd collected from a nearby brook. To help calm him, she fed him spoonfuls of the honey wine she'd kept secreted in her saddlebag. And she sang to him, the same nighttime lullabies her father had crooned to her when she was a child.

She kept her vigil by his side, watching him sleep under the buffalo-hide coat. She listened to his incoherent ranting and wept because, like Guthrie, she too had experienced soul-wrenching hurt.

On the third day, Sheen had exhausted herself.

"Wake up, Guthrie," she said with a heavy sigh. "We need to leave this place."

She had water from the stream, and she'd gathered enough small branches and twigs to keep the fire going. Though she had eaten a little, the two loaves of bread had gone stale, and the few potatoes she'd stuffed inside the gunny sack had sprouted eyes. There was enough bacon to last one more day. She was thankful for the chilly air. At least the cold kept weevils from hatching and spoiling the small sack of flour.

Each day she had removed the hobbles and led the horses to the stream to drink and then out to the fringes of the forest so they could graze.

And she listened, always, for the sounds of intruders—both human and animal.

After a short nap, Sheen rose, feeling refreshed except for the grumble in her stomach. She patted the area as if notifying her insides she recognized the problem.

As she gave her situation some thought, she realized there was no one to stop her from mounting up and riding far away from this place. Who was there to stop her?

She made her plan. Leave a loaf of bread and half the potatoes for Guthrie, and since she wanted to travel light, she'd also leave the jar of honey, the strawberry preserves, and the remaining coffee.

If she could manage her way back to the homestead, she would rest for a day, collect the few coins she'd put by, and then ride the hundred miles to town. There she would purchase a stagecoach ticket to anyplace where she might live in peace.

With that in mind, Sheen set out to boil water for a quick bath. She'd been wearing the one clean dress she'd packed in her saddlebag. The other dress had seen better days, soiled and stained with blood and ripped in many places. She'd washed it with little result in removing the stains. She'd given slight care to her appearance, but even under these dire circumstances she'd done her best with what was at hand.

Sheen dared a quick look at Guthrie, still sleeping peacefully on the ground. She unbuttoned the dress and slipped it off her shoulders, then dipped a large piece she'd torn from the ruined petticoat into a pot of warm water. She longed for the warmth of her fireplace, and an allover bath in the large galvanized washtub she'd traded from old Mr. Tatum.

****

Soothing sweet sounds surrounded Guthrie. The song pleasing his ears was a call for him to wake and see the angelic face of the woman with the dulcet voice. He forced an eye open. Bright sun caused him to shut it.

The beautiful voice continued, and he opened both eyes, squinting now to adjust to the light. When he moved slightly, the gash on his neck rebelled and he attempted a curse, but his voice wasn't there.

His mouth was dry, parched like cured summer tobacco, and he realized he hadn't spoken for days. How long had he been here like this—unable to move, unable to speak—and where was he?

He lifted the heavy buffalo-hide coat, pushing it from his body. Then, with great care, he turned his head and slanted his body to peer at the source of the song.

There he saw a woman, more like a slip of a girl. Her back was to him, her hair falling like a long sheet of red satin, her skin the color of fresh cream.

Memories flooded in then, and it all came back to him. Private O'Hanlon had told him about a fairy doctor. Hoping to capitalize on her powers to help him find his daughter, he'd intruded on the girl's home and forced her to come with him.

He recalled his buckskin gelding falling on him and the months spent at Fort Smith recuperating from a broken collarbone and several fractured ribs, and then, remembering the mountain lion's attack, he reached up and touched the painful wound on his neck.

He took his eyes off the girl to survey the surroundings. His gelding and the pinto mare stood hobbled. The foal suckled its mother.

Guthrie felt weakness overcome him. He didn't like the feeling. He shifted his focus back to the thin girl, bathing by the fire, and that captivating voice.

It was Sheen.

She'd been the one to ease his pain with soothing melodies. She'd been the creature he'd imagined cooling his fever, bathing his body with tender touches.

She lifted her arms up, pouring water, rinsing away the lathering bubbles from the bundle of russet hair. Then, as if reading his thoughts, she turned ever so slightly and stopped humming.

In that instant, Guthrie caught sight of the slope of one breast, small yet perfect for her body. Round and full, with a rosy tip that lifted skyward.

His body stirred at the feminine image she portrayed. His groin tightened, and even through his fatigue his manhood stretched, growing to near full proportions. But when she moved again, turning her head around toward him, he quickly closed his eyes.

"Guthrie?" she called out, and he heard the thread of hope in her voice. She'd been alone caring for him all this time. She must have known he'd moved. Yes, she was a witch gifted with the second sight. She'd known he was watching.

He grunted a greeting, not trusting his voice to work properly.

"You're awake."

He opened his eyes. With her back still to him, she drew her arms through the sleeves of a dark green dress. Nimble fingers buttoned the front as she approached, her hair dripping wet and the dress clinging to her still-damp skin.

Those rare blue-green crystalline eyes watched him. He met her stare but let his gaze roam down a bit, noting the outline of her hips and legs. He knew now what lay beneath that garment, unlike the first time he'd seen her and thought her lacking in feminine assets. Good thing he was too damned weak to take advantage of his lusty yearnings.

She knelt beside him and touched a cool hand to his forehead. Tears filled her eyes. "Guthrie, thank God. Thank God."

He tried to clear his dry throat. "W-water." He spoke so weakly he barely recognized his own voice.

She moved swiftly. "Of course. I could only get a few drops between your lips. I've been praying."

She'd prayed for him. The thought disturbed his conscience.

Guthrie watched as she uncorked the canteen. She used one hand to help lift his head, and the other to place the canteen to his lips. "Drink, Guthrie. There's plenty more, for I found a small brook of clear running water not far from here."

Guthrie choked on the first sip. She used the edge of her sleeve to wipe his chin, and helped him to another, and he sipped more slowly.

"Didn't know water tasted so good."

"Are you hungry?"

Drowsiness nipped at Guthrie's mind. He tried to stay awake but his eyes refused to obey. They closed of

97

their own accord, and the next thing he knew, a low nicker brought him bolt upright, his hand reaching for the pistol that wasn't there.

Guthrie shook himself, annoyed by his lapse. His stomach grumbled and his taste buds responded to the aroma coming from the campfire.

Sheen squatted beside him, a cup in her hand. "I see you've decided to rejoin the living."

"Smells like potato soup."

"Aye, and with wild onions."

"How long have I been out?"

"Today is the third day. 'Tis worried about you, I was."

Guthrie reached up and touched the bandage on his neck. "I wasn't hurt all that bad. I don't understand what happened."

"The wound in your neck was deep, to be sure." She hesitated as if uncertain to speak her mind. "I believe the fever took hold because the wound in your heart is much deeper."

When he didn't answer, she shoved the cup of soup toward him. "Eat. There's bread and honey, too."

"And coffee?"

"Aye."

"The songs you sang were nice, even though I didn't understand the words."

She smiled as she gazed into the warmth of his eyes. "When bad dreams visited me, my father sang them away with lullabies from our homeland."

Guthrie held the cup forward for a refill of soup. "I apologize."

"For kidnapping me?"

"Yeah, that too. I shouldn't have lost my temper,

before. When I thought you were reading my mind."

For a moment the two stared at each other. "Will you take me back home, then?"

He tilted his head, studying her. His eyes shifted from her face and he remembered the gruesome scar that lay hidden beneath the high collar of her dress. He chose not to answer her question.

He reclined against the saddle. "You came from Ireland. Your father brought you to America and settled in Boston. The scar on your neck isn't all that old. How did you survive a hanging, and who tried to hang you?"

Sheen looked away, hoping to hide her face. "You'll listen, to all of it?" She turned back to find him watching her.

"I'll listen."

She drew in a deep breath and blew it out slowly. "Even as a child I knew which roots and herbs and wildflowers had curative powers. Another gift I inherited from those before me. I collected and dried the flora, and the town doctor bought what he needed from me. The extra money helped with the rent on our wee house.

"One day, after school, I went to the woods to collect wild lettuce and burdock. I'd stopped hearing the spirits, and they had stopped plaguing me. Maybe that's why I didn't hear him."

As if collecting her emotions, Sheen stopped and concentrated on the folds of her skirt. "He grabbed me, tearing at my clothes, his hands touching and pinching, his mouth slobbering. I beseeched him to stop. When he didn't, I raked his face with my nails."

A silent sob shook Sheen's shoulders. She sat quiet as if lost in her remembrance. Guthrie prompted, "Did he...hurt you?"

Sheen nodded. "Not in the way you're thinking."

"Who was he?"

Breathing out a very long sigh, she said, "The preacher's son."

"How old were you?"

"I'd seen my thirteenth year, and he was eighteen. Luther Ulmarr was his name. He told his father I had cast a spell on him and then enticed him into the woods. That very night, the Reverend Ulmarr and his deacons paid a visit to our house. They held their torches high and made vile accusations.

"Maybe it was the flames from those burning sticks that brought back the memories of my mother being burned at the stake, and most assuredly when the Reverend quoted from the Bible. He said, 'Thou shalt not suffer a witch to live.'

"Heeding the warning, we collected all we could pack, loaded our wagon and that very night left town, never to return."

The strain and the sorrow seemed to swallow her up.

"Enough, Sheen. I see how much it troubles you to remember."

She rubbed her throat. "Until you hear it all, you will not be satisfied. But know this. That terrible night my mother died, a little of me died with her."

She reached for the coffeepot and refilled their cups. "Father and I traveled to the town of Salem. It was there the voices and the faces of ghosts began to taunt me until I opened my mind and let them in. It is a mistake I shall regret for the rest of my life. In doing so, I caused my father's murder."

Chapter Ten

Sheen tried to block the tears, but they came anyway. She allowed herself a few moments of grief and then set her mind to finishing her story.

"Our cottage stood apart from the others in the village, and I felt that set *us* apart, although ours was exactly the same as the others, a rectangle with walls of whitewashed cob.

"It didn't take long to realize the people of Salem were a superstitious lot—the rich no less than the poor. My da forever cautioned me to keep my thoughts to myself.

"Shortly after my sixteenth birthday, the voices sought me out." Sheen stopped long enough to soothe her throat with a sip of tepid coffee.

"It began innocent enough. Some boys playing a naughty prank stole Widow Edwyn's cat and tied it far into the woods so no one would hear its mewlings. The widow was beside herself until I led her to the poor frightened animal.

"Another time, the ghost of a murdered man wanted me to tell his fiancée where he'd hidden the money he'd saved for their wedding.

"Then one morning I went to a place in the woods where I'd never before ventured, to collect wild mushrooms and wildflowers. There was a smell of decay all about me. A smell of death."

Sheen clamped her hands over her ears as if to shut out the voices. "I ran to a deep crevice, an old cistern, and peered down into the darkness, with so many images inside my head coming at me all at one time."

Guthrie stared at her, and she noted the regret in his eyes. She sat still while he watched. Then heaving a shuddering sigh, she continued. "The dead were all little girls between the ages of six and eleven. Five little girls who would never celebrate another birthday.

"Their murderer had lured them away with promises of penny candy. He did unspeakable things to them, before and even after he'd snapped their necks, and then he tossed them into the hole.

"The spirit named Charity said they knew I would come. Each child wanted to go home, to have their mothers stop crying and wondering what had happened to them."

Guthrie gritted out, "Did the gho...er, spir...did they know who killed them?"

"Yes. It was the storekeeper."

"I don't understand the connection between you discovering a child killer and a lynch mob trying to hang you."

"You will, Guthrie. You will."

The air turned cold suddenly, as though the winds came out of the icy mouths of the dead from the North Country. Sheen shuddered. Guthrie laid a branch on the fire and then lifted the quilt to her shoulders.

Her thoughts had veered away from the facts and the logic and left her steeped in memories and grief.

Guthrie laid a gentle touch to her hand. "I can't imagine the kind of strength it takes for you to face the images in your head, to hear their voices, to survive it and build a life."

Taking comfort in his touch, she placed her hand atop his. As if momentarily lost, he'd opened a tiny door to his mind and she peeked inside. What she saw wilted her heart.

"There is no going back for you, Guthrie Tanner. And there is no going forward with your life until you come to terms with your loss."

She lowered her eyes as she removed her hand and tucked it inside the folds of the quilt. "Forgive me. I've intruded on your thoughts again.

Guthrie simply nodded, allowing her to know he'd not taken offense. "You were telling me about the little girls."

"Aye. I forgot all about collecting herbs and ran home to tell my da about the voices, and the hole and the wee lassies.

" 'Sheen,' he says to me, 'You must tell no one.' "

"But, Father, the little girls know who killed them. Their spirits cannot rest until they are given a proper burial and the killer is punished. With or without you, I'm going to the constable. 'Tis the right thing to do."

" 'You bring trouble to yourself, Daughter. I do not need to hear voices to tell me this.'

"Shamefully, I agreed to keep quiet. No one had ever spoken of the missing girls. This made me think the murders had happened long in the past. I was wrong. One child per year over a period of five years."

Sheen laughed and the roughest edge of her anger smoothed. "That very night the spirit of Felicity Ann Trumble came to my room."

Sheen recounted the child spirit's warning that the storekeeper had taken another little girl, Ella Rigby.

"Felicity pleaded with me to stop him. She said he'd taken Ella to the hole in the woods. Torn between obeying my father and saving the child, I slipped from my room and ran to the constable's office.

"He didn't believe me. Told me to go home, to stop playing *witch*. Reluctantly, I had just opened the door to leave when Farmer Rigby nearly bowled me over as he huffed inside the office. Hysterical he was, about his wee lass missing.

"We set out for the woods, the constable, Farmer Rigby, and me." A shuddering sob wracked over Sheen. "I didn't save her. We were too late. Another child's life lost. But when we came upon him, a strange thing happened. I saw it, Constable Firth saw it, and so did Farmer Rigby.

"The angry spirits, there were dozens of them, soldiers both young and old, even animal spirits, filled the woods with a horrible keening. Usually ghosts have no strength to do physical harm, but I think the years of moldering and then waiting to have their bones found gave them the power to lift the storekeeper and drop him into the deep crevice.

"There was not a mark on him when his body was retrieved. I think he died of fright."

Sheen caught herself clutching her hands together, deliberately unlaced her fingers. Faith and begorrah, she wasn't a lass of sixteen years any longer, a girl to be mortified by the disapproval of the man who sat across from her. She let the silence hang for a moment. She knew the value of silence, and of timing.

Her eyes mild and level, she said, "My story has gone on too long and the day is growing to a close. I can see the disbelief, the doubt in your eyes. Now, if you please, I am hungry and will prepare our meal."

She rose to her knees, but Guthrie grabbed her arm. "A little hard to chew on, I'll admit. Sounds more like a fairytale from a book than reality. "

She looked at the chiseled planes of his face and found them more compelling than before. Her voice was calm and soft. "At least let us make a fresh pot of coffee and have some bread and honey."

"You talk, I'll make supper."

"As you wish." She began again. "After the little girls' remains were properly laid to rest, villagers came, wanting me to contact their dead loved ones. But not Prudence Brownlow, the storekeeper's wife. She openly accused me of practicing witchcraft. Mostly people ignored her until a few months later a farmer's herd of swine died from a fever, and another's cows got hoof-'n'-mouth disease. Then the widow Edwyn died of the bloody flux.

"A few days after her funeral, a rabid dog walked right down the middle of town, drooling and frothing at the mouth. It latched onto the parson's leg. The constable had to lock the poor man in a cell until it was for certain he had the hydrophoby. And all the while Prudence Brownlow continued spreading her evil lies about me.

"When the parson died, the superstitious folk of Salem, all those who'd come and paid coin to make contact with their dearly departed, turned against me and my da, more vicious than the rabid dog.

"On the night of the full moon, the witching moon, we were dragged from our home. Our hands and feet bound, and as if we were contaminated with the plague, we were tossed into a freight wagon and driven to the outskirts of town.

"That's when they put the nooses around our necks. My da looked them each in their accusing eyes and said he prayed God forgave them for hanging two innocents.

"The last thing I remember was seeing Prudence Brownlow's wicked smile. At her nod, one of our neighbors busted the horses on their butts. I heard an unmistakable snap, and thought it was my neck. It wasn't. It was my father's.

"My noose had failed and I dangled in midair, gurgling and strangling.

"God had spared me, but not my father." Sheen lifted a hand to her throat. She shuddered, and closed her eyes as if reliving the memory. "By odd coincidence, a gypsy circus arrived just as the lash was put to the wagon horses. One of the Roms leapt from his wagon and grabbed my legs, lifting me upward and relieving the pressure of the rope around my neck.

"Later, I was told the noose had embedded so deeply in my flesh the Roma men decided to cut the rope and leave the loop as it was until they could get me safely away from Salem.

"The gypsies also cut down the body of my father. They buried him and placed a large boulder over his grave. I was too ill to know this until much later.

"Though the *Patrinyengri*, the clan's woman who knows herbs and healing, tended my wound, the rope had nearly bitten through my neck." Sheen again reached up and touched the collar of her dress. "You've seen the scar."

Her eyes met Guthrie's and she knew the empathy between them. There seemed to be a bond there that she had not felt before.

"I traveled with the circus for two years, earning nickels and dimes as Madam Zorvina, teller of fortunes, seer of futures. It was a good living.

"For a while I embraced my gift, and then I came to hate it. What good is this curse that possesses me if I couldn't use it to save my dear father?"

It seemed her voice echoed inside her ears. She barely remembered Guthrie placing the cup of coffee in her hands. So deep in her grief, his voice sounded far away when he spoke.

"How did you come to live alone in the middle of a Montana prairie?"

Her lips trembled open. "We were on our way to Bozeman when we passed the homestead. Although the place was abandoned, in complete shambles, it had good water and plenty of grass.

"The circus animals needed to rest, and so did the performers and roustabouts. Gypsies are not well liked or trusted by *gaje*, the white man. We shared that in common. Except when performing, they prefer to rest as far away from towns as possible. I think that's why I felt at home with them. Yet I knew when they had rested and were ready to move on I wouldn't go with them.

"The men helped make the cabin livable, and repaired the holes in the barn roof, and so many other repairs for which I remain grateful. The women sewed curtains and made blankets for my house. Each family donated a piece of furniture and more, buckets, enough food stores to last several months.

"For three years I lived in peace. The spirits' voices left me alone. I was happy in my solitude. I had my animals to comfort me, the occasional visit from old Mr. Tatum the peddler, and once in a while I traded with the Kootenai.

"My soul had begun to heal. I thought at last I could live out my days without the human or ghostly spirits interrupting my life.

"All was well until a month ago when I heard a child crying for her daddy. A few nights later Abigail paid me a visit, and then you came."

Memories rose up against Sheen. She let herself weep, and when she was dry, Guthrie handed her a damp cloth to refresh her face.

Guthrie blew out a breath. "I'm sorry for your hurts, Sheen. I'm even sorrier for being one of them."

Her mind went dull for a while. She was aware in a secondary way that Guthrie had decided to talk about Abigail.

Chapter Eleven

The fireflies were out. Guthrie watched them bumping their lights against the dark as he fought the knot in his stomach.

He clenched his hands into tight fists and braced himself against the tide of unwanted memories. "I used to think I was ready for this. I didn't know it would hurt so much." His voice faltered, "Did Abigail suffer?"

Sheen witnessed the emotions that stormed into his eyes. "Her last thoughts were of you."

"Hellfire, girl. I'm not some town namby-pamby that needs mollycoddlin'. I'll ask again. Did...she... suffer?"

Sheen's voice sounded like a whip snapping the air. "You already know the answer. You buried her. Yes, she suffered. All the while she fought her attackers, she screamed for you, and when she knew you weren't coming to save her, she pleaded with her daughter to run...to hide."

Sheen tried to relax her tense shoulders. "There, are you satisfied?"

Guthrie closed his eyes and sat there until the red wash of fury dulled. "I thought hearing it would help. It doesn't."

He pinched the bridge of his nose between his thumb and forefinger. "You said you heard a child calling for her daddy. Was it my Rachel?"

"Truly, Guthrie, I don't know. The night the voice came to me, I also heard many horses' hooves. Close, as if running through my yard. The next day, I checked. There were no prints. The child could have been Rachel." Sheen shrugged a shoulder. "I'm sorry."

Guthrie labored through reliving the horror of finding his wife's broken and abused body. "After the war there was nothing left of Oakwood Manor except burned buildings and charred fields. The carpetbaggers came and gobbled up all the plantations for back taxes.

"Abigail never wanted to leave South Carolina, but I saw the West as a place to begin a new life. I told her she was my wife and duty bound to follow wherever I went. I figured once we picked a spot and settled in, she'd grow to love Montana. Every day I promised to build her a house bigger than Oakwood Manor. She hated the heat, the cold, the snakes, everything.

"When she was pregnant, I should have honored Abigail's wish to return to Charleston. She had an aunt she could have lived with until the baby was old enough to travel.

"I don't know why I didn't send her back—stubborn pride, maybe, or fear of losing her."

His voice broke and he looked at Sheen, whose eyes were shiny with tears glistening on their surface.

"When I returned to the ranch, she was lying in the yard all bloody and broken and bruised. I don't know how long I sat in the dirt holding her...hours, maybe. When I finally came to my senses, I bathed her.

"While washing away the dirt and the blood, I didn't know which was worse, imagining the agony she suffered at the hands of those red savages or knowing it was my fault she died.

"Abigail had brought a peach-colored ball gown with her. She referred to it as her way of hanging on to a reminder of what civilization was like. I laid her to rest in that gown."

He attempted a smile, and succeeded only in twisting his mouth into an expression that hovered on the edge of pain.

"In the end, because of my stubborn pride, I lost them both...my wife and my daughter."

He stood and slapped his fist against the palm of his hand. "Damn, sure could use a shot of whisky right about now."

****

The loud smack of flesh against flesh caused Sheen to wince. The sudden hiss of temper, the dangerous flash of his, had her clasping her hands. She felt a pang of guilt, and of sympathy. It was odd to realize she didn't feel fear or trepidation as she usually did around angry men. "Sit down, Guthrie."

"What?"

She reached for her saddlebag and withdrew a corked bottle and handed it to him. "Here, because you look like you need it."

He accepted the bottle, pulled the cork, and sniffed, then gave her a quizzical glance.

She merely shrugged her shoulder. "'Tis no magic potion, if that's what's worrying you. 'Tis honey wine. I'd thought to use it only for emergencies."

He allowed his gaze to linger on her face. Sighing as if in profound relief, he dropped to the ground and took a long swig from the bottle.

Saying nothing, she rummaged inside the leather bag again and removed a small tin box. "Chamomile tea," she said when she opened the lid. "And just so you know, that's the only bottle of liquid spirits." She busied herself with filling a pot with water and setting it on the glittering embers. "I'll make us a cup of soothing tea."

"'Preciate it." He popped the cork back into the bottle, sighed, rolled his shoulders.

Without an upward glance, she said, "How do you know it was Otaktay and his warriors who killed Abigail and took Rachel?"

"Woman, do you have to know my every thought? It wears me out."

"That is why you've forced me to come with you, isn't it? To find him and rescue Rachel?"

Guthrie scanned the mountains to the north. "One solid year I've searched every hole, nook, and cranny for that red devil, until snow and lack of ammunition and food forced me down from the high country." His voice rife with loathing, he shifted his gaze to Sheen. "It's like the mountains swallowed up that heathen and his renegades. And, yeah, that's why you're here. I didn't live up to my promises where my wife was concerned, but I'll keep hunting until I find Rachel or until I draw my final breath."

"That first day, when you rode into my yard, why didn't you ask for my help? Why didn't you tell me about Rachel?"

She possessed an uncommon beauty, certainly more vivid and lively than that of the translucent paleness of Abigail. He leaned slightly closer to study her more carefully. "When a man lives by his cunning while hunting an animal, he becomes an animal himself."

Instead of commenting, Sheen reached up to hand him a cup of chamomile tea laced with honey wine. She kept her voice quiet. "You didn't say why you are so certain it is Otaktay you are seeking."

In one long draw, Guthrie gulped down the tea made cool by the wine. He drew a sleeve over his mouth. Disgust rode hard on his face as he looked at his open palm.

"You don't have to say it, Guthrie. I already know."

"Nothing is safe from you, is it?"

"You sought me out, remember? When you open your mind, I see what you've already seen. Otaktay left an upside-down bloodied handprint on Abigail's breast. It is his victory sign."

Guthrie threw the tin cup. It bounced off a nearby pine tree. In a rage, he stood and turned in a three-hundred-and-sixty-degree circle. Once more he glanced to the north. There was no turning back now. He wasn't about to stop for anything short of the end of the world. "Get some shuteye. We'll ride before daybreak."

He looked down at Sheen. Her face tilted up to him, the lips inviting. She seemed to understand the hunger in his eyes as she stood and touched his cheek, let her fingers trace the hard lines of his face, then abruptly turned and walked to her side of the fire.

Slumped inside his bedroll, he lay unmoving, a man weary of travel, contemplating more.

"Abigail, I am so sorry," he whispered. "I'll set things right."

Maybe somewhere in heaven she noticed him and, deep in her celestial soul, blamed him as he blamed himself. A wind tugged at him. A weary smile tugged at the corners of his lips. Perhaps that was his lot in life, to follow the wind.

Eyelids heavy, weighted with sleep, closed at last. And Guthrie slept, the bitter taste of revenge lingering in his heart.

Chapter Twelve

Clouds, rambunctious in a southern wind, billowed over the farthermost rim of Wolf Mountain, patching the land with drifting shadows. A breeze gushed upward out of the mountain valley, washing the rim in a cooling surge of energy.

Sheen sucked in her breath and thrust her hands under her armpits for warmth. The air was clear, and her range of vision extended all the way southward to the Powder River.

She watched Guthrie studying the land below. What she could see of it, before the valley doglegged off to the north and disappeared behind another ridge, appeared devoid of life. At least human kind. Not devoid of game, she hoped, and her stomach growled in assent. It seemed the mare understood her rider's thoughts and pawed the earth, causing a plume of snow to be whipped away by the wind.

For a quarter of an hour Sheen followed Guthrie along the twisting bank through emerald shadows. Now and then he paused long enough to let the horses paw through the snow searching for the sweet grass that lay beneath. And she looked on in envy, knowing that unless he managed to surprise a deer or was lucky with a makeshift trap, there would be beans and poor conversation for supper. It had been a week since either had burned their tongues on a cup of good strong

Arbuckle.

The recollection was so vivid she could almost smell the fresh pot bubbling over an open fire.

Almost? She sniffed the spring air and discovered the scent of roasting meat and the unmistakable aroma of coffee.

"Guthrie?"

Holding up his hand to signal for quiet, he reined up the gelding and peered through levels of light and shade, of gloom and slanted sunlight, and at last they both caught sight of tethered horses against an overhanging bluff, a lean-to shelter, and a distant figure of a man squatting by a fire.

"Let's hope he's in a mood to be sociable, Sheen."

"No, we should ride on."

A brief flash of anger crossed his face. "I'm hungry, and so are—"

She cut him off. "I'm not hungry enough to lose my life. These are bad men."

Guthrie loosened the Hawkins .54-caliber rifle from the boot. "Stick close to me and don't talk. We'll eat, make sociable, then be on our way."

"Guthrie?"

"Damn, woman, what is it?"

"The one who looks like a bear...he has a gold locket. It has a picture of a little girl and a woman inside."

Guthrie stared hard at Sheen, disbelief in his eyes. "Hellfire. How do you know... Never mind."

Sheen closed her eyes. What she saw frightened her. She met Guthrie's stare. "He'll want our horses and will kill to get them."

She didn't tell him she had seen what the man

would do to her if he succeeded in killing Guthrie.

"I'm not a tinhorn, Sheen." Guthrie turned away from her, a deliberate insult. He trotted the gelding at a brisk pace straight for the camp. He splashed across the creek, making enough noise to announce their arrival. As he drew closer he heard the singing. The man was singing in French, his voice deep and melodic.

As Sheen approached, she made out other peculiarities of the camp. There was only one man about, although the horses indicated others.

The singer had stretched out against a deadfall, using a spiny gray tree trunk for a backrest. He wore a beaver cap on his head, with a feather protruding from the crown. A short man, with the widest shoulders and the most massive chest she had ever seen, his black beard was laced with silver, his face a gnarled map of flesh, the face of a man who had spent a lifetime brawling. He wore buckskin breeches and a shirt with black and red stripes ringing his incredible girth. At his throat hung a gold locket.

The hilt of a revolver jutted from the broad leather belt circling the man's waist. He continued singing as Guthrie and Sheen rode up to the campfire.

Guthrie waited for an invitation to dismount. He exaggerated his southern drawl. "Me and my woman smelled your coffee."

"*Bonjour, mon ami.* I am Phillippe Arnou." He bowed from the waist. "I am Holy Hell with the ladies and just plain hell to my enemies. Step down, friend, and pretty lady."

A haunch of venison spattered the cookfire with grease. Arnou positioned himself so the log was to his right.

Guthrie alit from the saddle. He walked over and held up his hands to assist Sheen. He whispered. "Stick close."

The Frenchman rested his elbow on the weathered wood, arm crooked upward.

Guthrie realized the man was inviting him to arm wrestle. He shrugged. Amusing Arnou was a small price to pay for a meal.

"Where's the rest? You can't ride all those horses."

"Ahh. A perceptive man. My companions are checking the traps."

Guthrie sat opposite the Frenchman, close enough to smell grease on Arnou's shirt. He gripped the man's massive paw and looked his opponent square in the eyes.

"My name's Guthrie Tanner."

"And your woman?"

"Miss Sheen O'Reilly."

"Oh-ho. So she is not your wife. Maybe I'll take her for myself."

The Frenchman reached out and captured a long strand of Sheen's hair. "Lovely name. I find myself partial to women with red curls."

The fancy scrolled A inscribed on the locket dredged up memories of the day Guthrie had given it to Abigail. "Wrestle you for the locket."

The Frenchman grinned. "And if I beat you, I keep the locket...and the pretty lady."

The words ground through Guthrie's teeth. "Over my dead body."

"I am happy to oblige, *mon ami*."

Arnou exerted his strength. Guthrie's arm muscles bulged. He gritted his teeth. Arnou's jaws clamped shut. With excruciating slowness Guthrie's arm gave ground until at last it snapped backward over the log. The Frenchman retained just enough pressure to keep Guthrie prisoner.

"Bern, Jakob!" the Frenchman called. With a sinking feeling Guthrie realized the man had purposely trapped him, imprisoning his gun hand.

Two men emerged from the surrounding forest. Both were lean dark men of average height and build. As they approached, Guthrie noticed the younger of them was dressed like a farmer in a faded plaid shirt, bib overalls and brogans, while the other man wore faded Union-blue pants with a yellow stripe down each leg. Plaid-shirt appeared to be no more than a boy of sixteen, though his homely features centered around wild eyes.

"Hey?" Guthrie winced, trying to reach across his body for the holstered revolver. Arnou merely increased pressure on the right hand. Guthrie gasped and quit his struggle. The youth grinned and, leaning over, removed Guthrie's pistol.

In all the excitement it appeared the Frenchman had forgotten about Sheen until she stepped from behind the pinto. Her feet braced apart, she held the Hawkins .54-caliber against her shoulder. "I-I'm very nervous, so if any of you move, I will pull the trigger."

Guthrie rolled free, his right arm dangling at his side. "What the hell is this, anyway?"

"Ah, *mon ami*, an exercise in caution. You will forgive my rudeness, I trust." He spoke to the lad in overalls. "Jakob, give our friends some coffee."

"Don't cotton to lookin' down a rifle barrel. Let 'em get their own dadgum coffee."

"Jakob killed his Bible-thumping pa. He don't like obeying orders." Arnou's arm slashed out, and a knife buried itself in the dirt just below the squatting youngster's crotch.

The boy called Jakob glared at the Frenchman for a moment and then reached for two cups and the coffeepot. He grumbled beneath his breath but passed a cup of coffee to Guthrie.

Guthrie clenched his jaw against the pain when he lifted his arm. "I'll take my woman's, too."

As he savored the rope-thick brew, he peered over the rim of the cup at the necklace around the Frenchman's neck. "The locket—mighty pretty. I'll trade you the pinto colt for it."

"Guthrie, not the—" He cut his eyes toward Sheen's protest, saw her energy nearly spent, and watched her jaw clamp shut when he sent her an expression that said, *Trust me.*

"What about it, Arnou? You willing to take the colt for that gee-gaw?"

"Aw, no, *monsieur*." The Frenchman fingered the necklace. "Traded a Sioux brave two horses for this fine piece of jewelry. No, it's not for trade."

"So happens I'm tracking a band of renegades led by a Sioux named Otaktay. You wouldn't happen to have run across his trail?"

"Aw, *oui*, Kills Many. Mean sumbitch. What's your business with him?"

The sensual movements of the Frenchman's fingers sliding the locket back and forth on the gold chain ignited a fury in Guthrie's belly. He held the cup toward Sheen and took the rifle in exchange. He gave her a look that didn't take a mind-reader to interpret.

One that said—stay on guard.

"He stole something that belongs to me. I aim to get it back."

Arnou cut a portion of the venison and held it out to Sheen. He smiled and licked his lips. Shifting her weight, she set the cup on the ground, then took the food from the knife blade and passed the sizzling meat from hand to hand until it cooled enough to tear off a chunk and swallow it.

"Whatever my old friend Kills Many took from you must possess great value, does it not, *mon ami*?"

Though he was hungry enough to consume the entire shank of venison, Guthrie held his peace.

The Frenchman shrugged as he cut another slice of meat and handed it up to Guthrie. "Maybe it is this trinket? I see in your eyes it holds meaning for you."

The man called Bern walked past the Frenchman toward Sheen. He stuttered, "L-last person to p-point a gun at me was a gawdern j-johnny reb." The tip of his finger pressed against her nose. "Y-you don't never p-point no gun at me again, b-bitch."

Guthrie knotted his hand into a fist as he watched red spots dabble Sheen's cheeks. Caution kept him quiet. These were dangerous men, and riding out of this encampment alive depended on keeping a level head.

"No need for your man to insult my woman, Arnou."

"Aw, *monsieur*. I, Phillippe Arnou, have not always been among men of such low station. No, I was born to a higher position and often dined with French aristocracy." He reached beneath his shirt and withdrew a silver flask. It was embossed with a family crest. He handed the flagon to Guthrie, who stared at the offering a moment, unscrewed the top and took a sip. Brandy warmed his belly.

Guthrie returned the container. "What happened?"

Arnou looked past Guthrie, motioning the Yankee deserter away from Sheen. He slammed his fist into the palm of his hand as if a black mood had overtaken him. "An unfortunate misunderstanding between myself and the suitor of a young lady. A misunderstanding that forced me to flee France."

The Frenchman walked to Sheen and stood close. Much too close. He ran the edges of his fingers down her cheek. "On second thought, I will make a bargain with you, *monsieur*."

Guthrie's expression clouded. "I'm listening."

"The colt and the woman for the necklace."

Guthrie glanced over at Sheen, who was studying him with open apprehension. He could read her thoughts. She was wondering whether or not he would accept the trade.

"No dice, Arnou."

Sheen visibly relaxed.

"Think, *monsieur*. You are making a mistake. I am blood brother to the Sioux. I know how Otaktay thinks, and he will pay me what I want for this red-haired beauty. But a stranger like you..." The Frenchman laughed outright as he drew a finger across his throat.

"Not if I kill him first."

"You are indeed a fool, *mon ami*." Then, cupping Sheen's chin, Arnou turned her face to his roughly and took her mouth.

All hell broke loose.

The plaid-shirted boy named Jakob crowed like a rooster. He jigged around the Frenchman and Sheen, flapping his arms up and down. "Cockadoodle-doo. Shee-it. Let me have a go at 'er. Ain't never had me a re-fined woman a'fore."

Guthrie lifted the Hawkens and thumbed back the trigger. Before he pulled off a shot, Arnou shoved the barrel upward. The shot went wild.

Sheen bent low and without thought of burning her hands, swept a cloud of crimson ashes into Arnou's face. As he clawed at his eyes, she reached forward and snatched the locket from his beefy neck.

Guthrie swung the heavy rifle around and smashed the barrel again the Union deserter's temple. Levering another slug into the chamber, he pulled the trigger, leaving a fist-sized hole in the plaid-shirted boy's chest.

There was no mistaking the urgency in his voice when he shouted, "Get to the horses, Sheen."

"One question before you die, Arnou. Did Otaktay have a child with him—a little girl with blonde hair? She'd be about six years old."

The Frenchman clawed at his burning face. He uttered a string of curses in French and, slipping out a knife hidden in his leggings, lunged at Guthrie. "Die, *batard*, die."

Sheen sprang away as the shot exploded behind her.

Phillippe Arnou's mouth twisted into a clownish grin. He held out his hand, the fingers wet with blood.

Guthrie stripped each man of his gunbelt and emptied the loops of their cartridges. He used his knife to slice a generous slab of meat from the charring venison.

"Guthrie," Sheen shouted as she rode up, leading the sorrel gelding. "He's got a gun."

The Hawkens answered the Colt's roar, and the man wearing union blue pants sprawled backward.

Guthrie removed the slicker from his saddle and wrapped it around the venison.

Sheen glanced at the macabre scene. "I don't think I could eat any, knowing how we came by it."

He secured the slicker in place. "No need letting good food go to waste. You get hungry enough and you won't care where it came from." He looked around at the three dead men. "Besides, they won't miss it. Check their cache. See what other food they might have."

She furrowed her eyebrows and pierced him with a firm look as she slid from the saddle. "Stealing from the dead gives me the shivers."

With long, hurried strides Guthrie went to the tether line. After a quick scan of the three horses, he cut the ropes securing a pack donkey and two of the sorriest pieces of horseflesh he'd seen in a long time. The best of the three was a short-legged roan built to carry a stocky man. Guthrie figured the gelding belonged to the Frenchman.

He led the animal to where Sheen waited. After tying the roan's reins to the tail of his sorrel, Guthrie mounted. "C'mon, let's make tracks."

Chapter Thirteen

A coyote howled balefully in the distance. Its lonely cry carried on the night air, unanswered. Ghostly battlements of clouds drifted before a sky thick with stars. Twenty miles from the Frenchman's encampment, Guthrie signaled to stop.

"Up there is a cave."

"How do you know this?"

"Spent a year of my life in these mountains. Found it by accident when I was on the run from a Pawnee scalping party."

"No."

"What do you mean—no?"

"Caves hold wild animals and evil spirits."

"O'Hanlon said you were a fairy witch, talked to animals, and I already know you talk to the dead."

"Not *witch*—in Ireland those who communicate with animals are called fairy doctors."

"Bah, fairy, witch, doctor. It's all chicanery."

"Then tell me again why you've forced me to come with you. A true nonbeliever would have laughed at your Private O'Hanlon's drunken blathering."

"Don't make me tie you across your saddle, Sheen. I'm cold, tired to the bone, hungry, and in no mood for Irish stubbornness."

"Oh, all right. 'Tis no choice I have but to do your bidding." She mumbled under her breath, "If I were a true fairy doctor I'd turn you into a mouse."

"I heard that."

Sheen smiled. Still she couldn't shake the sense of dread threatening to consume her.

They started up the gradual slope. Riding the sure-footed mare, Sheen found the going relatively easy. She followed Guthrie as he guided the horses over fallen trees and around moss-covered boulders that rose to block their course in the dark.

She scanned the surrounding forest and noticed a parting in a stand of pines and in the clearing, an unremittingly dark patch of shadow, deeper than the night.

Guthrie pointed. "There."

The shadow became a cave with a mouth that arched higher than a tall man's head.

"We'll lead the horses in, Sheen. Last time I was here the floor was slick as an ice-covered pond."

He dismounted and handed the reins to her, then searched about and gathered together a nearly straight branch and enough dry grass to make a torch. He drew his revolver.

"Wait here while I check to see if there's any wild animals and *evil spirits*."

A sardonic smile lifted the corners of her lips. "May your tongue sprout hair for poking fun at what I know is true."

He felt the sting of her words, and at the same time the pulsing of his blood as her nearness tantalized him.

****

The cave ran deep into the hillside and half as wide. The domed ceiling vaulted upward to a spiked canopy of stalactites.

Sheen carefully made her way in awe and apprehension, wary of bear and mountain lion. She shivered, chilled by the cold air that filled the chamber. The mare's warm breath against her neck gave Sheen a bit of relief. The horses' hooves against the stone floor echoed, and the light from the torch Guthrie carried cast eerie shadows on the cave walls.

Her boots slipped on the wet surface, and she almost fell. The biting chill found its way through her coat. She couldn't wait to sit by a fire to thaw out.

Sheen counted to fifty—the number of steps she'd taken inside the cave's mouth. "How much farther, Guthrie?"

"Here's good enough. Too dark to see how far back it goes."

He walked to her side, and when he handed the torch to her, her emerald eyes sparkled in the light, sparkled and at the same moment were limpid and watchful. It struck him she was a lovely young woman with her fawnlike gaze and long red hair framing a childlike face.

"Don't fret yourself, the cave is safe. I'll tend the horses and gather wood for a fire."

"I'm going with you, to hold the torch."

He started off into the woods, and she followed, lighting enough of the forest floor for him to gather deadwood for a fire. When his arms were full, they returned to the opening. Sheen entered hesitantly. When they had a campfire crackling at the mouth of the cave, she relaxed enough to venture partway inside.

To her mind, the dark recesses of the chamber continued to house spirits who whispered indignation at the intrusion.

She huddled close to the fire, and while Guthrie unsaddled the horses and went out again to gather grass for feed, she poured water from the canteen, added grounds to the coffeepot, and set it on the outer rim of the small blaze.

Though her stomach felt as if it were gnawing at her backbone, the thought of eating any of the dead men's venison reviled her. Nonetheless, she sliced two generous pieces to warm in the iron skillet while she mixed flour, a pinch of salt, and water for fry bread.

Her body fatigued, her mind in a turmoil, she hummed an Irish lilt, a song taught by her father when she was but a wee lass.

The forgotten locket inside her coat pocket now called to her. She rubbed her hand against the trinket's hiding place.

"Oh, Mamai," she sighed, "I wish you were here to guide me."

She ignored the necklace and hummed another ballad. While she crooned, she tended the food. Though she refused to admit Guthrie was right, the pangs of hunger cramping her stomach outweighed the circumstances of obtaining the meat, a sack of coffee, salt, several tins of peaches, and one of cream. A small fortune, to be sure.

Using Guthrie's skinning knife, she ran the razor-sharp blade around the lid to open a tin of peaches. She added the juice, water, a pinch of salt, and a generous amount of sugar to a large scoop of flour. She dumped the peaches into the iron skillet and poured the flour mixture over the fruit.

"With a little Irish luck, we'll have a cobbler fit to satisfy any sweet tooth, for certain."

"Smells good." Guthrie squatted near the fire. "Horses are hobbled and fed. We can rest easy tonight."

An awkward silence fell between them as he removed his weatherbeaten hat and sat staring into the fire.

Beneath her lashes, she watched the flames cast a shimmering glow that played on the golden highlights of his hair and his windburned, tanned features. It didn't seem possible that he'd grown more handsome.

She filled their plates with food, thankful he made no comment about her eating the venison.

"Been a long time since I've had a meal this good." Guthrie eyed the frying pan. "Mind if I scrape up that last little bit of cobbler?"

Sheen smiled her consent as she emptied the remaining coffee into their cups. "'Tis a fine compliment when a man cleans his plate and the pot."

He stretched his long legs upon the floor across from Sheen. Flames danced between them.

"You've found us a good place, Guthrie."

"It'll do."

****

Sheen closed her eyes. Guthrie studied the clean, almost haughty lines of her face, the firm, slim outline of her body beneath her beloved quilt.

He became conscious of a very real desire. Now that he could see her relaxed in sleep, under different circumstances he would cradle her in his arms and make love to this woman who was inching her way into his heart.

Chiding himself, he placed the Colt revolver close at hand. Working the lever of the Hawkens underneath the barrel to free the spent cartridges, he reloaded the rifle with bullets from his saddlebag.

"Guthrie, what will happen tomorrow?"

"Thought you were asleep."

She answered him with a yawn.

"We'll head to Otto Werner's trading post. Maybe he's had some news about Otaktay since last time I visited. Get some rest. We've a long ride ahead of us."

Guthrie set the rifle aside. He stretched his full length and inched nearer to the fire, warming his backside against the chill emanating from the depths of the cave.

****

Sheen struggled in her sleep. The images slid into her head, along with shapes, sounds, and scents. There were hands squeezing her heart so it beat in hitchy strikes. She fought to find herself in the confusion, in the pain. In the terror.

Abigail!

Oh God, not her. Not her.

A child is crying. A name goes unanswered. Thunder splits the mind, horror rises in the throat. He runs, and the name on his lips is repeated over and over like an echo and never stops.

He flings the door wide. And steps inside, searching the shadows, Abigail doesn't answer his call.

Finding her at last, sprawled at the edge of the cornfield in a garish semblance of sleep. But who will wake her from the sleep of blood?

She can't be dead. My fault. My fault.

A cry starts deep in his soul, deep where the hurt lies longest. Unleashed now, it claws the throat in an anguished wail, in an outpouring of betrayal and fury and insufferable torment.

Raging.

Raging.

Sheen's eyes opened wide and unfocused. Her throat convulsed as if parched.

Closing her eyes, she opened herself, overriding her instinct for self-preservation. She didn't struggle when the images shifted, solidified.

Light spills down the icy slope. She sees a drop-off and a dark pit, which in the flickering illumination reveals a rocky bottom covered with bones, the remains of animals that blundered into the cave and fell prey to the icy slope. Rib cages and tusks and various appendages jutted from the ice, a graveyard that bore witness to the sudden stark tragedies of prehistory. Shuddering, she hears the anguished roars and violent ravings of the beasts imprisoned in the pit, doomed to die a slow, starving death, and the sounds mingle with her soul.

Her boots slip and slide for a sickening moment. I don't want to do this. I don't want it.

I can't see. Can't.

The strain and the sorrow swallowed Sheen up as a child's voice invaded her sub-consciousness. She again opened her mind.

Daddy, they hurt Mommy. I'm scared.

Rough hands bind the child's wrists. She is lifted into the arms of a half-naked savage. His flesh is dyed crimson, and his pony painted with symbols of upside-down bloody hands.

I want my daddy. I want my daddy.

A dirty hand clamps over her mouth.

Quiet, little frog.

Sheen sat up and screamed, "White Frog!"

Guthrie caught her, lifted her. She was limp as the dead. "Sheen, wake up."

Even as he bent to lay her next to the fire, she stirred. When her eyes opened, the world remained dark and unfocused.

Sheen lifted her hands, ran them over her own face. She needed to feel the lines of her own cheeks, nose, mouth. She needed to remember who she was.

Guthrie started to speak, then stopped himself.

Confused, she stared at him. "She isn't there now."

"Who, Sheen?"

She reached for her coat and stuffed her hand inside the pocket. When she thrust her closed fist toward Guthrie, he said, "What is it?"

She slowly opened her hand and in the palm rested the delicate gold locket embossed with the letter A.

"Her name is White Frog."

His brow furrowed in confusion. "Who? I don't understand."

"Guthrie." Tentatively she touched a hand to his. "I'm sorry to bring this back to you, but you have to know. Her name is no longer Rachel. She is—White Frog."

"H-how do you know this?"

"She was here. Otaktay and his warriors spent several days inside this cave."

"But I...I was here, too. Why didn't I see signs?"

"Your heart was closed to the spirits. There was no one to guide your instincts."

Guthrie picked up a rock and hurled it into the darkness.

She stepped back from him then, in that deliberate way of hers.

She remained still, knowing he needed to collect his thoughts, his emotions.

"Does it always come on you like that? Out of nowhere?"

"Most times."

"It hurts you?"

She'd seen and felt Guthrie's anguish, his soul-wrenching grief, his helplessness. "It wears me out, makes me a little sick, and sometimes I live their pain, their horrors."

"I'm sorry for that, Sheen. Sorry for a lot of things."

Guthrie Tanner was a man who had lost touch with his true self. An apology, she knew, had cost him.

"You said her name is White Frog. Do you know where those murdering vermin have taken my Rachel?"

Tears slid down her cheeks when she looked into his eyes. It tugged at her heart, knowing the hope in the sea of blue would turn to frustrated hurt when she answered him.

His sigh was deep and filled with anguish when she said, "No."

He looked down at the locket, then closed his fist over it. "Thank you for this."

"'Tis no way of knowing how long our journey will be. We should rest now."

"When you were having your...your vision, you kept ranting about a deep hole with bones. Did you see it here, inside the cave?"

Sheen gazed off into the darkness. A deep shudder shook her as she pointed. "Aye, back there. 'Tis an ancient place, a place of death."

"I'll light the torch."

She knew there was no use arguing the point with him. If he was determined to face danger from the icy cavity, he would need a way to protect himself. And with that thought, she said, "There is ice, and the way is slippery. The torch will only cast shadows that will deceive you. Morning is soon enough to satisfy your curiosity."

He sidestepped her, then without another word walked away and into the starry night.

Chapter Fourteen

Guthrie woke to Sheen's melodic singing and the aroma of strong coffee.

Love, 'tis the fairest flower
That blows on a summer morn,
But 'neath the sweetest blossom
Lies the sorrow of the thorn.

Bolting upright and grabbing for his revolver, he glanced across the smoldering coals of last night's campfire to find her back to him.

He relaxed and watched the embers, like molten rubies, crackle and crack asunder, scattering jewels of fire.

****

Sheen stopped singing. She felt Guthrie's despondency as if it were her own. And something less corrigible. Guilt. Shame. She could feel it swelling and festering in him like a malignancy.

Tears stung her eyes, but she willed them away. Using the hem of her skirt to protect her hand from the pot's hot handle, she filled two cups with coffee.

"At bedtime, Abigail would sing Rachel to sleep."

She rewarded him with a smile. "I didn't mean to fill you with sad memories."

He reached into the skillet for a piece of meat. As he chewed, he stared into her eyes. Not lazily, but with a steady look. "Seems like a lifetime ago."

Her heart went out to him for all he must have suffered over the past year.

"Do you still intend to explore further inside the cave?"

"Why do you ask when you already know the answer, Sheen?"

She cast him a somber look. "It's been a year."

He nearly sighed.

They supped in silence.

While Sheen wiped the utensils clean and stowed them in the gunny sack, Guthrie said, "I'll saddle the horses. Not knowing what we'll find, we may need to make a fast getaway."

Scattered thoughts filled Sheen. She rose unsteadily, handed him the sack, and watched as he secured it around the horn of her saddle.

She closed her eyes and drifted. *The sound of laughter rises high and bright, a child's careless joy.*

There by the edge of the corral, Rachel stands, shading her eyes from the sun with a tiny hand and waving with the other.

Hey, Daddy. Hey, I was waiting for you a long time.

Freckles sprinkle the bridge of her nose. Hair the color of corn silk, tied with a blue bow, cascades down the center of the child's back.

Mommy's mad 'cause supper is cold.

Strong hands reach out to lift the child into his arms. He laughs and tweaks her nose. He bends down to pluck a single wildflower that dared bloom next to a fencepost.

He holds the yellow flower to the child's nose. You think this will make Mommy smile?

Eyes shadowed and still glazed from the dream stared back at Sheen. Her own eyes. Too late to turn back, she thought. It always was.

She thought of her own mother and how she'd soothed away a child's fears. Sheen thought of everything, dreading what mysteries the deepest parts of the cave held for them, and longed for someone to quell her own anxiety.

"Sheen?" Guthrie's strong hand gripped her shoulder.

Still dazed, she twisted from his grasp and stepped back. She shut off the images as her eyes met his.

"What were you seeing?"

She winced, but managed to compose her face. Remaining silent was her best defense, she decided.

"Damn, if I hadn't been so hell-bent on leaving South Carolina, none of this would have happened. God knows, I should have listened when Abigail begged to leave Montana."

"You wanted the best for her."

"Yes, I did."

"It scares me—going into the cave."

"It scares me, too. But I can't let it go, Sheen."

"I know. Part of you dreads what you'll find and the other part fears nothing is there except ancient bones and another dead end."

Guthrie lifted his eyebrows. "Are you always right?"

Sheen shrugged.

Guthrie lifted the torch. He stuck the end into the hot ashes until the dried thatch blazed.

She watched him. He seemed eager to be on his way. She forced herself to relax as she followed on his boot heels.

Ten minutes passed, or perhaps thirty. She lost track of time. Her gaze focused on the ground, the interior walls, the monotonous dripping of water as she followed the meandering path behind Guthrie.

Like being caught on a merry-go-round gone out of control, Sheen watched every moment of flashes before her eyes, as if she awaited her own brutal end. Oh, yes, she knew it now—all the signs building to this moment had been there.

But like some deaf, dumb, and blind fool, she followed Guthrie into the bowels of hell.

The cave ran more than three hundred feet deep into the hillside. The domed ceiling loomed far above, nearly eighty feet, she judged. Stalactites hung like monstrous rows of teeth ready to clamp shut. Massive columns of ridged limestone connected floor to ceiling. Through this cold primeval vault, Guthrie carefully made his way.

Low sounds, sounds of excruciating pain, rumbled inside Sheen's head. Clenching her hands into fists and steeling her spine, she took a deep breath, forcing down revulsion and fear.

"Guthrie—"

His named echoed throughout the cave: *Guthrie, Guthrie.*

"There's a hole. A deep one, just ahead of you. It's filled with bones."

The ground suddenly sloped away. Guthrie's boots slipped and slid for a sickening moment as the torch he gripped reflected a chasm of darkness.

Wrapping one arm around a stalagmite, she instinctively reached out with the other hand and grabbed Guthrie's coat. She braced her feet and prayed. For several sickening seconds it seemed his weight would pull them over the edge and into the abyss.

The heels of his boots firmly planted, Guthrie lifted the torch. Light spilled down the icy slope. "You can let go, Sheen."

"You're sure?"

He whispered hoarsely, "Yep. All the same, I'm beholden to you for saving my hide."

Her mouth dry, she released her arm from the stalagmite and eased closer to his side. The torchlight flickered over a drop-off and a dark pit.

As she'd seen in her dream, the illumination revealed a rocky bottom covered with bones. Not all of them were from animals.

"Horrible murders were committed here. Men lured to their deaths for the want of their pitiful possessions."

"Indians are superstitious, Sheen. Otaktay and his warriors would consider this an evil place. Maybe it was another cave you saw in your vision."

Eyes like teal pools stared up at him. "He was here. Rachel was here, but not *here*...at this place."

She glanced at the stalactites, columns, and limestone outcroppings.

Guthrie stood silent and lowered his gaze to the floor. "Then where?"

****

A bumblebee explored the cave. It hovered over Sheen's hand for a moment and darted upward when she moved.

"Funny," Guthrie thought aloud, "buzzing bees and damp dark caves don't go together."

Sheen lifted her hand for silence. He watched the

expression on her face as she listened to the droning insect. She stopped her inspection and turned to him. "We should follow the bee."

A frown flashed across his countenance. "So you're talking to insects now." His heart plummeted.

Guthrie did not try to understand the source of his growing anger. He wasn't ready to accept another dead end, another disappointment of not finding his daughter.

Sheen stood proud, her delicate chin held high in defiance of his sarcasm. "'Tis only by accident the poor drone lost its way, Guthrie. But 'twill be no accident for it to follow the same path back to the hive."

Guthrie held the torch high. He scanned the darkness. "All right, the creature seems to have disappeared. Which way should we go, *witch*?"

She folded her arms over her breast. "So, 'tis back to name calling, is it? The devil take you, Guthrie Tanner, for 'tis certain no one else will be havin' you."

He winced at the bite behind her words. "I'm sorry, Sheen. I don't know what gets into me."

"'Tis not your apologies I'm wanting. Only your respect."

Once again, he'd made a mistake where this woman was concerned. He shuddered with shame, and it turned the lingering taste of morning coffee in his mouth to bile.

Realizing she wasn't thinking of her own safety as she strode away from him, he called out, "Wait."

He held the torch to light her way. For what seemed a lifetime they walked, bracing their heels to keep from losing their footing on the narrow path leading downward, until reaching a point where the chamber ended abruptly and the rocks jutted from the earth like an army of angry fists. Sheen stopped.

The bumblebee flitted close enough for Sheen to hear its hum. For a split second the insect lit on the back of her hand and stretched its wings before taking flight again.

It made sense now. She had called on her mother for help. *Thank you for pointing the way. Perhaps I am a true fairy doctor, after all.*

Sheen filled her lungs with fresh air as the distant shushing grew to a deafening roar that echoed inside the chamber's granite walls. She yelled to make herself heard. "It sounds like a great cascade of water."

"A waterfall. Damn, Sheen, we're behind a waterfall."

Determined, he barged his way around a particularly thick barrier of rock, Sheen fast on his heels, and they came to an opening between two boulders. The broken-off knuckles formed a natural cave and made way for a waterfall haloed with colors of the rainbow and creating a mystical tranquility.

Sheen turned in a complete circle as if taking in the natural beauty. "'Tis the perfect hiding place. One could live here for a long time with all their wants provided."

Guthrie's gaze focused on the stone floor like a bloodhound. "Was she here...my Rachel?"

Sheen closed her eyes. She was silent for such a long time Guthrie feared she'd fallen into a trance.

He laid a gentle hand on her shoulder. "Sheen?"

"Aye, she was sitting on the ground, trying not to cry. Only babies cry. And she was not a crybaby. But the tears leaked out despite her bravado. She'd skinned her knees and her elbow and the heel of her hand when she jumped from the horse and tried to run away. The scraped skin burned and seeped blood. She wanted to go to her daddy and get hugged and petted and soothed. He would kiss her knee and make it all better."

When she finished speaking, he heaved a weighty sigh.

She heard his breath in her ear and peered at him. "She lost a shoe. It's there."

He walked to where Sheen pointed. His muscles trembling, his pulse pounding, with an ache of joy and loss in his heart, he spotted the scuffed toe of a small brown leather demi-boot wedged tight between two rocks.

He held the shoe as if it were delicate and breakable. "I always meant to buy her a new pair. Rachel had outgrown these and said they pinched her toes."

Sheen touched the back of his hand with her fingers. "I'm sorry."

"Don't be. I was actually afraid we'd find her...bones. Do you know how long ago Rachel was here?"

The sorrow in Sheen's eyes reached deep inside of him. "I've no way to tell. Judging from the green mold growing on the leather, it's been a long time."

He shook his head in disbelief. "I was this close to finding my little girl. Damn, Sheen. Damn it all to hell."

He handed her the shoe. "Take care of this while I go get the horses."

Taking her hand, he helped her balance as they made their way through an arch formed over the stream that had dug a deep groove into the rock until the waterfall and brook joined together.

Sheen closed her eyes against the bright sunlight but lifted her face to catch the rays' warmth.

"There's no snow, and it feels like summer. How can that be, Guthrie?"

"I've seen it like this before. Last February there was snow in the valley but the weather was warm enough to walk around in shirtsleeves."

He, too, lifted his face to catch the sun's warmth. "We've traveled most of a month. It must be April by now."

"'Tis plenty of grass and living waters. If we are to travel much farther, the horses will need a good grazing."

"Nope, we'll push on as soon as I find a way to bring them to this side of the mountain."

"You yourself said it's been over a year since the Sioux took Rachel. By the time you make your way to the other side and return with the horses, it will be too late in the day to travel."

He wanted to find someone and use his fists, use his fury. "Son of a bitch." He hissed it between his teeth.

Taking her hand, he placed the rifle in it. "Do you know how to use this?"

Sheen blinked. "It isn't in me to hurt the living. I've never wanted to learn."

"I hope the day never comes when you have to pull a trigger," Guthrie said, quietly, still cupping her hand.

She nodded her understanding. "I'd rather have the skinning knife. The meadow is a veritable garden of food."

"Stay inside the cave, Sheen. It's safer." Somehow

143

he knew telling her to stay put was like talking to the wind. He unsheathed the large knife and held it hilt forward.

Her chin high, her voice even, she said with sincerity, "Be safe, Guthrie."

His belly clenched at the trust that finally shone from her darkened eyes. He didn't deserve her. But, deserving or not, he wanted her.

****

Sheen watched Guthrie as he climbed upward, one boulder at a time, until he disappeared over the mountain. The day was warm. Her body felt sticky beneath the coat. She undid the buttons and removed the heavy garment. She wrinkled her nose as she whiffed the acrid odor. "'Tis a good washing it needs. As do I. For we both smell as musky as a billy goat."

Standing completely still, she closed her eyes and listened. There were no voices, from the dead or the living. Nothing to imply her privacy would be intruded upon if she bathed.

"What good is a bath without soap?" She lifted her skirt and traipsed uphill until she spotted a patch of red flowers shaped like beads on a stalk. Lifting the hem of her skirt, she gathered into it several handfuls of Indian paintbrush. She would crush the flowers and use the juices to shampoo her hair, soap her body, and wash her clothes.

She also spied wild onions and poke salad along the stream banks. And there was tansy, and valerian. Everywhere she looked a storehouse of plants grew, including fresh mint. She gathered a goodly amount of each. Never know when such herbs will come in handy, she thought.

The onions she would make into a soup, and she'd steam the poke salad. She'd brew tea and steep it with the mint. She would also crush the fragrant leaves to freshen her body after she bathed.

Sitting on the grass, she removed her shoes and stockings, then stripped down to her camisole and pantaloons before testing the water with her toes. Thinking how good it felt to be free of her encumbrances, she stretched and scratched.

Wearing a satisfied expression, she walked to the deepest part of the swirling pool and dove in.

Chapter Fifteen

After a two-hour climb to where the horses remained saddled and waiting inside the stone chamber, Guthrie rode down a narrow gorge and through stands of pine and cedar until the cliff drew back and horses and rider came to the green valley at the end of the trail.

The sun had settled its warmth upon the meadows where wild flowers swayed in the breeze and grasshoppers arched above the tall grass, their wings rattling; hungry sparrows and buntings and blue jays swept down to intercept the insects in midair.

Guthrie sat back among the trees and watched the meadow below. He blinked his eyes as he spied Sheen curled in a bed of rich green grass, dressed in her undergarments, her hair fanned out around her shoulders like a red cape. As much as he wanted to frown, he couldn't help the smile that lifted the corners of his lips.

Lazy minutes ticked past. Lost in introspection, he was content to sit and watch her sleeping.

The pinto colt seemed to sense his mistress. He squealed out a loud whinny and, leaving his mother's side, trotted down the embankment, splashed across the stream, and went to stand over Sheen.

Guthrie watched the startled way the woman sat up, the lovely lines of her face bunched in momentary fright. Then how the alarm faded, and her eyes crinkled with laughter.

She stood and wrapped her arms around the young stallion's neck and cooed endearments. Guthrie longed for her arms to embrace him, to hear whispered words meant only for him. His heart sped for a moment.

All the way back he'd sought the peace of the forest in hopes of calming the turmoil in his spirit. And now, here before him, was another object of turmoil. How could one so slight and delicate cause so much disquiet?

He'd shed the buffalo-hide coat and tied it behind his saddle. Reaching into his shirt pocket, he removed the gold locket, caressed the letter A with his thumb.

A heavy sigh lifted his shoulders up and down. *Abigail, oh, my sweet Abby, without looking at your picture, I'm losing you. It's getting more difficult to remember the sound of your laughter, the way your eyes lit when you were happy.* He harrumphed—*when you were happy.* In reality, he couldn't remember the last time he'd done anything to please his wife.

What he remembered most was the argument they'd had the morning he left to round up strays. He finally promised a trip to town—three days' travel, a day of shopping, and another three days back home— even though he rationalized to himself that he couldn't afford to lose that week away from the ranch.

In all honesty, he feared Abigail would buy a stagecoach ticket back to South Carolina and take Rachel with her. And so for the rest of the day he concentrated his efforts on busting steers out of the brush and pushing them back to the main herd. There would always be another time, he'd reasoned, to make the long trip to Billings.

He remembered his father had once said, " 'A man has to live with his regrets, son.' "

Until the day he found Abigail's broken and bloodied body, he'd never fully understood the true meaning of his father's words.

The pinto mare tugged on the lead rope. She huffed a squeal as if not wanting to be away from her foal. Guthrie tightened his grip. The sorrel and roan geldings pawed the ground as if eager to be on their way.

A voice interrupted his reverie. "Guthrie... Guthrie?"

He'd been so lost in thought he hadn't noticed Sheen slipping into her dress. Now he watched her nimble fingers plaiting her hair into one long coppery braid.

The breeze shifted, bringing a tantalizing aroma of smoked fish to tease his taste buds. His gaze moved to where Sheen had fashioned a roasting spit. Two large trout sizzled over smoldering embers.

He was dog-tired, and his belly felt like it had grown to his backbone.

Gigging the sorrel gelding forward, Guthrie needed more than food. He needed comfort—the kind only a woman could give.

****

Sheen stepped back into the shadows of the black cottonwood trees. And she listened to his thoughts. Guthrie had unwittingly opened his mind. His sadness and self-recrimination was overwhelming. Now she understood why finding Rachel had become more than obsession. Without his child, he'd lose the remnants of Abigail's memory. He'd lose himself.

She ached to reach for him, to hold him tight, to

give him reassurance that together they would find his daughter. But, fortunately, good sense took hold. It wouldn't do to encourage feelings that couldn't be realized. She had enough to deal with, and so did he.

She lifted her lips in a smile, her eyes meeting Guthrie's with warmth.

"I've collected Indian paintbrush. It makes a fine soap. The water is cold enough to prune your skin, but I'm thinking a scrubbing is good for what ails you."

He chuckled, approaching her. "What I need more than a bath is a bottle of white lightning."

"I'm afraid I don't know this white lightning."

"Moonshine, Sheen. Good ol' home-brewed South Carolina moonshine. It'll make young boys think they're men and old men kick up their heels."

She wrinkled her nose as he stood close. "Foolish blarney, if you ask me. The truth is you smell like ye've wallowed with the pigs. I'll finish supper while you give yourself a good washing."

She reached into her pocket and withdrew a handful of red flowers from the Indian paintbrush plant. "See to it you give your clothes a scrubbing, too."

"You gonna watch, Sheen?"

Red heat mottled her cheeks. "Be off with you. I've cooking to do."

"Horses need tending first."

She followed him to collect the gunny sacks that held the cookwares and the remains of their food supplies, helped him unsaddle the horses and tether them so they could graze.

And then she watched from her hiding place as Guthrie walked to the stream and stripped down to his long johns. To hold back a gasp, she clamped a hand over her mouth when he slid the long underwear down over his hips and kicked them aside as they passed his ankles. His thighs were rock hard from hours astride a horse. The muscles in his back corded when he stretched his arms over his head. He was a powerfully built man, strong and broad.

Seeing him naked heated her flesh, and her traitorous mind thought of other delights. What would it be like to lie with him and experience unmeasured lust?

Her body remembered the one and only time he'd kissed her and fondled her breast. The remembrance was so strong her bones felt as if they were melting at the sight of him.

She wondered at her musings for him, a man who was mostly a stranger and certainly not a friend.

He turned and looked directly at the place where she hid. Fingers of fire heated her cheeks, knowing she had been discovered. But he seemed not to care, instead, he stepped up on a boulder and, like a graceful bird, dove to disappear in the crystal blue depths of the swirling pool.

While he bathed, she opened his saddlebags, where she found a clean set of clothing that she left on a large rock at the edge of the pool.

Afterward she busied herself with steaming the poke salad and wild onions. Brewing water for mint tea, she also opened a can of cream, added sugar, bruised a few mint leaves, and then poured the mixture over the peaches to simmer into a sweet concoction.

Occasionally she glanced beneath her eyelashes toward where Guthrie stood waist deep in the pool using the delicate red beaded flowers to wash his clothes.

When he walked out of the water and seemed to deliberately take his time spreading his garments over bushes to dry, she continued to marvel at the sight of him.

Chapter Sixteen

Guthrie's hair was still a little damp, so the gilt edges of it stood out. Licking the spoon, his blue eyes lazily content, he quirked a half-assed smile.

"Back on the plantation, the darkies knew about herbs and such. Never put much stock in it, though. Figured it was some kind of ju-ju they practiced. How'd you learn all this stuff about using flowers and plants for food and soap?"

A thin wind rattled the leaves of the cottonwood trees. Sheen shivered and reached for the coat that smelled like fresh sunshine.

"In truth, I don't know how this knowledge comes to me. My da said I had a natural gift like my mother and my *maimeó*, my grandmother. He used to say his own dear mamai was a plain woman with no special skills except for being fertile and producing a brood of rosy-cheeked children."

This brought a chuckle from Guthrie. "Have you never found a man to love, Sheen?"

She swirled her cup and watched stray tea leaves spin in circles, wondering how to answer his question. She took another sip, then sat quiet, rolling the cup between her hands.

"Aye, a young Rom. His name was Besnik. He accepted me as I am, even though I worried about future children. What if our daughters were like me—

cursed. Unlike the gadji, the outsiders, the Roma value all children regardless of how they are born."

The silence between them grew until Guthrie said, "Sheen?"

She expelled a shuddering sigh. "Like everything good in my life, he too died. Besnik was an acrobat. As part of his new act, he decided to add a series of somersaults to his high-wire act." She set the cup aside as she shrugged her shoulders, her voice matter of fact. "He lost his balance. The fall broke his neck."

"Did the gypsies cast you out?"

"Nay, they did not. I was tired, tired of traveling, tired of living, tired of reading futures, just plain tired. Surely you understand."

He doused the embers. Rising, he offered his hand. "Let me love you, Sheen. Let me soothe away your hurts and free you of your doubts. Let me love you."

She did not take his hand. She stared into his face, her eyes unreadable.

"And what if your seed takes hold in my belly and produces a daughter? For it is ordained from all the women before my *maimeó* that female children will possess the second sight. What I have is not a gift, Guthrie. Nay, 'tis a terrible curse and a heavy burden for a child. No matter what my body desires, I will not share your bed."

Guthrie laced his fingers through her own. "Sheen..."

"No, Guthrie, please don't." She pulled away.

He hesitated, then gritted his teeth. "You cannot expect a man, any man, to spend day and night with you and not... Sheen, there is more between us now than either you or I will admit. Despite your reasons, you and I share a connection between a man and woman that's...that's..." He let out an exasperated sigh and ran his hands through his hair. "Hellfire, I'm not a poet. The words escape me. Don't you know how beautiful you are?"

She shook her head. "'Tis the moonlight talking and leprechauns putting such fancies in your head. You pursue me hoping I'll concede my heart. I'll sleep in the cave. Alone."

Guthrie scooped her into his arms. "Not if I have anything to say about it."

She bucked and fought. "No! Would you force an unwilling woman?"

She beat her fists against his chest as he stomped toward the cave. He held on tighter, his arms locked around her like a vise.

"For weeks you have cooked my meals, even tended my wounds when the cougar attacked me, yet you've lain on the other side of the fire from me. You retrieved Abigail's necklace from that murderous thief, Arnou, and you found this place, and my baby girl's shoe."

Inside the cave, he set her on her feet. Folding his arms over his chest, he said, "Do you really think I would repay your kindness by forcing myself upon you? Have I been so horrible or mistreated you in any way that would make you think I'd hurt you? I've never forced a woman, and it stabs my heart to see the doubt in your eyes, Sheen. It will snow tonight. We'll sleep here."

She pierced him with a look that spoke her distrust.

He stalked from the cave to gather wood for a fire. "If it'll make you feel any safer, I'll sleep outside with the horses."

Sheen, breathing hard, leaned her head into her hands. The thought of spending the night without him left her cold. She wanted him, the man who had kidnapped her, called her a witch, a man she didn't fully trust. Damn him.

****

Guthrie stomped out of the cave. He kicked the coffeepot and sent it flying. At least the horses would keep him company.

If she found him so unappealing, then why did every signal he could sense tell him she wanted him as much as he wanted her, despite her protests?

Damnation, would he ever understand a woman's mind?

He propped against the saddle, stretched his legs, and wrapped the blanket tightly around his body.

The pinto colt stood over him and nickered. Guthrie stroked the horse's velvety nose. "When you get old enough to kick up your heels, I hope the mares won't try to outrun you."

Guthrie sneezed. A deep shiver shook him, but it was better than sleeping with the witch inside. He closed his eyes.

The vision of Sheen standing in the firelight filled his mind. Her gentle curves, her burnished hair spilling down her shoulders... He wanted to bury his face in that place between her neck and earlobes, to kiss the softness of her silken skin and breathe in her scent.

A cold flake splattered his forehead. He shifted his position and threw his arm across his eyes.

Damn it all to hell. Why did she have to look the way she did? The ache in his loins was more than just the cold. It was lust, pure and simple.

More flakes dotted his forehead. He ran his hand across his face and looked up. He shivered.

Hellfire. He refused to lie here suffering in the cold when a warm, dry cave beckoned a few steps away. At this point all he wanted was sleep. Snow or no snow, tomorrow he planned to set out for Otto Werner's outpost, where he'd soothe his hankerings with a bottle of rotgut.

Sheen sat up when Guthrie stormed into the cave. Her lips parted and a gasp slipped past.

He met her glare directly. "It's damned cold outside." He dropped the saddle to the ground, shook the snow from his hat, and flopped down next to the fire. "You stay on your side of the fire, and I'll stay on mine."

Sheen lowered herself back down, hugged the quilt close to her breast, and closed her eyes.

He could hear her breathing, and he watched the rise and fall of her chest from the corner of his eyes. Her scent of mint reached out to tantalize his senses.

"Guthrie," she whispered, "had we met under better circumstances, and if I weren't cursed...but now it's too late."

He couldn't resist her anymore. Gathering his blanket, he shifted to lie next to her. A warm current rippled over him, emanating from the point where their shoulders touched. Guarded desire shimmered in her green eyes, eyes that asked a question and probed his soul.

Guthrie lowered his mouth to hers. Sheen did not pull her head away but let her lips open just enough for him to taste her. Mint tea and peaches.

He stopped and pulled back, staring into her eyes, giving her the opportunity to push him off or roll away.

She lay perfectly still, and then he felt her hands sliding up his back, until her fingers buried in his thick blond hair. She pulled his face to hers. "Faith and begorrah, may the leprechauns dance on our graves," she muttered against his lips.

He moved on top of her, her softness warm and inviting. He explored her mouth with his tongue and let his hands roam, lowering the quilt. "I want to feel you, Sheen, and see you. Will you let me?" He slowly removed the heavy blanket and unbuttoned her dress. He slipped the camisole off her shoulders and exposed her creamy, rounded breasts, nipples erect and jutting.

Sheen shuddered. He feathered kisses down her neck and brushed the tips of her breasts with his lips. Arching her back, she pressed herself against him, warmth spreading from between his legs to his belly. It made him ache for more. He didn't want this to stop, wanted it to last forever.

He wanted this amazing, tantalizing woman he'd called a witch.

****

An owl screeched in the night. A coyote howled, and off in the distance another answered the plaintive cry.

In an instant, Sheen pulled away, struggling to cover her breasts. She clasped the bodice of her dress to her chest. Confusion and alarm stole across her face. "I've forgotten myself and who I am. Aye, and I have forgotten who you are and what it is you want...truly want. It isn't me."

Guthrie groaned, and lay as stiff as a pine log.

157

Minutes passed, and then he raised himself and kissed her softly on the lips. "I want you, Sheen O'Reilly. I don't pretend to understand these powers you have, but I don't fear them. My father used to say the things we feared most made us strong. You're a strong woman, Sheen. Don't use your gift as a barrier between us. With the patience of a man who knows what it takes to gentle a nervous filly, I will wait for you to come to my bed willingly and with an open heart."

He grabbed his blanket and settled beside the fire. His head lolled back against the saddle and he stared at the stalactites, knowing sleep would evade him tonight.

Sheen turned to face away from him. "Don't kiss me again. You speak of wanting me, but you do not speak of...love. I know from your ramblings when you sleep, and when you unknowingly open your mind, that your wife still holds your heart. You say you will wait until I come to your bed. You will wait a long time, for I am not Abigail."

The air in the cave suddenly turned cold, brittle.

Utter devastation flooded the last of Guthrie's checked reserves. He rose to chuck another log on the fire. "No, by damn, you're not Abigail, *Sheen* O'Reilly. If you were, you would not be here. And neither would I."

Though she tried to suppress the sob, it reached Guthrie. He seethed, the veins at his temples throbbing. He clenched his fist. "Tomorrow, no matter how deep the snow, we'll leave this place. You and I, Sheen, will find Otaktay and rescue my daughter. Until then, I will do my best from now on to keep myself in check where your person is concerned. But no more flirtatious looks from beneath your eyelashes, and no more rubbing your body with mint or whatever the hell other plants you know about. It will make things easier for both of us."

When she answered him with silence, he sighed and rolled to his side. Damnation, he looked forward to a good stiff drink of whiskey. Hell, the whole bottle.

Chapter Seventeen

"Damn it all to hell!"

Guthrie's aggravated curse woke Sheen. She rose quickly and, wrapping the quilt around her shoulders, went to join him at the entrance of the cave.

Standing beside him, she hugged herself around the middle and looked out to where the waterfall tumbled into the pool.

Snow fell.

Thin, featherlike slivers streamed down and were quickly covering the ground. She marveled at the beauty, the flakes coating everything in sight. Evergreens glistened and, tipped with white frost, appeared almost magical. She didn't need second sight to know snow meant trouble and a delay in Guthrie's plans.

"Are we trapped?" She thought about the ramifications of remaining in the cave with him for another night.

He reached down and grabbed his gear. "Not if I can help it. Let's get the horses saddled and make tracks."

"How far is it to the outpost?" Hot shivers coursed the length of her from his scrutiny. She moved away from the opening to heft her own saddle.

"If you're willing to do without morning coffee, not stopping for a noon meal, and if a blizzard doesn't set in, we might make Otto's by nightfall."

"What about the horses? Won't they tire?"

"They're good stock, Sheen. Besides, we have Arnou's roan to ride while resting either the sorrel or your mare."

"I'm not a predictor of weather"—she drew in her bottom lip—"but I have a feeling all is not right at Mr. Werner's. We should make haste before the snow gets too deep."

Guthrie raised an eyebrow. When he peered into her eyes, she wondered if he could see what was going on inside her head.

He grabbed her saddle. "C'mon, Sheen. Let's get the hell out of here."

****

Miserable and numb, Sheen spent the rest of the day and evening hunched against the cold. In spite of the steady down-drift, the snow didn't bank deep enough to keep the horses from traveling at a steady pace.

Guthrie had stopped long enough to slap his saddle on the roan gelding's back, and for Sheen to take care of her private needs.

She rested her chin against her chest and closed her eyes. The argument they'd had the night before, in the cave, kept creeping into her brain like a disturbing dream.

Wind kicked up, blowing frigid air into her face. It was enough for her to prod the mare alongside Guthrie. "How much farther?"

"Not as far as it has been."

Sheen spoke softly to Moon, encouraging the mare to press on as the northern air grew increasingly colder.

"Just a little bit longer," she encouraged herself and the horse beneath her.

Two hours later, Sheen's heartbeat sped at the sight of smoke spiraling in the distance. She sighed and darted a glance at the few crude surrounding buildings that made up Otto Werner's outpost—a smokehouse, a barn and corral, a small log cabin, an outhouse, and the trading post, a two-story structure with a snow-covered roof.

Relieved they'd made it this far, she reined Moon to a halt in front of the livery. Guthrie reached up and helped her out of the saddle.

"I'll see to the horses, Sheen. You go on inside and warm yourself. Mrs. Werner will likely have a pot of coffee brewing."

Exhausted, she closed her eyes and thanked her mother for small miracles, then unhinged Guthrie's arm from her waist. She tried to keep her teeth from chattering when she spoke. "Death is happening inside the house, Guthrie. I don't want to go in without you."

"The hell you say...Indians? Maybe that accounts for all the empty stalls. Damned thieving renegades. And where the hell is Burt?"

Leaning heavily against a stout post, Sheen prayed the ominous feeling threatening to consume her was merely fatigue.

"Not Indians. Put the horses inside the stalls... Hurry, we should hurry."

The last horse secured, Sheen nearly tripped over the hem of her dress as she ran to keep up with Guthrie's long strides. He tried the iron latch. "It's locked."

Using his fist to pound on the thick wooden door,

Guthrie shouted, "Otto...Otto Werner. It's me, Guthrie Tanner. Open up."

Seconds ticked by. Impatient, Guthrie said, "If he doesn't open up soon, I'm smashing a window and going in."

Sheen pressed an ear against the door and listened. "I hear footsteps."

Guthrie cradled the Hawkens in the crook of his arm, his finger on the trigger. Moonlight cut across to highlight Sheen's worried frown. "The only enemy inside is not mortal. You won't need the rifle."

A whiskered man, late in age and burly in stature, opened the door. "Ach, Guthrie! Tanks be you're here. Mine vife..." His hands were gripped into tight fists that reminded Sheen of two large hams.

A shrill scream from an upstairs room threatened to curdle Sheen's blood.

"Mine vife... The baby is come too soon. I send that no goot Burt for der doctor. Ist ten days gone. Vhy, oh, vhy, do I choose to live too far from a settlement? More than a hundert miles. I am dumm...dumm."

Sheen shifted her glance from the worried German to Guthrie, whose expression reminded her of a gigged frog and just about as helpless.

"With your permission, I have midwifery skills, Mr. Werner. Perhaps I can help."

"Ya, Ya. Dis ist goot."

She barked orders. "Guthrie, I need my bag of herbs. Mr. Werner, I will need you to heat lots of water, and also get me a stout needle, the kind used for mending saddles, and four strong leather thongs."

She tapped a finger against her lips as if taking a mental inventory of her needs. "Do you have cord, the kind to tie packages with?"

"Ya, Ya. I hab everyting you need."

"Mr. Werner, 'tis no time I should think of food, but Guthrie and I haven't eaten since last night. Would it be too much if I made a pot of coffee?"

"Mine dear *fraülein*, vhat ever you need I vill get for you und my friend Guthrie. Go, now, see to mine vife."

Sheen patted his arm and offered him a reassuring smile.

"Guthrie, don't stand there catching flies. I need my herbs—now!"

She started up the stairs, and when the burly German followed, she scolded, "No, Mr. Werner, right now, your job is to do what I've asked, please."

After taking two steps, she turned and asked, "What is your wife's name?"

"Mine vife ist Cheyenne. Her name, Dyani. Her English is goot. But she ist like me, not so young anymore. Maybe too old for to hab'n a baby."

"Don't worry, Mr. Werner. I'll do all I can for your wife and child."

"*Danke, fraülein.*"

****

Sheen entered the room at the top of the stairs and walked to the bed. A pair of frightened eyes looked up at her, and a voice filled with pain asked, "Otto?"

"He's downstairs in the kitchen. I'm Sheen O'Reilly, and I'm a midwife."

"D-did Burt get back with the doctor?"

"'Tis snowing. I'm for certain they'll get here as soon as possible." Sheen moved closer to the bed. The lantern light showed a woman with skin the color of smooth mahogany, beautiful but now past her prime. She feared Mr. Werner was right about his wife being too old to birth a child. "Do you mind if I examine you? I promise to be gentle."

The woman nodded.

"Mr. Werner said your name is Dyani. 'Tis a pretty name. May I call you Dyani?"

A groan was Sheen's only answer.

She lowered the blankets. "I'm going to ask you to pull your knees up as far as possible, and then I'll need to lift your nightgown. 'Tis important for me to know how much you are dilated."

As she worked Sheen talked, her voice low and even, in hopes of keeping the woman calm. It was as she suspected—the sheets were stained red.

A ewer filled with water sat on a stand next to the bed. Unbuttoning the cuffs at her wrists, Sheen pushed the long sleeves up her arms. Longing for a bar of lye soap to cleanse away germs, she filled the basin and rinsed up to her elbows. Rather than using a towel, she flailed her hands back and forth to air-dry them.

Running a hand over the distended belly and then down the sides, she gently parted the Cheyenne woman's legs. "Dyani, this may hurt at little. I need to see how far the baby has dropped. Draw in a deep breath, and hold it until I tell you to blow it out."

A look of alarm shot across Dyani's face, then vanished.

Sheen inserted her hand inside the womb and probed. Her worst fear was realized. "You can breathe now."

The woman stirred feverishly on the bloody mattress. Sheen sponged her lips with water, squeezed a few drops between them. Dyani moaned piteously.

Dyani's eyelids quivered then opened. Her eyes were glazed with fever. "The Great Spirit has punished me by taking all my babies. I have prayed he can let me keep this one."

"The baby is strong." Sheen hoped she had not told a lie.

Looking over her shoulder when the door opened, Sheen lowered the woman's gown. Wiping her hands on a towel, she rose and went to meet Guthrie. In a low whisper, she said, "The baby is turned the wrong way. How sharp is your skinning knife?"

"For God's sake, Sheen, what are you planning to do?"

"I'm going to cut the baby from the mother's womb."

"What the hell... No! You'll kill them both. And if Otto doesn't peel my hide for bringing you here, I shudder to think what Dyani's brothers will do to us."

"If I don't do this, Mr. Werner's wife will bleed to death and the child will die, too. There isn't much time, Guthrie. I need your help. But if you are not man enough, then I'll do the best I can—alone."

He stepped back as if she'd slapped him. He scrubbed hands over his face. "Okay, tell me what to do."

"I need lots of lamps to light the room. You'll need to run whiskey over your knife, then set a flame to it to purify it. If there is no soap, wash your hands with whiskey, then flap them in the air like this." She showed him how to air-dry his hands. "Do you have my bag of herbs?"

"Right here." He pulled the leather pouch from his

coat pocket and handed it to Sheen. She said, "Follow me to the kitchen. I must brew a tea of valerian leaves. It will help Dyani sleep."

Outside, the wind swirled, caught a branch, and hurled it crashing through the kitchen window. Shards of glass cut Otto Werner's hands. Through the open window, the screaming wind reminded Sheen of Ireland and wailing banshees. A shudder raced up and down her spine.

The flames in the lamps jumped and wavered, and some went out while the German and Guthrie rushed to secure a bearskin rug over the broken window.

Sheen steeled herself as she carried the cup of valerian tea up the stairs to the pregnant woman. A thin wind rattled the shutters, and Sheen looked toward the window. Catching a momentary reflection of herself brought a frightening flash of childhood memory— memory of herself hiding inside a straw man and wondering why the bad men had set fire to her *mamai*.

When she was older, her father had recounted the tale of how her *mamai* had cut a babe from its mother's stomach. He'd said, "The grim reaper spared the *báibín*, but nay the *bæn*." Branded a witch, Keelin O'Reilly had paid for her sin in the most horrible way.

And now she was following in her mother's footsteps. Sheen's trembling had nothing to do with the cold. She forced her legs not to buckle as she made her way up the staircase and into the bedroom.

Her voice was hoarse as she handed Dyani the cup. "Drink all of the tea. In a few minutes, you will relax. Don't fight it. Just close your eyes and sleep. It will keep you from feeling the pain."

"My baby?"

"I will do all that is in my power to bring your wee bundle into this world alive, kicking and screaming."

Except for the howling wind outside, all inside was quiet, as if the house waited...anticipated.

When the Cheyenne woman's eyes shut, Sheen leaned close and listened. "She's fully asleep and will not awaken for at least two hours. We must work quickly."

She looked at Guthrie, who nodded and tried to offer a smile of reassurance. Otto Werner crossed himself and uttered a prayer.

"Mr. Werner, Guthrie, no matter how tired your arms may get, I need you to hold the lamps high and hold them steady. I must have enough light to see what I am doing until completely finished.

"And Mr. Werner, are you strong enough to watch me cut the baby from your wife's womb?"

He nodded. "I...I tink so, ya."

"You won't faint?"

Though his trembling was visible, he promised to stand stalwart.

"I will need you and Guthrie to hold two lamps high by the table while I ready Dyani."

She lifted each of the woman's legs and tied them securely to the bedpost with leather thongs. To make certain she did not thrash about with her arms, Sheen tied each wrist to the bedrails.

She hummed a tune that was no tune. Her fingers touched the pulse at Dyani's throat, then her forehead, then pulled up and released each eyelid.

Guthrie and Otto Werner stood like statues with the lamps, but their eyes followed Sheen's every movement.

She pulled a folded leaf from her pouch, and sprinkled its powdery contents over the woman's belly. Then, wetting the powder to create a paste, she rubbed it into the skin. "'Tis valerian paste. It will make the skin numb so that she does not feel pain when I make the cut."

Her teal eyes looked first at Otto Werner then at Guthrie. "She may scream, but she will not feel pain. You must not move. The light is vital. Do you understand?"

Before either man could reply, she took the skinning knife, passed it over the flame of the table lamp, and stroked it the length of Dyani's belly. The Cheyenne woman's scream was like the cry of a lost soul.

Before the sound was gone, Sheen held a blood-covered baby in her hands. She took a strip of clean sheet and swabbed the inside of the baby's mouth, then she placed her lips against the tiny opening and gently blew once, twice, three times.

"*Mein Gott!* Der babe, it ist like the others—dead." Otto Werner exhaled a deep sob.

"Buck up, man. Let Sheen do her work."

A whisk of the knife cut the cord, the baby was laid on the folded sheets, and Sheen was back beside Dyani. "Hold the lamps closer," she said, her voice crisp with authority.

Her hands and fingers moved quickly, sometimes with a flash of the knife, and bloody bits of membrane fell to the floor beside her feet. She poured a dark fluid between Dyani's lips, then a colorless one into the horrible deep slash in her belly. Sheen's humming accompanied the small precise movements as she sewed the wound together.

"Mr. Werner, wrap your wife in these clean sheets and those warm blankets while I wash the child," she said. "Guthrie, you can cut the bindings from her ankles and wrists."

Sheen returned with the baby swaddled in a soft blanket. "Congratulations." Her chuckle brought an answering lusty cry from the baby, and the infant boy opened his eyes. "Meet your son, Mr. Werner."

It was difficult to see a man the size of a grizzly bear shed tears, but weep he did. "Mine beautiful baby boy, ve have vaited so long for you, your mama and me."

The German looked at Sheen, "*Danke, Fraülein* Sheen. I can never repay you enough."

The new mother lifted her head from the pillow. "Otto, our baby, is it—"

"He is a strapping good boy, mine vife." Otto placed the child in his mother's waiting arms. "Ve call him Jurgen after mine brudder for who died before his first birthday, and White Antelope after Dyani's father."

"Both are strong names." Guthrie wrapped his arm around Sheen's waist and held her close to his side. He whispered, "You are an astonishing woman who never ceases to amaze me."

She couldn't help the pleasure that lit her face.

Eyes the color of shiny coals looked at Sheen. Dyani smiled. "*Néá'eše, ma'heona'e.*"

Otto stood over his wife. He caressed her cheek. "She ist tired and forgets a bit of her English. She say, 'Thank you, medicine woman.' "

Sheen acknowledged the compliment with a slight

dip of her chin. "Dyani should rest now. Especially while the baby sleeps."

Guthrie cast a knowing glance toward Sheen. A twinge of joy pricked her heart for the hint of pride he'd tried to mask.

The German bent down and kissed his wife's forehead. "Iss a proud papa you've made me. Sleep, mine vife."

He turned from the bed. "Ho-kay." Keeping his voice low, Otto Werner rubbed his hands together. "Come, mine friends, I open a keg of ale brewed like in der old country. Ve make merry, ya!"

"I believe I'll have a tot of whiskey." Sheen needed to celebrate three victories. One for her mother, one for herself, and one for the pure consuming love that had come to Otto and Dyani Werner after a lifetime of emptiness.

Chapter Eighteen

A day became two, a week's procrastination led to another. Sheen found excuses to remain at the outpost. First it was the need to prevent the deep cut in Dyani's stomach from becoming festered, and then the tending to baby Jurgen while his mother healed.

For a man who had lived on the move for more than a year, Guthrie took little enjoyment in having time on his hands.

"You grow itchy, mine friend."

Guthrie forced back his irritability. "Should've been on the trail days ago."

"*Nein.* Your old enemy had to hole up for der winter same as you."

Opening and closing his fist, Guthrie said, "Would Dyani's brothers have word of Otaktay's whereabouts?"

"On the day of Jurgen's birth, I send smoke up der chimney announcing my son. Wounded Knife has no love for dat sumbitch. Ven he come, I vill ask."

"You are a good friend, Otto."

"I vorry, Guthrie. Ist too long since Burt ist gone for der doctor."

"How 'bout I ride out, see if I can pick up his tracks? Could've run into some trouble." Restless, he stood and stretched and sauntered away from the fireplace.

"Ya, sure. I go, too."

"Better you stay here, Otto. I don't trust how a bunch of randy trappers come down outa the hills to trade would treat two lone women."

Though seeming to regret the necessity of remaining behind, the burly German conceded to Guthrie's reasoning.

Outside, the morning was sunny and the winds had died down, so that the warmth lingered, offering a day that was pleasant and filled with promise that spring had finally arrived. Guthrie followed his friend to the barn.

"What month is this, Otto? I've lost track."

The German counted on his fingers. "Ack, it is April almost gone. Soon der trappers vill come down from der mountains mit many furs to trade. Dyani's family vill come, too. Ve *haben* big celebration."

The last of the melted snow ran from the eaves of the barn and dripped on the wet ground. A pine smell filled the fresh air. Guthrie forced back his old rage.

Otto rubbed his chin as he and Guthrie entered the barn. "Vhat about *die fraülein*? Who ist she?"

"She's an unusual woman with unusual talents, as you have seen."

"Come, come, Guthrie. Ve be friends long time. Vhy ist she mit you? She ist not your lover and she ist not your vife."

Guthrie slapped a saddle on the sorrel's back. Otto's words went unanswered, and the German wisely picked up a shovel to muck out stalls.

Leading the horse out of the barn, Guthrie glimpsed Sheen striding across the yard. "You're leaving," she said as if out of breath.

Straight-backed, with her auburn hair parted in the middle and bound in thick braids, she filled out the wash-worn calico dress with an appealing firmness.

"Going to look for Burt."

"I see. You are leaving without food, and"—she worried her bottom lip with her teeth—"without saying goodbye?"

He shaded his eyes with his hand and looked at the sun to tell the time. "Figured I'd get what I needed on the trail."

"Coffee, too?"

A noisy crow flew by overhead. Guthrie shook his head. "Reckon I can wait long enough for you to put together stores for a few days."

Sheen agreed with a hard nod and headed across the yard toward the house. And, much to Guthrie's surprise, she cast over her shoulder, "Saddle the roan. I'm coming with you."

"What? No, you're staying here"—he lifted his eyes toward the sky as if searching for words—"where it's safe."

Sheen whipped around and, with hands on hips, stomped back to face him. Her words spewed like molten lava. "You, who broke into my home, forced me to ride hundreds of miles in the cold and face down savages, who took me into a camp of murderers, made me spend the night on the hard floor of a damp cave— You, who have continuously called me a witch, dares now to care for my safety?"

Her eyebrows winged upward as she smirked. "There's a name for men like you."

"Yeah, you said it before. Bastard, right?"

"No, hypocrite."

He brushed back a lock of hair from her cheek, traced the frown lines along her lips. She was a lovely gift, one he didn't deserve. He didn't know when he'd fallen in love with her or how he would go about winning her heart. "True, all of it true."

She pushed his hand away. "Don't look at me like that. It muddles my brain."

He could not resist the urge to touch her again. "I thought Dyani and the baby still needed you."

She stared. Longing filled her face. "Saddle the roan, Guthrie."

He didn't know what tomorrow would bring or if they would find Burt alive or maybe scalped, but for the moment the crack in his heart didn't seem so wide.

****

Sheen felt like she was on fire. Her skin tingled where Guthrie had touched her. As much as she hated to admit it, the attraction between them was too difficult to deny, too hard to keep in check.

She hustled inside the trading post, sprinted up the stairs, and knocked before entering the bedroom.

Sitting in a rocking chair and nursing her son, the Cheyenne woman was a vision of contentment. "Dyani, I am going with Guthrie to help look for Burt."

"I treasure your company, Sheen. It is often lonely without another woman to share secrets with. You have brought happiness to this house. Won't you stay?"

"If your handyman is injured, he'll need my doctoring skills."

"It is not my nature to be selfish, Little Sister. Of course, you must go with your man."

Sheen gave the Cheyenne woman a quizzical look. "Guthrie isn't my man. He is rarely nice to me. I-I hate him."

"I have seen the way he looks at you, and the way you look at him." Dyani lifted her lips in a knowing smile, her eyes meeting Sheen's with warmth.

"Oh, go on with you now. 'Tis nonsense you're talking."

Dyani's laughter reminded Sheen of tinkling bells. "Hate is a powerful emotion, Little Sister. It will grow into love when you least expect it."

Sheen waved away the notion. "'Tis high time I get my feet moving. There's food to ready, and my bedroll, too."

Bending down, she hugged her new friend. "Don't lift anything heavier than the baby while I'm away. Gently wash around the wound and then pat the skin dry as you've seen me do. You should be all healed and ready for the stitches to be removed when Guthrie and I return."

"May the Great Spirit keep you both safe, my sister."

A shudder prickled the hairs on Sheen's arms. She reached to touch the crucifix between her breasts.

****

Midmorning, Guthrie and Sheen rode up the rutted path toward the hundred-mile stretch to the nearest town. In Sheen's estimation, it could hardly be called a road, simply two narrow ruts that seemed to lead nowhere. Riding in the lead, Guthrie twisted in the saddle often and frowned.

"What have I done to cause such scowls?"

"It's not you, Sheen. It's the canopies on these saplings. Makes me edgy when my view is blocked."

"How far are we from the outpost?"

"Two hours, depending on how the crow flies."

"How will you know where to look for Burt?"

"He'd follow this cut all the way into Billings. Weather was passable when he left to go for the doctor. Otto said Burt was riding a sturdy mount. If something happened to him along the way, we—"

"We'll find his body." She finished the sentence for him. "You think he's dead, don't you?"

"Out here, anything's possible. Best keep alert."

There seemed to be no more reasons for talk. He watched the sensual way Sheen's body moved, as if one with the horse, while he freed his imagination to paint tempting pictures.

Yes, he could see it in another time and place—he would ride in after working cattle all day, and she'd greet him at the door, her mystic green eyes welcoming, a tender smile curving her mouth as she stood on tiptoe to kiss him.

It was only a dream. He wanted it. He wanted Sheen. Cursing himself, because he loved Abigail and had pledged to love none other, he rubbed his chest to ease the pain within.

****

Sheen had already sensed Guthrie's thoughts, the turmoil of his emotions. The truth of it echoed in her head like an earsplitting gong.

Oh, Guthrie. I feel your anguish, your blind devotion to Abigail, and the maddening drive to find your wee daughter. I know the guilt you've heaped upon your shoulders. Aye, and the burden is a heavy one.

The rest of the day went without incident. Repeatedly Guthrie checked behind them. Not once was there any sign of Pawnee, Sioux, or Burt.

Sunset found them in an arroyo. "We'll camp here for the night. There's a stream. We can make coffee."

"Is it safe to build a fire?"

"The walls of the arroyo will shield the flames from prying eyes."

Guthrie saw to the needs of the horses while Sheen prepared a simple meal. An hour later, she sat warming her hands around a cup of Arbuckle.

"I'd forgotten how wonderful the simple things in life can be," she said wistfully. "A bed, a stove, a tub."

"You'll experience them all again soon enough," Guthrie promised.

"Aye, so 'tis you who now predicts the future?" Guthrie didn't miss the mischievous twinkle in her eyes.

They sat draining the coffeepot and savoring the cold sandwiches she had prepared before leaving the outpost.

Guthrie sat Indian-style with his legs crossed. Leaning his hands toward the fire to catch the warmth, he was reflective for a moment. "Sheen, that day I rode into the yard, if I'd asked for your help in finding my daughter, would you have agreed?"

He thought it took a long time for her to answer.

"I think in some deep corner of your mind, you knew I would say no."

She saw the frustration in his face at her answer, and the weariness.

"Why wouldn't you have said yes?"

"I knew you were coming... Well, not *you* specifically. All my life people have used me to get what they wanted and then turned on me." She nearly

178

backed off, her voice as sharp as honed tacks. "You believed me a witch, you believed I had magical powers, and I didn't trust that you wouldn't treat me as cruelly as all the others, once I'd helped you get what you wanted."

Without thought, she reached up and touched the high collar that hid the hideous rope burn on her neck.

He uncurled and stepped over the fire, then crouched down so their eyes were level. Wanting to touch her, he knew now wasn't the time. "I'm sorry, Sheen. Once upon a very long time ago, I considered myself a gentleman. I was raised to treat women with the highest regard."

He pressed his fingers to his eyes. "This is a poor excuse for an apology, but I am truly sorry for the way I've abused you, and for the way people have taken advantage and then hurt you. I wish I could take it all back. I wish I knew how to make it right between us."

The flames reflected the anger and self-loathing in his expression.

She touched his face, saw the man, and saw the boy he'd been. "It's time to forgive yourself. I have."

He looked at her, a strange new light in his eyes. "Thank you," he said huskily.

With nothing more to be said, Guthrie returned to his side of the campfire, lowered himself against the saddle, and settled the wide-brimmed hat down to the bridge of his nose.

Sheen pulled a wooden comb from her pack and dragged it through the tangles in her hair. She closed her eyes, in part from the pain in her scalp and in part to keep the tears behind her lashes from spilling down her cheeks.

Chapter Nineteen

The night seemed overlong to Guthrie, lying awake, his gaze seeking the stars for hours, awaiting the gray light of dawn on the horizon. He reached over and tossed a handful of twigs on the fire and listened to them crackle, burning orange and blue. In the soft light, Sheen looked ethereal as she slept undisturbed and wrapped in her patchwork quilt.

He sighed at the memory, sweet and not too distant, of when they'd come together in the cave. The sensation of her body against his was so strong he felt the wickedness of his own smile. He now knew how the bees must have felt when they were drunk on the peach juice from his mother's orchard.

Sheen had allowed him a sampling but had refused to give the fullness of her nectar.

He groaned and rolled to his stomach, his man root begging for relief.

****

The images were sliding into her head, Guthrie's images and shapes, and sounds and scents. She understood what he was saying, felt a surprising joy to know he was experiencing her.

The sound of his strained breath rose and floated down to her. They were standing face to face.

I care about you, Sheen. More than words can express. Let me hold you and show you how much.

180

Splaying her fingers, she slid her hands down his chest and meshed herself with his thoughts.

Do you know how safe, how right I feel when you hold me?

Ah, Sheen, do you know that your skin carries the fragrance of sunshine and honeysuckle, and just breathing it in makes me ache. It makes me want to taste you...everywhere.

Their thoughts roared to life. Like a runaway fire. Heat spread through her body, stealing her breath and leaving her panting shallowly.

You like the thought of my hands and mouth on you. I can picture it happening. Do you feel me, Sheen, like I feel you?

His erotic whispers won shiver after delicious shiver from her. *Yes...oh yes, Guthrie.*

Behind her closed lids she pictured them in the pool by the cave. Smiling in confidence and trust. She wore a gossamer nightgown and he wore the night.

She reached up to him and he lifted her high off the ground, so high she felt dizzy with delight and threw back her head to laugh breathlessly. The sound turned to a sigh of pleasure when he pressed his lips to the deep V between her breasts.

Curling her fingers in the silvery highlights of his hair she whispered, *More.*

He turned his head to the side and brushed an openmouthed kiss to the inside curve of her breast. Then another few inches over. Then another. With each progressive kiss, he freed her body from the gown, until the filmy material slipped from her shoulders.

Beautiful....so beautiful.

Kiss me. Let me feel your mouth, here. Her nipple

beaded at the thought of how it would be, and when his mouth covered her, she trembled from the rush of ecstasy that swept through her body like a summer storm. His lips suckled, his tongue stroked, and even though the dual sensations won a gasp from her, she cupped the back of his head and drew him closer.

The night air was cool on her moistened flesh when he turned to offer the same caresses to her other breast. Then the silky gown slid down to her waist and over her hips, leaving her completely exposed. His mouth claimed her, and heat spawned anew.

I can feel your heartbeat against my womb.

Are you afraid...of my seed growing inside you?

Nay, I am not afraid.

Then I can feel your heartbeat inside my mouth.

The provocative admissions intensified Sheen's desire, allowing yet a new self-confidence. She twisted and pressed closer, her body restless to learn everything. All-powerful, all-patient. Guthrie fulfilled each yearning.

He lifted her higher. His kisses grew more ardent and their bodies became like one long torch whose blinding flame reached toward the heavens.

Want me, Sheen, my beautiful witch. Need me.

I do. I do.

Touch me.

And he lowered her so she could. She shifted her hands that had been on his broad shoulders to his suntanned, fierce face. She directed her fingers over the crowsfeet that lined the edges of his eyes, and the scar above his eyebrow, and with each caress his stormy eyes burned with a deeper passion, virtually stealing her breath. When she followed each caress with a soft kiss, his own breathing grew strained, and his muscular body turned rigid, as if he were fighting pain.

Why are you hurting, Guthrie?

It's from wanting you too much.

I want you, too.

Then kiss me. Kiss me as though I were the only love in your life.

What about Abigail? How can you be the only love in my life when you still hold on to her?

She watched him seek the truth of those words.

She could feel him fighting the anguish that went beyond emotion, deeper than blood, all the way to that sacred part of the soul that cursed him to a life of perpetual torment.

I want both of you?

Nay, I will not compete. I am flesh and blood. Abigail is a memory. You must choose.

How?

I have already told you...forgive yourself...release the guilt. 'Tis time to stop punishing yourself for what you could not prevent. It was Abigail's time to leave this earth. It is your time to live.

Her gentle reminder freed him, as she had intended. Magic claimed the night, and with the tender violence he'd been repressing, he kissed her. And kissed her. Long, draining kisses that made them both tremble and soon had them straining to get closer.

Joy grew into unbearable agony.

Sheen let Guthrie lower her to the soft carpet of pine needles. Her hair caressed his skin like raw silk as he skimmed a trail of kisses up her legs. Then it obliterated the world like a moonless night as he rose above her.

The blue of his eyes burned into hers, and his hard, hot flesh probed with irrevocable intent. But it was his tender care that gained him entry.

Sheen's breath caught at his sensitive possession. Instinctively she arched to welcome him deeper. Behind closed lids the red tide of pain yielded quickly into an indigo pool of sensation and pleasure.

She heard him whisper and groan her name. She had no voice, no thought, only the unbelievable sensation of being fully and completely possessed.

Then he began to move.

It was all grace and power, and she quickly felt their mutual, irrepressible need to race toward oblivion, to reach that plateau of ecstasy they'd fought against for so long.

Then, in that breach of consciousness, as the heat and light of satisfaction united them in some psychic universe, Sheen opened her eyes.

The shock of being awake stole her breath away.

The haze of her vision cleared. She saw Guthrie asleep, the wide-brimmed hat covering his face, his ankles crossed.

Smiling through her tears, Sheen recalled Dyani's words. *Hate is a powerful emotion, Little Sister. It will grow into love when you least expect it.*

And Sheen knew it was true.

She ached to touch him, to put her hands on his body as she'd done in the dream. Shoving irrational thoughts aside, she rolled to her back and gathered the quilt until it touched her chin.

****

Something was wrong—dreadfully, horribly wrong. Sheen looked around and frowned. She did not know this place. What's more, it had no part in the dream she had just shared with Guthrie. She didn't want to be here and wished she could rouse fully from this trancelike state.

But the vision went on in spite of her distress.

Help me... I'm down here... Somebody, anybody... Do you hear me?

The excruciating pain gripped him, jerking him upright and forward. He lost sense of time and place. His voice grew weaker.

Sheen felt the man's panic. He didn't like where he was. Didn't want to be there.

There was blood. Lots of blood. And belatedly she smelled the unmistakable odor of death.

What did this mean? What had she picked up on this time?

It wasn't until the aura of deep anguish continued to press down upon her that she allowed herself to consider a different source, and attempted a telepathic connection.

What is your name? Tell me where you are?

In the distance an owl hooted, but otherwise the night remained hauntingly silent.

Please. Do you hear me? Who are you? Where are you?

It was like asking snow not to be cold. No matter how hard she listened, how open she made her subconscious, there was no answer.

Surprisingly, despite her active mind, she did sleep well. Her only disappointment was that she had not learned who was calling out in such despair.

Chapter Twenty

Startled from an all-consuming slumber, Sheen fought the hand shaking her shoulder. A voice murmured.

Her wild red hair shining in the early morning light and dark green eyes aflame with alarm, wide enough to swallow the sun, caused a slow smile to spread across Guthrie's face.

He called her name. "Sheen...Sheen, wake up."

Her voice rasped, "Guthrie? What's happened?"

He rocked back on his heels and grinned. If ever Sheen O'Reilly looked like a witch, she did at this moment. Still rumpled from sleep, she bolted upright.

He gripped her shoulders. "You were jabbering away in your sleep. Couldn't understand a word of it, but whatever you were saying sounded mighty serious."

She wrapped her arms defensively around her body. "I must have been dreaming."

He took her trembling hands and folded them around a cup of coffee. "Sounded more like a nightmare. Maybe the Arbuckle will soothe your jangled nerves."

"Aye." She lifted the cup to her lips.

He gave her a searching look. His voice was quiet as he watched color suffuse her cheeks. "You want to tell me about it—the dream?"

She took another sip of coffee as if to steady

186

herself, then coughed to clear the morning hoarseness from her voice. "I heard a man calling for help. He is hurt and in a place where no one can find him. I tried to communicate with him, but he...he didn't hear me."

She was breathless when she finished talking.

"You said—he. Did you see his face?"

Shrugging her shoulders, she sighed. "I only heard his voice. He sounded very weak, and in terrible pain."

Guthrie shook his head. "Do you think it was Burt?"

"I can't be for certain. Old ghosts seem to follow me everywhere."

"You said he was where he couldn't be found. Can you describe this place?"

She stared beyond Guthrie's shoulder, then closed her eyes and moaned.

"What is it, Sheen? What did you see?"

She stared into space. "Blood. Lots of it. And death, too." Coffee sloshed over her trembling hands. "It's screaming. Oh, Guthrie, it's horrible. I-I can't shut it out."

Guthrie removed the cup from her trembling hands and set it aside. Then, gently pulling her to his chest, he cradled his arms around her, resting his chin on top of her head.

He crooned to her as if she were a frightened child. "Ssh, hush now. You're safe with me."

Reluctant to leave the comfort of his arms, Sheen felt the pinch of something fastening onto and tugging at her soul. "I know I am safe with you, Guthrie, and for that, I thank you, but we have to go now. He's dying."

A deep expansive silence fell over the surrounding

woods. No birds sang morning songs, and none flew over the bright blue and cloudless sky.

****

Sheen turned in a complete circle. Her eyes wide, she stared as if studying an invisible crystal ball.

"There." She lifted her skirt and ran.

"Wait!" Guthrie grabbed the Hawkens, and while he sprinted to catch up to Sheen, he levered a cartridge into the rifle's chamber. He grumbled aloud, "Damn woman, charging headlong into who knows what, bound to get us both killed."

She raced through a copse of jack pines, twisting and turning and following an invisible trail.

And when she thought her lungs would explode for the need of air, the horror of her vision rose like a stark reality to greet her.

She jammed her fists to her mouth to keep from screaming. Her stomach revolted at the sight of the mutilated and maggoty remains of the carcass that still wore its saddle, the sickening stench so foul she fought the urge to retch.

She couldn't bear to see such things. "Oh, sweet mother, the poor creature."

Guthrie came to a halt to stand next to Sheen. He turned her in his arms. "Don't look at it, Sheen."

She felt truly sorry for the animal. "What did this?"

"Hard to say—grizzly, wolves, cougar. Whatever it was, this ole pony put up a helluva fight."

"Poor horse. It appears other animals have been at it, too."

Guthrie glanced at the area. The ground around the dead animal was stained a burnished brown. "I'd say the screaming you heard in your dream and the blood you saw came when this fella was fighting for his life."

He took a step closer and inserted the rifle barrel beneath a broad leather strap, then tugged until he was able to drag the saddlebag from the saddle.

Squatting, he unbuckled the strap, opened the flap, and reached inside the pouch. He removed a small sack of coffee, a box of .44 caliber slugs, a clean shirt, and a bar of soap.

Ignoring the queasy feeling from looking at the carnage, Sheen met Guthrie's gaze. "Do you think this was Burt's?"

Guthrie held the flap up for Sheen to see. Burned on the underside of the leather was the initials—BAR. "Reckon so. Didn't know his full moniker—just Burt Ramsey."

"But why would a grizzly or whatever go after the horse and not the man?"

Squatting on his boot heels, Guthrie surveyed the area surrounding the dead animal. He stood and walked a ways, looking at the ground as if searching for clues.

He tipped back his hat and scratched his head.

"What is puzzling you, Guthrie?"

"Even after ten days, the ground is still torn up." He squatted again, then brushed his hand over a clump of pine needles, gently pushing them aside. "Well, I'll be damned."

"Guthrie?"

"Hoof prints, and lots of them. It appears Burt met up with a party of renegades about the same time as a grizzly decided to attack."

"How do you know it was a bear?"

He pointed. "Pine needles covered over the paw prints."

Standing, he shifted his weight from one leg to the other before using the toe of his boot to scuffle away more debris. He picked up several pieces of dried pellets. "Bear scat, and from the difference in size, I'd say this was a she-bear with cubs. Coming out of hibernation and with babies to feed, she's hungry, and mad at the world. That deadly combination would make her attack anything that got in her way—especially if she sees it as food."

"Wouldn't the Indians have killed the bear?"

His voice held a hint of mockery. "Why? To save Burt so they could scalp him? Not likely. Besides, many tribes revere bears as their ancestors."

"Were these Pawnee or Sioux?"

"No way of knowing for sure."

Sheen hugged herself as if warding off a chill. "We're only a few hours from the outpost. It's frightening to know they were so close."

Guthrie tossed away the spoor. "Yeah, we'd better get a move on if we're going to find Burt."

"Sweet mother." A chill ran through her, into heart and bone.

"Sheen? What is it?"

"I can't explain." She cocked her head to one side. "Listen."

He gave her a puzzled look. "I don't understand. What am I supposed to hear?"

"Nothing. Nothing at all, because the birds aren't singing. It's as if all the creatures are waiting for us to make a discovery."

She cupped her hands around her mouth. Before she could call out, Guthrie admonished, "No!"

Struggling to keep her temper, she said, "Burt can't

have gotten far. Wherever he is, if he hears his name, maybe he will answer."

"Yell out his name, Sheen, and every Pawnee or Sioux within ten miles will come out of the woodwork, and then it'll be us fighting for our lives."

"How will we find him?"

"Look for what's out of the ordinary. If he's hurt, look for blood, or broken twigs, places where the ground has been disturbed."

Sheen held the back of her hand to her forehead. "I was right. This is a place of death."

The sun was warm on her back. She shed her coat and draped it across her arm. "Will our horses be safe if we leave them while we search the area for signs that might lead us to Burt?"

Reaching up and scratching the shadow of whiskers on his cheek, Guthrie didn't hesitate. "It's best not to risk it. Just as easy to lead them behind us as to leave 'em. C'mon, let's break camp."

By midmorning, Sheen and Guthrie had tied their bedrolls and war bags to their saddles and were leading the horses away from the camp. Guthrie warned, "Death smell is still pretty rank. It will most likely spook the horses. We'll cut a wide berth away from the carcass."

Then he added, "We'll cover more ground if we split up. But, Sheen, keep me in sight at all times. Never can tell who or what might be hiding behind the next tree."

With her bottom lip caught between her lips, she gripped the reins, leading the roan gelding away from the site of the dead horse.

The morning seemed endless as she moved slowly,

searching the ground for clues of Burt's whereabouts.

She glanced every few seconds to where Guthrie walked a hundred or so yards to her left. There were times when he seemed to disappear in the shadow of the trees.

Every nerve in her body seemed to shriek as she walked through the pines. The dark place in her dream haunted her. Ten minutes passed, or perhaps twenty. She lost track of time, especially when she succeeded in locating several bushes with broken twigs that interested her.

Her gaze focused on the ground, she felt like a bloodhound as she followed the meandering path, so rapt in her discovery that she forgot about keeping Guthrie in sight.

In the woodsy shadows, the firmness of the ground changed. Moisture wet the hem of her skirt and sucked at the soles of her shoes.

Without warning, the gelding whinnied and planted it feet with such force the reins were jerked from Sheen's hand. She let out a yelp as her feet slid out from under her.

A sound, similar to a loud belch, erupted beneath her. Before she had time to react, the ground quivered and then collapsed, leaving Sheen desperately clawing into the mud and pine needles to keep from being sucked away.

Her stomach rolled and fear rising from her belly, she screamed, "Guth...ree!" Oh, sweet mother, she prayed. Let me see him once more before I die.

Chapter Twenty-One

The desperation in Sheen's cry caused a chilly finger to race from the nape of Guthrie's neck to the base of his spine. In a quick glance about, he spotted her roan gelding placidly nibbling at snatches of grass.

A thousand thoughts raced through his mind. Rattler? He dismissed the thought. The ground was still too cold for snakes. Renegades, grizzly, cougar? No, the roan was too calm.

In one effortless motion, Guthrie swung into the saddle and raced the sorrel toward where he had last seen Sheen. His breath caught in his chest as he leaped to the ground, dropping the sorrel's reins.

Brief, terrible, and unmistakable, a shelf of earth had dislodged, leaving a gaping hole. Guthrie tested the ground for stability as he inched his way toward the opening. He bellied down on the muddied pine needles and sharp burrs to peer into the darkness.

His heart pounded like a sledgehammer. It made his ears ring. "Sheen?"

"Down here. I can see you."

Guthrie inched closer. He squinted until he spotted her dangling in mid-air.

"Are you hurt?"

"No, but it's so wet that I'm afraid the root I'm holding will pull from the earth."

"Try not to wiggle. I'll get the rope."

"I'm not sure there's time."

His mind reeled. He'd lost one woman he loved because he'd allowed his own stubbornness to rule his decision to avoid taking her and his daughter to town.

For whatever reason, he'd been given a second chance at love. He'd be damned if he lost Sheen before he had the opportunity to win her heart.

He weighed the length of time it would take for him to sprint to the horse, remove the rope, tie it to the saddle horn, then return to the hole and lower the rope to Sheen.

The urgent squeak from her throat shifted his decision. He prayed the ground was solid enough to hold both his and Sheen's weight. He scooted closer to the edge of the fissure until his shoulders extended over the gap. Using one hand to grip the muddied ledge, he leaned into the gloom and extended his right arm.

"Sheen, reach up and take my hand."

****

The spiny stem Sheen grasped hurt her palms and fingers. She felt faint. Her breath whistled through her nose.

"Sheen, reach up and grab my hand."

"What if I fall?"

"You won't."

"I'm afraid."

Guthrie's body blotted out the sun. She reluctantly released one hand from the straggly root and, obeying his command, reached upward. A squeak rose from her throat when the sodden earth shifted and the root loosened.

She stretched until her arm felt as if it would pull from the socket. "I can't reach any higher."

A shower of dirt rained on her face, stinging her eyes, and she guessed Guthrie had scooted closer to the edge. A wave of relief washed over her when their fingertips met. She felt the power in his hand and, for a moment, thought he might crush her fingers as he sought a firmer grip.

It wasn't enough.

"Don't be afraid, Sheen."

His hand groped hers. She knew if he could clutch onto her wrist that with his brute strength he would pull her to safety.

And just as the steel of his fingers sought to imprison the palm of her hand, she gave a little bounce to offer him more leverage.

Time seemed to stand still for a mere second. The burdened earth, saturated from melting snow and spring rains, released its grip on the stringy piece of root.

Realizing she was no longer suspended in space but falling, Sheen plunged down. The scream she heard was her own.

Air swooshed from her lungs as she landed in a crumpled heap. She lay still, allowing the shock of pain to ebb from her body. Gradually, she tested her legs, then her arms. Deciding no bones were broken, she sat up. Dizziness overtook her and the space around her rotated. She blinked her eyes and swallowed, waiting for the world to right itself.

Longing to cradle herself in Guthrie's arms, she groaned, tears welling in her eyes.

****

Guthrie felt as if his heart had stopped. "Sheen, answer me! Are you hurt?"

He listened, then called again. "Sheen?"

195

Loretta C. Rogers

There was but one alternative, and that was to climb down inside the hole to rescue the girl. When she didn't answer, he feared she had broken her neck in the fall.

Unmindful of the cold, wet mud soaking through his shirt and pants, he shoved to his feet and forced himself to calmly approach the fractious sorrel. As the horse backed away, Guthrie seethed inside but spoke in soft, even tones to the animal.

"You sorry piece of crow bait, now isn't the time for testing my temper. First opportunity I get, I'm trading your sorry hide for a horse that appreciates a good feed and a gentle hand. That is if I don't put a bullet in you first."

Heat itched Guthrie's scalp when, as he was within inches of grabbing the reins, the horse once again backed away.

Guthrie spoke between gritted teeth. "Damn it all to hell, horse, you're trying my patience."

The standoff between Guthrie and the sorrel gelding seemed an eternity. Casting a glance over his shoulder to where the placid roan stood, Guthrie already knew there was no rope attached to Sheen's saddle.

He unholstered the Colt revolver and pointed it at the sorrel.

"It'll be a mighty inconvenience getting back to the outpost with one horse. But I don't have the time or the inclination to play games with you, Jughead."

Guthrie used his left arm as a brace to steady his gun hand. The click from thumbing back the trigger seemed to get the horse's attention.

The animal flicked its ears forward, gave a little

196

squeal, pawed the ground, and then much to Guthrie's surprise walked forward.

"Well, I'll be damned. If I'd known all it took was threatening to shoot your sorry hide, I'd have done it a long time ago."

Holstering the revolver, Guthrie grabbed the reins that dangled to the ground. He gave the horse an affectionate slap on the neck, dismissing the fleeting thought of hobbling the gelding. He'd deal with the horse when Sheen was safe. With trembling fingers, he loosed the rope from the saddle strings.

Locating a sturdy pine closest to the hole, Guthrie tied a bowline knot around the tree. He gave a sharp tug, testing its strength. Rapidly coiling the length of line until he reached the tip, he tied a noose at the end.

With the coiled rope looped around his arm, he pulled leather gloves from his back pocket and slipped them on to protect his hands from rope burns, then sprinted toward the cracked earth.

He fashioned the noose around the arch of his boot, secured the knot, and, using caution, lowered his body over the ledge and into the dark abyss.

Over the past year he'd learned a bit about caves. They opened in places least suspected. One like this probably ran parallel to the mountains and had remained hidden and undisturbed for centuries. He also knew caves had walls, and unless the hole dropped straight down and opened into a larger chamber he should be able to touch a wall with his foot. Reaching out with his left leg, his boot connected with a solid surface. Balancing himself and using the strength of his hands and arms, he rappelled downward until his boots hit the ground.

Glancing upward, he estimated the distance from the surface to where he stood to be a good twenty feet. A far drop for man or animal, and especially for a slightly built, fair-boned woman.

There was a momentary silence. No sound except for his own breaths. "Sheen?"

Then he saw her, as she took a step forward and stopped, apparently overcome by dizziness. "Guthrie, I'm here."

When she reeled, he bounded across the space, clasped her outstretched hands, and pulled her to him. He pressed his face against her hair and stroked her back. The warmth of her body sent a charge of desperation and need through his heart.

Pressing her close, he said, "The last thing I saw was you lying on the ground, not moving."

"Oh, sweet mother, I was for certain the leprechauns had spirited me back to Ireland, and away from you."

His voice was a husky whisper. "I thought I'd lost you."

He felt his own heart beating, heard it thudding in the silence as she looked up at him, hopeful, with emerald eyes that shimmered with desire.

He kissed her lips, then hesitated. "As much as I desire you, Sheen, our first time together should be special. Not a quick tumble on a cold dirt floor, inside a cave. You deserve a soft bed with clean sheets in the finest hotel, and roses and champagne."

She closed her eyes and clutched him tighter. The disappointment in her voice was evident. "Aye, it sounds wonderful, to be sure. Alas, we must still find poor Burt."

And though she had smiled up at him with the words, that smile now vanished. She closed her eyes and moaned.

Guthrie scooped her into his arms. "You're hurt. C'mon, we've got to get you out of here and back to the outpost."

She said nothing, but her hands linked together, a sure sign of tension.

"No, Guthrie. 'Tis true, I am a little shaken. But we can't leave. He's here, and there's not much left of him."

"Burt?"

"Aye."

"Are you sure it's him and not some other...spirit?"

She crooked a smile, and closed her eyes. "This is the dark place I saw in my dream. The ground did break away, as I saw it do. Aye, this is where we will find Burt."

"You said there's not much left of him. I hope that means he's alive, and not eaten by critters."

"I mean he's barely holding on by a thread, and if we don't reach him soon, he'll die."

Guthrie thought if he were to know this woman for a lifetime, she would always remain a mystery to him.

"I'm learning not to doubt this mystical power you possess, Sheen. Lead the way."

"Do you think anyone from above will hear us if we call Burt's name? I wouldn't want to bring danger to us."

Guthrie chuckled. "Remember me telling you that Indians are a superstitious lot? Well, if a band of Sioux or Pawnee were up top and heard voices coming from the bowels of the earth, they'd think the devil himself was after them, and they'd hightail it out of here as fast as they could whip their ponies in the opposite direction."

She managed a laugh.

He looked at her then. "Maybe I should call his name. If Burt hears your angelic Irish brogue, he might think he's died and gone to heaven, and then really give up the ghost."

Sheen conceded. "Such thoughts! You are a sinful, sinful man, Guthrie Tanner."

Guthrie cupped his hands around his mouth and called. The name echoed throughout the underground cavern.

When the reverberation had ended, both Guthrie and Sheen stood stock still and listened.

Nothing.

"He's down here, Guthrie. It's almost as if I can feel the life draining from his body. He's too weak to answer."

"Mighty dark to go traipsing about into the unknown. Never know what'll meet us around the next turn."

"Aye, but we have to try."

She looked tired, he thought. He wanted to kiss the tautness from her mouth, to hold her until she fell asleep. The longing to touch her twisted in him like a knife in a wound.

He said, his tone expressionless, "Take my hand and stick close."

And then he called again. "Burt...Burt Ramsey, if you're alive, sing out. If you can't, try to let us know where you are."

"He couldn't have gone far, Guthrie. Before I

tumbled through the hole, I spotted several broken twigs and was following them without heed to where I was walking. Maybe the same happened to Burt, but in a nearby place."

"Anything's possible, Sheen. Could be he got lost trying to find his way out."

Except for calling the handyman's name intermittently, Guthrie and Sheen walked in silence. Time seemed to stretch into forever.

And then the sound came. A faint but repetitive tapping.

Guthrie shot a glance at Sheen. "Burt, if that's you, tap three times."

They listened and were answered by a tap...tap...tap.

"If we're close to you, tap once."

When the answer came, Guthrie said, "Damn, Sheen, I wish we had some food. Poor feller's probably half starved."

"If only we had a lantern to light our way, it would help make traveling a little faster."

Guthrie reached into his pants pocket and withdrew the tin holding his matchsticks and removed one. When he flicked the head with his thumbnail, the sulfur flared. He shielded the flame with his left hand. "It isn't much."

The faint light showed a low shelf. "We'll have to crawl on our hands and knees. I'll go first, Sheen."

The flame burned down to scorch Guthrie's fingers. He quickly dropped the match.

"Be careful, Guthrie."

The tapping started again. This time the sound was louder. "I believe he's on the other side of this crawl space, Sheen."

"Then we must hurry."

In less time than it took to count to ten, Guthrie called to Sheen. "Come on through. I'll hold the match up so you can see."

Sheen gathered her skirt between her legs. The hard surface of the floor scraped her hands and knees as she crawled through the low opening and toward the wavering spiral of orange flame.

Guthrie took her hands and helped her stand.

"He's here, Guthrie...over there." And she pointed.

A shaft of light from above pinpointed the frail figure propped against a large rock.

In two quick strides, Guthrie squatted next to the injured man. "How bad are you hurt?"

"Bad enough, I reckon. Broke my leg when I fell from up yonder." He pointed upward to where the sky was obliterated by a stand of brush. "Dang leg's busted in two places. Tried to hold onto the side of the wall. Thought I might use my arms and one good leg to climb outta here. Must've sprained my ankle. 'Tween a busted leg and a bum foot, couldn't make it. Pain's been real bad, Guthrie...real bad.

"Sure as hell thought this place was my tomb. I don't know how you found me, but I'm mighty proud you did. Leastwise, I won't have to die alone now."

Sheen squatted beside the man. She lifted his hand into hers. "I'm Sheen O'Reilly, Mr. Ramsey, and we are not going to let you die. As soon as Guthrie climbs to the top and gets to the horses, he'll figure a way to get us out. Then I'll make you a fine broth."

"Miss O'Reilly, I'm beholden to you."

She patted his hand. "You can rest easy now, Mr.

Ramsey."

"Burt," Guthrie said, "Is that the only way out of here?" He pointed to the opening above them.

"Don't rightly know. I was runnin' for my life. Thought I was runnin' through a pile of brush, lookin' for a place to hide, when the ground dropped out from under me and I landed down here."

Sheen shot Guthrie a scowl. "Time's wasting, Guthrie."

He nodded. "Boulders look as if they're stacked about right for climbing. With a little bit of luck, I should make it to the top without much effort."

He motioned Sheen aside, and gripped her shoulders. "I don't like leaving you."

"Don't worry about me. How will you get Mr. Ramsey out?"

He kept his voice quiet as he spoke. "It's a two-hour ride back to the outpost, and then another two hours back here. Maybe between me and Otto, we can figure a way. Only thing, Sheen, do you think Burt will last four more hours?"

She touched her hand to Guthrie's. "I don't know how he's lasted this long. It's a miracle gangrene hasn't set in. The bone is sticking through his pants leg. I'll need my herbs and the sack with the cookware and food, and then we'll be fine until you return."

His brows lifted. "You're a brave woman, Sheen O'Reilly."

And then he went to squat next to the injured man. "Burt, you hang on, ol' man. As soon as I get to the horses, I'll return in two shakes of a lamb's tail with food. Sheen, here, has doctoring skills. She'll take good care of you while I ride back to the outpost to get Otto.

Between him and me, we'll get you out of here."

"I'm beholden to both of you." Burt offered a weak smile. "I've got me a real hankering for a cup of Arbuckle."

Guthrie unfolded his lanky body to a standing position. "You've got it, friend."

Sheen followed Guthrie to the stack of boulders that he planned to use as a stairway to the outside world. She raised her gaze to his steel-blue eyes. She whispered, her voice nearly cracking, "Be safe, Guthrie."

He answered her with a nod and didn't look back until he had scaled the rocks and reached the top. Before disappearing from sight, he turned and gave her a salute.

**** *

Sheen busied herself setting a small fire. She collected water from a nearby pool and then brewed a pot of coffee.

Lifting the old man's head with one hand, she held a cup to his mouth. "I'm sorry you've suffered such pain, Mr. Ramsey. I've steeped an herb in your coffee to give you a bit of ease. 'Tis not very hot. I didn't want you to burn your mouth."

He choked on the first sip and then sighed after he'd consumed the entire cup. She was amused to see how he cradled his cup and sipped as if the Arbuckle were pure liquid gold.

"Don't remember when I've had better coffee. 'Preciate it, ma'am."

"Lie back and close your eyes, Mr. Ramsey, while I make us a nice strong broth."

"Ma'am?"

"Aye, Mr. Ramsey?"

"In the whole of my life, I don't recollect anybody ever calling me Mister. Sounds kinda odd to my ears. Reckon you could call me Burt?"

She offered him a gentle smile. "On one condition...Burt."

"Yes'm?"

"That you not call me ma'am or Miss O'Reilly. My name is Sheen."

"Right pretty name, ma'am."

His eyes fluttered shut and his breathing fell into a smooth rhythm, and Sheen knew the herb had taken hold. Burt was resting peacefully.

She leaned down and pressed her ear against his chest. The beats of his heart were barely discernible. She prayed Guthrie and Otto would return without delay.

As day ebbed into the night, a three-quarter moon hovered over the cave's stovepipe hole. Its brilliant beam illuminated the small chamber.

Sheen glanced at the injured man. His sleep was deep. The herb had worked its magic.

Gathering her skirt, she stood in the circle of light, stretched her arms upward, and closed her eyes.

She swayed to the music. Music heard only by the ancients and the fairy doctors. The time of the witching moon drew closer.

A shadow temporarily blocked out the light. An owl belled in the night. Another answered.

Teeth chattering, Sheen went down to her knees. A little girl's cries battered her ears.

Sheen whispered the name. "Rachel."

Chapter Twenty-Two

Otto Werner's outpost stood quiet under the midday sun. Horses dozed in the small corral. Sparrows flitted in and out of the stable's hayloft.

Sheen sat in a rocking chair on the porch looking beyond the animals and the lush green of the distant snow-capped mountains. The spirits had spoken to her. It was time to find Otaktay, destroy his evilness, and return little Rachel to her father.

She drifted back a few days to their daring rescue of Burt. They had placed his emaciated body on the flat bed of an old wagon. Otto had fastened a rope knotted at each corner, and as the burly German used the horses to pull the slab of wood upward, Guthrie climbed the rocks, steadying the makeshift stretcher with one hand. Sheen followed.

The way proved hard. The worn soles on her boots slid and she bruised and scraped the palms of her hands grasping the rough, porous rock to keep from plummeting to the bottom of the cave.

She silently called to her mother and grandmother to give her strength. It was only when a bumble bee lit on her hand, its tiny wings fanning the air, that Sheen knew she was safe. They were all safe.

Ten days had passed since their return to the outpost. So much had happened. Burt had agreed to have his injured leg re-broken and set so that it would knit back together properly. He would walk with a permanent limp, but he was happy to think he would not be a burden to anyone.

It was that day also when he related the near miss with Otaktay and his band of warriors. As if warding off a chill, Burt had pulled the blankets tighter to his chest and shivered as he recounted his harrowing experience.

"I never did like that patch of woods. Too dark and spooky. Well, sir, me and my pony was loping along, mindin' our own business, when next thing I seen was them salivatin' jaws of a she-grizzly and her yearlin' cub a-pawin' the air right in front of me.

"Poor ole Buck, that's my horse, you know, he was plumb skeered and reared up so high he fell over back'ards. 'Bout the time I got my senses back, I spotted that murdering Otaktay and a whole passel of his braves come a-barrelin' through the pines.

"Weren't nothing I could do to save poor ole Buck. But I tell you, he was puttin' up a purty good fight. I figured I was caught between being et alive or scalped. Didn't cotton to neither choice. Only thing I knew to do was light a shuck under my feet and try to find a hidey hole. I found one, all right.

"Don't know how long I was unconscious, but when I come to myself, I can tell you, the screams from Buck shivered my spine. He were being kilt, and there I was somewhere underground with a busted leg and no prayer of gettin' out alive."

Burt had reached up and wiped a tear from his weather-wrinkled cheek. "Won't be 'nother like Buck. We rode a-many a mile together. I was proud to own him."

Guthrie had asked, "Which direction did Otaktay ride in from?"

Burt scratched his sparse gray hair as if trying to remember. "Everythin' happened in a blur. I recall thinkin' how I hoped he hadn't attacked the outpost. 'Specially with the missus near her birthing time. Come to think of it, he was ridin' towards me."

"You mean he was coming at you from the same direction as the bear?"

Burt frowned up at Guthrie. "Well, ain't that what I just said?"

"In all the confusion, how can you be sure it was Otaktay?"

Burt leaned forward and spoke in a hushed voice. "I seen that devil eye of his'n. All white and turned back'ards. It were him, all right."

The old man's shoulders shook with laughter. "I remember lookin' over my shoulder, and them injun ponies were a buckin' and crowhoppin' somethin' fierce. Even old Many Kills himself got dumped." And then Burt harrumphed. "Shoulda broke that murdering scoundrel's danged neck, 'cause I spied fresh scalps hanging from his war lance."

Guthrie looked across the bed at Otto. "He could have attacked Fort Smith, or a settlement between Billings and the fort."

"Ya, I tink if der grizzly hadn't attacked, Otaktay vould be comin' here. He ist enemy of Dyani's people."

Guthrie had slammed a fist into the palm of his hand. Sheen knew revenge ate at his soul.

****

The Cheyenne woman's lilting voice shifted Sheen's attention back to the present.

"It will take time before Burt walks again. He is alive because of you, Little Sister. My son is alive because of you, too."

Sheen nodded, accepting Dyani's words of praise, and then her eyes widened and the blood drained from her face.

A frenzied excitement swept through the outpost. Dogs barked, horses in the corral whinnied and raced around the enclosure, and with rifles in hand Guthrie and Otto appeared from the barn.

Three warriors mounted on paint horses galloped into the yard and shouting, "*Ného'nâho'htsevâtse.*"

"Dyani, quick, we must arm ourselves."

The Cheyenne woman touched Sheen's arm and offered a reassuring smile. "Have no fear, my sister. It is only my brothers—Wounded Knife, Yellow Wolf, and Tall Buffalo."

"Whatever they are shouting sounds so fierce."

Dyani laughed. "They are saying, 'I have come to see you.' "

Otto walked to the center of the yard. *"Haa-hee,"* he said, lifting his palm upward to Wounded Knife, who dismounted. Yellow Wolf followed suit. Only Tall Buffalo remained on horseback.

"*Haa-hee*, Old Father," Wounded Knife replied. "It is good to see you."

"There is much to tell, mine brothers. Much to celebrate."

The man called Tall Buffalo pointed at Sheen. "The woman with hair like fire, she is the one with big magic?"

Otto answered. "She ist der reason Dyani and me haben our son. Her medicine ist strong."

The man who reminded Sheen of a piece of brown granite rode toward the corral, leading a magnificent black-and-white tobiano stallion, and a smaller horse, a brown-and-white pinto. He opened the gate and the animals followed him in.

Wounded Knife said, "The Great Spirit thanks the *ve-ho-e* for bringing Spirit Woman to our sister. For this, the stallion is yours, white man." And then he motioned to the one called Yellow Wolf, an old warrior dressed in shirt, breechcloth, and leggings. He stepped forward with a leather parcel in his hands.

Wounded Knife said, "My woman made this for you, Spirit Woman."

Sheen smiled at the man. "Thank you." She unfolded the package and held up a shirt trimmed with red beads in the image of a star. Between her fingers, the doeskin felt as soft as the petals of a delicate flower. "I don't know what to say." She did a small curtsey. "Tell your wife she honors me with such a beautiful gift."

Dyani pointed to the symbol on the shirt. "We are the Morning Star people. And now you are of the Morning Star, too."

Emotions welled inside Sheen as she hugged the Cheyenne woman. "It has been a long time since I've had a family. Thank you, Sister."

Wounded Knife huffed as if impatient with womanly emotions. He pointed to the corral. "My sister, we have brought small mare for our nephew. She is just weaned from her mother, and young like the boy. The two will grow together. Be good friends."

Dyani smiled at the old man. "Many thanks, my brothers. Come inside. We have roast venison, smoked trout, pickled quail eggs, boiled potatoes, fried bread, wild strawberries, and coffee."

While Sheen and Dyani went into the kitchen to set out platters of food, Otto offered each of his Cheyenne brothers a pouch of tobacco.

"Mine goot friend, Guthrie, has need of information, Wounded Knife. You answer, ya?"

The oldest of the three Cheyenne responded with a grunt and a nod. "What is your question, *ve-ho-e*?"

Guthrie joined the circle and sat cross-legged on the bearskin rug. He shifted his glance around to each man. Then he leaned forward with a lit match to light the pipe offered to him. Inhaling deeply, he savored the rich tobacco before blowing a smoke ring that floated delicately across the room.

The three elderly warriors exclaimed in awe at what magic the white man possessed to create circles of smoke from the inside of his mouth.

"Ah-ho, white man, tell my brothers and me how you make this magic." Wounded Knife spread his arms to indicate the two men seated on either side of him.

Guthrie gave a brief explanation of how he held the smoke inside his throat, and he then did another demonstration before passing the pipe to Wounded Knife.

It pained him to watch the old man's struggle to hold the pipe, and knew pride prevented him from asking for help. He silently prayed the old warrior wouldn't get choked on the smoke, and sighed deep relief when a fragile circle wobbled from the old man's throat.

One after another, Yellow Wolf, Tall Buffalo, and Otto experimented with creating circles of smoke.

Like excited boys, all the men cheered, with Otto bellowing, "Bring ale, mine vife! Ve celebrate more."

As the men drew in the tobacco and exhaled, then passed the pipe one to another, Guthrie said, "Do you know a Sioux warrior named Otaktay?"

Wounded Knife hissed. "Ssaah." He held forth his arms. The right one revealed a missing hand, and only the thumb and little finger remained on the left.

"Many Kills." He spat the name as if it were venomous. "Once I was a warrior who counted many coups. But Otaktay, as you call him, sought revenge when I hit him with my war cudgel and claimed his mighty stallion as my prize. For this, he took away my hands and my ability to hunt. The Lakota are our brothers. Many Kills is Santee clan. Even his name brings fear to his own people."

"It is said that Otaktay has a blind eye. How did this happen?" Though Guthrie's voice was soft, the tone was hard and flat.

"Saah." Tall Buffalo spoke. "Otaktay hates all white-eyes. When he was a young buck, he captured a white woman and brought her to his people. It is said that he rode her like a mustang and beat her just as badly. One time, she grabbed a stick from the fire and jabbed it through his eye. He slit her throat."

Guthrie was glad Sheen was in the kitchen with Dyani and had not heard about this vicious act of violence.

"How do you know this enemy of mine?" Wounded Knife wanted to know.

Guthrie lifted his gaze to look the man in the eyes. "Thirteen moons ago, Otaktay and his warriors raided my ranch. He raped and brutally murdered my wife and stole my little girl. Rachel was five years old. I've tracked Otaktay from here to kingdom come and never struck his trail. Then winter forced me down from the mountains.

"A few days ago, Otto's handyman, Burt, ran into Otaktay and his band of renegades. The only thing that saved the old man's scalp was a grizzly happened along about the same time.

"With him and his warriors this close, I figure Otaktay's intent was to either raid the outpost or head to his stronghold. Burt said there were fresh scalps hanging from Otaktay's war lance."

Guthrie studied the faces of the three Cheyenne brothers. All weatherworn men. All past their prime. Anger riffled through him as he clenched his hands into fists. "I want my little girl back in my arms. I want Otaktay dead. Will you help me find him?"

The Cheyenne were silent, with Wounded Knife probably thinking of the time when he and Otaktay had tangled and of the humiliation of no longer being a great hunter and warrior.

Deep down, where pain had dwelt for so long, Guthrie felt a piercing, stabbing hurt. He forced back the growl building inside his throat. With Indians, it didn't pay to get impatient.

He gazed through the window toward the Pryor Mountains and waited.

While his face remained as stone, sorrow leeched into Wounded Knife's voice. "I am no longer a great warrior. Today, I am a feeble old man who waits for the Great Spirit to call my name. My woman cries for our sons who walk with the All Father. She is beyond child-bearing age. There will be no more sons.

"Like me, Yellow Wolf and Tall Buffalo have lived many winters. We are old men. It shames us that we can no longer paint our ponies for battle."

Yellow Wolf said, "Tall Buffalo will lead our brother's horse to our summer camp. I will guide you to the secret stronghold known only to a few. There you will find Many Kills, if he does not find you first."

"How soon can we leave?"

The wails of a baby from an upstairs bedroom seemed to prompt the Cheyenne's answer.

"You will die soon enough, *ve-ho-e*." Yellow Knife held up two fingers. "When the sun rises over the mountains this many times I will show you the way. Now we celebrate the new life of my sister's firstborn child."

Chapter Twenty-Three

Sheen stood at the kitchen door, a tray laden with food in her hands. She supposed listening to the men's conversation wasn't really eavesdropping. After all, no attempts were made to lower their voices. What she heard caused her skin to slick with sweat, and her heart to bump and keep bumping. The deep timbre of Tall Buffalo's words echoed in her ears.

"Otaktay is tough as rawhide, and deadly with his gun and his knife. Heed my words well, white man. You must be more cunning than the enemy of my people. If not, you will die a death more horrible than my words can speak."

Against her will, Sheen's eyes closed. Her heart knocked against her ribs and her hands tightened on the handles of the tray. *No...no. I don't want to see.* She beseeched the vision and the voices inside her head to stay away.

Try as she might, the chattering images persisted. She tried to open her eyes. They refused.

Sun rays glinted off the razor sharp edge as Otaktay parried the broad-bladed knife from one hand to the other. The vicious expression never left his sooty eyes, even when he allowed a smile to grace his thick lips. His face bore several white-ridged scars, evidence of his many fights, although every man who had scarred him now lay in a cold, dark grave.

With swift movements, Otaktay used the knife to pop buttons off Guthrie's shirt. The warriors holding Guthrie chuckled fiendishly as he struggled against their grip.

In his desperation to escape, Guthrie called on brute strength to lever his body upward and, lashing out with his boots, landed a smashing blow to the center of Otaktay's chest.

The renegade's face went black and a large purple vein throbbed in his temple. He snarled, revealing dirty, yellowed teeth.

With one mighty swipe, the man known as Many Kills whipped the knife across Guthrie's neck. The two men who held him were sprayed with his blood. The warriors let go and Guthrie slumped into a heap.

Otaktay laughed manically, then leaned close and with his blind, disfigured eye stared straight at Sheen.

The sudden terror of it caused her to cry out.

"Sheen, can you hear me?"

The voice sounded as if it were calling through a wind tunnel. She tried to answer.

"Sheen, open your eyes. It's me, Guthrie."

She wanted to obey his command. She thought she looked up at him and smiled.

"Let go of the tray, Sheen. It's okay. I've got you."

She felt his breath near her ear, felt his hands steadying her. She opened her eyes, her muscles trembling, her pulse pounding, an ache in her heart. Her fingers hurt as she opened her hands and released the tray to Guthrie's custody. Her eyes shifted to the distressed look on Dyani's face as Guthrie handed the platter of food to the Cheyenne woman.

Concern filled Guthrie's voice. "What did you see,

Sheen? Tell me."

She sighed a weighty sigh, knuckled her eyes, and peered at him. Her throat convulsed as she spoke. "I can't tell you. It's too horrible."

"Was it Rachel? Did you see her?"

"Nay, Guthrie, I did not. Please, I need to lie down."

He nodded his understanding. "I'll be up in a bit to check on you."

As she turned to leave the kitchen, Yellow Wolf blurted out, "Whiskey. Otaktay likes whiskey."

She'd momentarily forgotten about Dyani's brothers. Old warriors. Too old to fight. Too old to protect Guthrie.

Tall Buffalo answered, "Saah, our old enemy favors the white man's firewater."

And then Otto said, "Ya, by Gott, we get dat savage betrunken."

Sheen looked into Guthrie's blue eyes. "It won't work, you know."

"What won't work?"

"Getting Otaktay drunk. He's much too smart. First, he'd steal the whiskey and kill all of you, then celebrate your deaths by drinking himself into a stupor."

Guthrie's breath came out on a shaky laugh. "Is that what you saw in your vision?"

Sheen moved to the stairs. Not bothering to answer his question, she lifted her skirt and was half way to the top when she stopped, hesitating a mere second before she turned. "Don't try to leave without me, Guthrie."

A smile twisted his lips, seriousness lit his eyes. "You know I don't like it when you invade my thoughts."

A light breeze caused the kitchen curtains to dance, twined up with the scent of wild honeysuckle. She was tired of the pain she suffered when she opened herself. Yet here she was opening herself to all that hurt again.

Though she knew he jested, the quip was lost to her. "If you want to find Rachel alive—" She left the sentence unfinished. Let him draw his own conclusions, she thought, and then she made her way up the remaining stairs, opened the door to her room, and closed it softly.

A wave of dread washed over her.

****

Guthrie's face grew somber. He continued to look up at the staircase for long moments after Sheen had vanished through the doorway to her bedroom.

He stepped back, shoved his thumbs inside the waistband of his faded leather pants, and then returned to sit with Otto and the old warriors.

Tall Buffalo was the first to speak. "Your woman, she is *winyan wanagi.*"

"Spirit Woman?" Guthrie's brow wrinkled into a frown. "How do you know this, Tall Buffalo?"

"Blue Elk, the medicine man of our village, spoke of the spirit woman with hair the color of fire. He saw the moon die and the earth blanketed in total darkness. On the night of the witching moon, the one you call Sheen will come full into her power. She is your greatest weapon. Listen to her and heed her advice, for she is the only one who knows the way."

Guthrie's heart pounded. No longer amazed to hear about magical powers, he was learning to accept them, as did the Indians, including these three warrior brothers and their sister, Dyani. "I don't understand. She will show me the way to what?"

As if they were one, the old men unfolded their aged bodies and stood. Tall Buffalo's aged voice cracked. "The day is dying and my old bones are tired. We thank you, Sister, for the food, and our brother for the bitter water that warms our bellies and makes us long for the days of our youth when we hunted the buffalo and spent endless nights pleasuring our wives. We will sleep in the barn with our horses."

The men moved toward the door. "Wait," Guthrie said, his mood souring at the old man's obscurities. "You didn't answer my question. What way will Sheen show me?"

Tall Buffalo held out a handless arm and pointed toward the mountains. "That which you seek, *ve-ho-e*."

Guthrie met the man's watery gaze with silence. Thoughts came rushing in. South Carolina. Abigail. Rachel. Sheen. Otaktay.

Revenge.

He strode away to his own room, and an overwhelming sense of loss consumed him.

The moon hung low beneath the scattered clouds as he stood at the second story window looking toward the mountains. The ground below was covered with a swirling fog. It glistened in the moonlight.

He watched the warrior brothers stride across the yard to the barn. With the animals confined for the night in their pens, all was quiet at the outpost.

And then he saw her. Like an apparition, Sheen appeared through the mist.

He let a sad smile lift the corners of his lips. Steel encased his heart, but it was no longer forged in anger.

He'd come to value Sheen. He might even love her.

The revelation shocked him. The realization told him he needed to know how deep the taproots of his feelings for her had grown.

The thought calmed him yet didn't help deflect the blame he'd heaped upon himself for the death of his wife and the abduction of his daughter.

Guthrie peered up at the darkened sky. Searching until the three-quarter moon came into view, he tried to recall what Sheen had said about the witching moon. Now the old warrior had spoken of it.

What the hell is a witching moon? The question ran through his mind. He didn't know how soon this phenomenon would occur, but he needed to be on his guard when it did happen.

He'd allowed his thoughts to ramble, and when he looked again, only the swirling mist remained where Sheen had stood. Deciding he'd imbibed one too many glasses of Otto's warm beer with whiskey chasers, he stepped across the room and wearily sank onto the bed.

****

Sheen rested her head against the goose-down pillow. She squeezed her eyes shut, but, no matter how she tried, she could not put aside the vision of Guthrie lying still on the ground, in a puddle of his own blood. A surge of panic rose from her stomach, and she fought the urge to retch. Her thoughts interrupted, she tensed as a light rap sounded against the door.

With the covers pulled to her chin, she watched through squinted eyes as a halo of light outlined Guthrie's large frame. He cut a handsome figure in the soft glow from the lantern that hung from the hallway ceiling. His broad chest strained at the seams of his blue chambray shirt. He spoke, his voice barely above a whisper. "Sheen?"

In the dim light, he was a dark shadow, all the larger now for the burden she knew he carried.

She held her breath, fearing any sound she made would bring him to her bedside. A thin wind rattled the shutters, and when Guthrie's boot heels echoed against the wood-planked floor, she scooted deeper beneath the blankets.

A jolt of pain shot through her soul when he bent and kissed her cheek. The sad roll of his words tugged at her heart. "Too much has been taken from me. I don't think I could stand losing you, too, and I can't leave without telling you I'm sorry that I forced you to come with me, but I am glad you're here. I would do anything to find my daughter and bring her home. I wish I could promise that I'll return to you."

He reached down and brushed his fingers over her hair. "When you had the vision tonight, the expression on your face told me otherwise. Rest well, my beautiful witch. I'll be long gone before the sun greets the day."

She sensed him turning away, sensed his hesitation, and sensed that what he was going to say would hurt her heart even more. "I promise if I survive whatever Otaktay puts me through, I'll return to you, and we will live in peace, together."

She listened to the gentle footfalls as he made his way across the darkened space. A glimmer of light bled into the room when he opened the door, and then she was shut in total darkness.

Slipping out of bed and tiptoeing to the window, she leaned her head against the chilled pane. She heard an owl bell and the night creatures singing their songs.

Her mind was racked with confusion and with anger. He feared for her safety and planned to leave without her. Guthrie was the kind of man women fell in love with. The kind she wanted to fall in love with. Once that step was taken, it colored everything you thought, everything you did, and everything you felt. In the bold hues of joy. In the drowning grays of despair.

Miserable and numb, she walked back to the bed, and covered herself with the thin, battle-scarred armor of that belief. Rolling to her side, she pulled her knees to her chest.

She had loved once, and he had died. So this step couldn't be taken. Not again.

The visions crept into her dreams and kept her awake most of the night.

Chapter Twenty-Four

From atop a tree-lined knoll, Sheen watched the dawn crest the horizon, the morning air clear and quiet, the pale blue sky feathered with delicate clouds. She inclined her head, sensing the gelding was getting restless. "Patience, Jughead. Besides, Guthrie will be along soon."

As much as she'd wanted to ride Moon on this journey, she knew better than to have a mare in the presence of a stallion. Guthrie had aptly named the fractious gelding she had chosen as her mount. The horse quivered and champed at the bit. It hunched its back, a signal she'd often witnessed when the horse would try to unseat Guthrie.

"Oh, no, you don't." Planting her boots firmly in the stirrups, she leaned forward and whispered into the wall-eyed horse's ear.

The gelding flicked its ears back and forth as if understanding the words Sheen spoke. She placed an affectionate pat to the sorrel's neck. "Aye, 'tis a good laddie ye'll be from this day forward."

No sooner had she spoken the words than she caught a hint of movement. A horse, fast approaching. The earth vibrated beneath its hoof beats. Guthrie sat astride, his long legs hugging the black-and-white tobiano stallion.

The gift Dyani's brothers had given Guthrie suited

him well. A spirited horse and a powerful man. Both exuded strength and danger.

She urged the gelding from the stand of aspens. As Guthrie drew closer, she knew by the expression on his face he was not happy to see her.

He hauled on the reins, and the stallion reared and snorted, his front feet slicing through the air, then pounding the ground. An ear-piercing whinny peeled from his throat.

Anger flared in Guthrie's eyes. Not at the mighty stallion. "Where the hell do you think you're going?"

Sheen straightened, her face transformed into that of a woman in control, who had decided what needed to be done. "The day will be long gone by the time Yellow Knife and his brothers sleep off all the alcohol they consumed last night. They didn't even stir when I saddled Jughead and led him from the barn."

Guthrie scowled, resisting any sort of understanding. "That's not what I asked you, Sheen."

To indicate her vexation, she drew a deep breath and slowly expelled it. "Sweet mother, 'tis as plain as the nose on your face, Guthrie Tanner. You need me, and we both know it. If you make me go back to the outpost, I'll just wait until you're out of sight and then I'll follow."

He huffed out an exasperated sigh. "I ought to haul you out of the saddle and tie you to a tree, but I suppose you'd use witchcraft to untie yourself and follow me."

A secretive smile traced across her lips. "And you might be right."

His voice took on a more serious tone. "I admire your courage, Sheen. I don't know what kind of powers you have or don't have. You already know we're on a treacherous journey. Otaktay is no ordinary Indian. He's not only cunning, but he has no soul. Which makes him even more dangerous."

Guthrie reached forward and lifted the crimson braid from Sheen's shoulder. For a second, it seemed he'd forgotten time as he fingered the silken strands. "You have beautiful hair. I'd hate to see it dangling from his war lance."

She tilted her head, studying Guthrie, and her face softened. "When we find Rachel, she will need your strength, but she will also need the comfort of a woman's arms."

Guthrie rubbed his neck. He peered toward the horizon as if allowing her words to soak in. "If you have magic, help me use it against Otaktay and his renegades."

"I've told you, I have no magic. And even if I did, how exactly do you propose I use it?"

"Dammit, Sheen, I'm a father searching for his daughter. The only powers I have are the abilities to ride, shoot straight, and use good logic. I've seen what you can do, and it defies anything I've ever witnessed. I'd call it magic."

"Aye, in Ireland, they call us fairy doctors— women born with the second sight and the ability to communicate with animals. But, nay, we are not witches. I did not ask for this curse. It was gifted to me many centuries before I was born. Now, do we sit here debating who or what I am, whether or not I have magical powers, or do we place our trust in each other?"

He glared at her. "Damnation, woman, you're like a pine burr stuck in the seat of my britches."

Her eyes widened into a smile. "Good. At least we agree on something."

Clucking the gelding forward, she pointed toward the mountains beyond where she had fallen through the crevice and where they had rescued Burt Ramsey. "There is where we will find your enemy."

"That's away from the Powder. Yellow Knife said we'd find Otaktay and his band somewhere along the river."

"You've searched the Powder River and beyond, and the reason you didn't find Rachel is because Otaktay's hideout isn't there. You've asked me to trust you. Now you must trust me, Guthrie."

Indicating she should take the lead, he muttered something under his breath, but loud enough for her to hear. "Damnation. Then where is he?"

Reining the sorrel gelding around to face Guthrie, she weighed her answer. A moment of doubt crept in. What if she was wrong? "Last night, I dreamed of a very large snake. Its body was as large around as your girth, and it had humps on its back."

Puzzlement filled Guthrie's face. "I've seen some mighty big rattlers in my time, but nothing like what you've described. What kind of snake was it?"

"I've only read about jungles, in a place called South America. There were drawings of strange people and even stranger-looking animals. The jungle is a place where this evil creature lives in the water. Like Otaktay, it strikes without warning and it crushes its victims to death. It is called anaconda."

His brief tender look sent a wave of warmth through her. "Yeah," he replied. "Come to think of it, Anaconda Butte does resemble a huge snake, and it's the perfect hiding place. A long line of mountain ranges, tall enough to hide smoke from campfires and to block out sounds from horses and people. There's plenty of grass, and in the center a spring-fed lake. I never could figure out why he didn't move his people from winter camp to summer camp like the other tribes. Now I know. Everything his people needs is at the Anaconda."

"Then we should make haste. How long will it take us to get there?"

"Going at a pace steady enough not to wear down the horses, I'd say a week." Saddle leather creaked beneath him as he shifted his weight. "The Anaconda is a long range of mountains. The trick is finding the right one, and the opening to his stronghold."

Sheen offered him a reassuring smile. "Don't worry. We'll find it—together."

****

After a long day of riding in the misting rain, Sheen was glad when Guthrie signaled to stop. "We'll spend the night here. I'll make us a shelter while you tend to the horses."

She tied the two animals to a tree and loosened the girths around their bellies. She had learned the necessity of not removing a saddle, especially if having to make a quick escape.

Grabbing the saddle bags and the food sack, she ducked beneath the blanket Guthrie had fashioned over two low hanging branches. The rain had stopped and streams of moonlight filtered through their meager shelter, casting feeble rays inside the damp interior.

"It's not fancy, Sheen. Wish it could be more."

He'd found wood dry enough to build a fire, and

the small blaze warmed the open space.

"It will do, Guthrie," Sheen said, pulling a frying pan from the food sack. "Do we eat a cold meal, or is it safe to fry some bacon?"

"Safe enough, I reckon. Coffee will taste mighty good."

She set about creating a sparse meal. Too tired for conversation, they ate in silence.

"You look all done in, Sheen. I'll clean up and set the pot for morning coffee. Rest while I try to find some more dry wood."

Sheen collapsed onto the pallet. And though it was late in the month of May, her feet and fingers were numb with cold and her soaking clothes stuck to her like a chilly second skin. Tiredness consumed her strength. She wilted, closed her eyes, and drew a deep breath, as if she could somehow force the dismal day to end. It was hard to imagine life as it was just a few hours ago, with a roof over her head and a comfortable bed with a pillow to support her head. She wondered if she would ever have a peaceful life.

Guthrie's words came to her—*we will live in peace, together*. And though she believed his words, she knew nothing would ever be the same.

The crunch of boots against leaves and underbrush sounded as he strode into the shelter with a bundle of sticks beneath his arm. He dropped the kindling to the ground, and settled beside her. "Tell me about fairy doctors?"

The question took Sheen aback. "Are you making fun of me?"

"Nope, just curious."

Sheen sat up and wrapped her arms around her

knees, hugging them to her. "Legend has it that fairy doctors are born only once every five years. And that once every one hundred years, a special fairy doctor is born."

"Are there men fairy doctors?"

"Not that I've ever known."

"How do you know you're the special one?" Sheen's face tightened like a bow being pulled. The look caused Guthrie to lift his hands as if warding off an attack. "Don't take offense, Sheen. I'm just asking. How do you know? Is it because your father put all of this nonsense in your head?"

The question drew a puckered frown to her face. She opened her mouth, then closed it again before something leaped out that she hadn't thought through.

She lifted her laced fingers and closed them again, like a prayer. Her voice came quiet yet deliberate. "Those who are chosen to be special are marked before birth, while still in the mother's womb. I carry the mark."

"You mean a brand like ranchers put on their cattle to identify them?"

"I've never quite thought of it like that, but yes, I suppose the All Mothers brand their chosen ones to identify them from the ordinary fairy doctors."

His eyes blue as hers were green, quirked into a half-assed smile. "The brand on my cattle is the circle T. It's burned on the haunch. What about yours—where is it and what is it?"

His hair was a little damp, so the gilt edges of it stood out, emphasizing the mischief in his eyes. Tamping down her fury, she cocked an eyebrow. "'Tis a wee fairy, her wings are spread, and she holds a tiny globe in her hands. And it is, as you say, on my—haunch."

"Before you get too angry with me, tell me about your special powers."

"Witches are evil. They take delight in doing harm, Guthrie." Her voice snapped at the end, like a whip's crack. "I am not a witch."

He acknowledged her reply with a bland smile. "Hold on, now. This time you're the one who said witch."

He reached for her skirt and she slapped his hand. "Don't," she warned.

"Seems like I keep sticking my foot in my mouth. What makes a fairy doctor special?"

"She doesn't come into her full powers until the night of the witching moon."

"What is the witching moon, Sheen? I want to understand who you are."

"There are things about myself and the powers I possess that even I do not understand." She pointed a finger at the fire and, instantly, small flames jumped from twig to twig. Sheen gasped. "I d-didn't do that, did I?"

Guthrie clasped her hands between his. He chuckled. "Well, at least we don't have to worry if we run out of matches."

Sheen withdrew her hands and tucked them inside the sleeves of her coat. "Not funny."

"No, it wasn't. You were going to tell me about the witching moon."

"My father said it would happen in my twenty-third year, at the time when the moon is full, and then the day will turn to night and all the world will turn black. There will be a mighty rush of wind, and the spirits of all my grandmothers will rise from the dead and give me their gifts."

Guthrie sat back on his heels and wrestled with his sleeves, attempting to withdraw his arms from the wet leather shirt. It was clear that he had no intention of asking for assistance.

Sheen barely had the strength to rise, but she stood above him and pulled on his sleeves until his arms were free.

"Sheen, have you ever heard of Hallowe'en?"

"You mean the time of Samhain?"

"I don't know about any Samhain, but what you're describing sounds like the story my grandmother used to tell about All Hallows Eve, when the witches brewed their magic spells in cauldrons and boiled little children who were naughty. We called it Hallowe'en, and it happens in October, not May. It's all a myth, Sheen. None of it is real. In all my thirty-one years, I've never seen the day turn to night."

"You're making fun of me."

"I'm not. Believe me, after the things I've seen you do, I'd never make fun of you. What I think is that your father filled your head with so much nonsense that you've come to believe it."

Furious, she heaved the wet shirt and hit him smack in the face. "Do not belittle my father, or poke fun at that of which you have no knowledge."

She strode from the camp, torn between getting on her horse and riding away or staying to help Guthrie rescue his little girl.

****

"Hellfire and damnation." Guthrie ran his hands

through his hair. His fate was tied to a comely witch who didn't want to be one and who had no idea of the effect she had on him. Never before in all his life had he resisted the urge to take a woman in his arms and kiss her senseless. Women had always been so willing. And then he'd fallen in love and married Abigail.

Damnation, he was cold and tired. He longed to feel a woman's supple and warm body next to his. Closing his eyes, he tried to visualize Abigail. The only face he saw was Sheen's.

****

Sheen stood on the fringes of the camp, wrestling with her emotions. All her life she'd been the victim of people's ignorance, and had the rope burns around her neck to prove what happened to those who were deemed different from others.

She thought about Guthrie and the things about him that made her heart go still, like the way his wet shirt clung to his well-formed chest and made her breath refuse to leave her lungs. No, it was something else entirely. It was that hint of vulnerability that made her want to return to the shelter and trace the long column of his neck and run her fingers through his thick, blond hair. A nameless pull that made her want to fill the space between them, though he stood barely a hand's breadth away. She wanted to breathe the same air he breathed. She wanted his warmth and his masculine scent wrapped around her and to feel the strength of his powerful and muscled arms.

She wanted to run her fingers across the scar that marred his shoulder, over his torso, lean and tight, narrow waist with rippling muscles on each side that met in a V and dove downward beneath the front of his leather britches.

Just as she thought she couldn't stand another moment of longing for him, he rolled the leather britches past his hips, down his muscular thighs.

Astonished and speechless, she studied him, all of him, unabashedly, though she knew she should look away. But she could not avert her eyes. Behind him, the low fire danced and cast a golden glow on his nakedness. His buttocks were as strong and as round as a stallion's, and his long hard legs as taut as bowstrings. There between his thighs rested...

Sheen's breath quickened. Goose bumps rippled up and down her arms. A strange sensation filled the pit of her stomach, and at the apex of her womanhood warm moisture formed. She bit down on the inside of her cheek to keep from looking lower. It wasn't seemly that she should inspect him so, but in truth, she could not tear her eyes away.

Unconscious of stepping forward, a twig snapped under her foot. The sound may as well have been a gunshot for the way she jumped.

A guttural sound rumbled from Guthrie's throat. He yanked his damp britches back up and stepped forward, consuming the last measure of space between them, his gaze never wavering from hers, and in an instant his arms wrapped around her waist.

He pulled her close. "Damnation," he swore under his breath. "I don't care what you call yourself, you really are a witch."

A small gasp slipped past her lips. Her breast molded against his chest, she felt his heart beating and the rush of his breath against her cheek.

"Sheen," he said, his voice ragged and husky.

"You've cast a spell over me. You've tempted me since I first laid eyes on you that morning I rode into your yard."

He tipped her head back by lifting her chin, then slid his hand up from her waist to cradle the nape of her neck. "I want to taste your lips, to feel their softness, and all they promise."

His mouth touched hers and her body trembled. She offered no resistance. She was powerless to stop him, and opened her lips to receive his kisses.

His tongue, wet and silken, tasted her. She leaned against him with languid relish, and let her hips meld into his. She wrapped her arms around his neck and threaded her fingers through his damp, slick hair. All of her senses centered on the pleasure of his mouth, and the thunderous sound of his heart beating close to hers.

Her brain hazy with desire, Sheen sensed his movement down below. His hard man root, growing larger, pressed against her thigh. It startled her, and yet she could not find the strength to protest. She would not protest. She returned his kisses, using her own tongue to explore his. Sweet mother! She did not have the will to stop.

Guthrie abruptly ended the embrace. He pulled his mouth from hers and set her from his arms, his eyes intense with lust.

A sharp cry of disappointment escaped Sheen's lips. The space between them felt cavernous and vast.

He stood there staring at her with his chest heaving, hands clenched into fists, and the fire crackling behind him. His arousal was evident and he made no attempt to hide it. He let out a frustrated groan and raked his fingers through his hair. "Damnation,

Sheen. Didn't anyone ever tell you what happens between a man and a woman?"

The makeshift tent suddenly felt warm. Hot. And the wisp of white smoke that drifted upward from the glowing embers made Sheen's eyes water. She put her hands to her neck and lowered her gaze, uncertain of what to say, regretting what she had just done. "My father never talked about what happens between a man and a woman. He only said that a man and a woman should never share a bed until they were properly wed. All I know about such things is what I have observed between animals when they mate."

Guthrie let out a long, ragged breath. "Sheen, there is a difference between sex and making love. Your father was right. Making love is what a husband does to his wife." His kept his voice even, though the tightness of his words belied his struggle. "The trials of what we've been through these past few weeks, and being in close quarters together, especially now, has caused us to drop the guard on our emotions. I promise I won't let this happen again. It isn't conducive to our plans for locating Otaktay and finding Rachel."

He held out his hand as if to shake hers. "Let's shake on it and swear to forget this ever happened."

Sheen swallowed. As if she could forget the flaming torch he'd ignited. As if denying what had passed between them would make her feelings go away. Well, if he could be so damnably detached and controlled, then so could she. What had occurred between them would never happen again.

"Of course, Guthrie," she answered coolly as she shook his hand. "'Twill never happen again. I'd never allow a man who isn't my husband to make love to me.

And since we are neither betrothed nor have any intentions of marrying, I'll thank you to never kiss me again."

She'd said the words hoping her indirect reference to marriage would prick his conscience. But she was surprised to see the hurt flash across his face, before his eyes narrowed with sullen anger.

He glared at her. "Sheen, when a woman studies a man with such intent as you did when I undressed, she invites such attention as that kiss between us. And more. Much more. Is that what you want?" he asked, in a throaty whisper.

Heat rose to her cheeks. "No, I, I..." She lowered her eyes.

She what? She didn't mean to look? More than anything, she *wanted* to look, wanted to see everything. Sweet mother, she was weak and could not promise to forget what had happened between them, even if his lips never touched hers again. She would never forget his kiss. And the sight of him naked would forever be burned into her memory. It would be a lie if she admitted she'd never see him in her dreams long after he'd used her magic to save his daughter and she returned to live alone on the prairie. That is, if they survived and lived to tell about it.

Chapter Twenty-Five

Guthrie eased down on the bedroll beside Sheen. "I'll take my share of blame for what just happened between us, but you shouldn't put your trust in men the way you did with me. It took every ounce of will power to keep from granting what you seemed to desire."

Sheen let out a little huff. "I don't wish for anything except to find your daughter and return home to my animals."

He reclined on his elbow and looked distractedly at the glowing red embers. The corners of his mouth turned in a slight smile. "Ah, but you do. I saw it in your eyes, my little—fairy. Beautiful eyes, like a meadow in spring, dark and shimmering green. They promise a place where a man could lose himself and take refuge from all his troubles."

He was teasing her.

Flustered, Sheen absently spread her wet skirts across her legs. "You flatter yourself, Mr. Tanner. Not every woman swoons with the flowery words that cross your soft lips."

Heat colored her cheeks. Why did she turn into a mutton-headed nitwit when he egged her on?

He tweaked her nose and laughed out loud.

Sheen looked away, but not before she caught a glimpse of the wicked scar that rode across his collarbone. She knew the damp and cold caused him pain and wanted to reach out and touch the welted mark.

She cleared her throat, forcing her thoughts toward getting warm. She scooted closer to the fire, turning her back to him and letting the warmth caress her hands and face as the pungent aroma of wild pine filled her head.

Without warning, a tingle prickled the inside of her nose. She turned her head and sneezed. And sneezed again.

Guthrie sat upright. "You'd better dry your dress and undergarments before you catch your death from the chill." He snatched his bedroll and tossed it to her. "Here, I'll leave you to your privacy." He strode from the shelter, wearing only his britches. "Call me when you're finished."

Relieved not to have to remove her clothing in front of him, Sheen kicked off her soggy leather boots and slipped the damp dress over her head. Her once-white chemise was now stained from where the dye in her dress had bled through. The damp garment clung to her hips and breasts and twisted around her legs. She let out a long breath.

Shivering, she stepped out of the chemise and reached for the blanket. Barefoot and naked beneath the canvas coverlet, she settled on the pallet and let the smoky warmth in the shelter surround her.

Thoughts of her father filled her. She wanted to hear his hearty laughter and feel the warm safety of his arms as when he held her as a child.

She pressed her arm across her forehead and closed her eyes, clinging to the hope that they would find Rachel—alive. Then she would return to her little house, her animals, and the sanctity of the prairie.

****

Guthrie strode from the shelter into a cluster of silver-barked aspen trees, where the horses were tied. He kept an eye on the campsite. God knows he couldn't trust Sheen to do as she was told and stay put.

To complicate his feelings further, he found her enticingly attractive. Alluring. He'd had to leave their makeshift camp because he could barely stand being alone and almost naked with her. He was glad his pants were wet and chilly. They kept the searing ache from his loins.

Hellfire. His fate was tied to a comely witch. No, he corrected himself, a beguiling fairy doctor. He shrugged. Witch, fairy doctor. Regardless of Sheen's explanation, he didn't see the difference. Guilt boiled inside his chest at the idea of bedding a woman who had clearly never been with a man. Sheen was not someone he wanted to dally around with. She was with him for one reason, and one reason only—to help find Rachel.

He rubbed his forehead. He needed to keep his lustful desires corralled. Spinning on his heel, he headed back to the camp. She had had plenty of time to change. Damnation, he was cold, and hunger gnawed at his insides. It wasn't food he needed. He stormed under the low-hanging blanket.

He found her snoring, curled up beneath the bedroll, feet poking out at one end and at the other a mass of dark hair spilling onto creamy shoulders, draping over the swell of her breasts.

Guthrie reached to brush a tendril from her forehead, then pulled his hand away. He had no wish to awaken her but felt the need to touch her hair.

Sheen stirred, reaching to scratch the tip of her nose. The blanket slipped, fully exposing one exquisite breast.

Heat pooled in his chest, and he squeezed his eyes shut. Hellfire. Why was he here? Had the fairy doctor cast a spell on him? Her voice resonated in his head, usurped his thoughts. He could recall almost her exact words.

I am no witch, Mr. Tanner. If I were, I'd cast a spell on you.

He'd nearly laughed aloud when she'd spoken those words the day he'd ridden into her yard. The day the crows had attacked his horse and the three-legged fox snarled at him.

He drew a breath. Struggling to command his mind, he longed for a glass of Otto's warm beer and a chaser of whiskey. He stretched out and reclined just close enough to Sheen to feel her body's heat but not close enough to touch her.

She moved, her bare leg slipping out from beneath the bedroll, her foot brushing against his. A slow burn spread up his calf, behind his knee, to his inner thigh, then higher. The ache between his legs suddenly grew hard and insistent, longing for release.

Then he saw it, the purple print of a tiny fairy, kneeling and holding a globe in her hands. The birthmark was just as Sheen had described.

Damnation. Forcing his eyes shut, he rolled away, wishing he could sleep.

****

A damp chill had settled beneath the sparse shelter. Sometime in the dark hours of the night Sheen snuggled against the man who lay beside her, his breathing slow and rhythmic. Her eyes snapping open, she suddenly realized his bare arm rested across her naked breasts. She didn't dare move.

Sweet mother. Why was he lying so close?

Carefully, she lifted Guthrie's arm and placed it at his side. Wrapping the blanket tight around her chest, she rose from the pallet. Guthrie groaned as she slipped into her boots, but he didn't move as she padded from beneath the shelter. She drew the brisk night air into her lungs, forcing herself awake. She scanned the woods, praying no Pawnee or Crow were lurking, then ventured forward, tiptoeing over the soft carpet of pine needles. The night hummed with crickets. A lone coyote howled far in the distant night. The gelding's ears pricked as she came to stand beside him and pressed her face into the hollow of his neck. Inhaling the familiar equine scent, she rubbed her cheek across his soft hair. "You're a fine horse, Jughead, now that I've threatened to turn you into a rabbit if you keep misbehaving. But I do miss Moon and her baby. 'Twouldn't do to bring the mare along, though. Not with the stallion. And Skye likes to wander off from his mother and get into mischief."

She smiled, but tears flooded down her face. Choking back a sob, she hiccupped once, twice, then wiped her palms across her eyes. "No more tears. He only thinks of me as a witch, and nothing more. Why can't he look at me the way he must have looked at Abigail?"

She scratched the sorrel's jowl. "You deserve a rest. But we've a long way, yet, to travel."

Guthrie stepped behind her. "So you threatened to turn my horse into a rabbit. I wondered why he was behaving so well."

Sheen started. Trapped between the horse and Guthrie's arms, she turned and faced his chest. "How long have you been standing there?"

He whispered, "Long enough to miss the warmth from my bed partner. Come back with me. It isn't safe out here. Never know if a scouting party is nearby."

Sheen ducked beneath his arms and clutched the blanket to her chest. "You were spying on me?"

His eyes roamed the length of her. He pointed to the blanket and glared his reproach. "Go back to the camp. You shouldn't have risked coming out here alone."

Acutely aware of his eyes on her, she spun around and stomped to the shelter. Once inside, she closed her eyes, taking a deep breath to fight off the pain of humiliation and restore her pride. Perhaps he had not seen her cry, or heard her confession. She dearly hoped not. It served no useful purpose. She clutched the blanket to her chest and squared her shoulders.

Sweet mother! Why did she care what Guthrie Tanner thought, or that he spoke to her as if she were a child who needed scolding?

Heavy footsteps approached. Sheen dropped the blanket and grabbed her chemise and dress. She pulled the damp garments over her head and tried to smooth her tangled hair. Guthrie marched into the shelter and sat down, stretching his legs. He said, "You're right, Jughead needs a rest. We all do. It is a long way to Anaconda Butte." He rested his hand on the butt of his revolver. "Go back to sleep, Sheen, and don't even think of leaving the camp. If you need to take care of necessities, I'll go with you."

Exasperated, Sheen let out a hissing sigh and lowered herself to her pallet. Night birds twittered sweet songs, but no matter how she tried, she could not force herself to sleep.

****

Morning came with a vengeance and shone brightly in Sheen's eyes. Glad to be awakened, she was surprised to find Guthrie and his bedroll gone. Panic wrapped its fingers around her heart, until the stallion snorted and stamped its foot.

Guthrie had banked the fire. He'd poured a cup of coffee and set a slice of thick bread on top, and had taken care to set it on a stone near the embers. This puzzled her. Where was the coffeepot, and the food sack?

Pouring water from the canteen, she splashed sleep from her face and was rolling up her bedding when Guthrie walked through the brush.

"No time for a meal, Sheen. Soon as you gulp down the coffee, and take care of your morning necessaries, we've got to get a move on."

That finger of panic jabbed her heart again. "Indians?"

"Yep. The horses were restless, especially the stallion. I did a little scouting. Looks like a large group of riders—roughly a dozen or so—passed during the night. Good thing we were tucked away. Pony tracks were unshod."

Sheen wolfed down the bread and chased it with tepid coffee. "Do you think it was Otaktay?"

"Maybe. The tracks point toward the Anaconda range. I've got the horses ready and the food sack secured."

Her cheeks burned as she handed him her bedroll. "Ten minutes and I'll be ready."

"We'll be traveling hard and fast, Sheen. You up to it?"

She knew the urgency of leaving this place. If it were Otaktay, picking up his trail and following was imperative. If it were Crow or Pawnee on a raiding party, it wasn't safe to remain here.

Lifting her skirts, she said over her shoulder, "What do you think?"

Chapter Twenty-Six

Guthrie and Sheen rode at an unforgiving pace, stopping long enough to catch a few snatches of sleep, with cold meals of jerky, water, and stale bread. For days neither of them spoke.

Now on the fourth day and in sight of the Anaconda Mountains, Guthrie was reflecting on following the day-old hoof prints leading toward the butte when a strident cry rang out.

Six bronzed riders had materialized from the tree line. They were too far off for Guthrie to see their faces, but he knew by their marking these warriors were Pawnee. He wondered if they were from the same band as that of the two men he'd killed weeks ago.

Voicing a collective howl, they bore down on him and Sheen like a pack of rabid wolves.

"Sheen, ride like the devil himself is after you." He extended his arm and pointed. "Make for that clump of rocks. Maybe I can hold 'em off there."

Wind whipped across Sheen's face. Eyes watering against the sting, she closed them. She imagined a wall, thick and high and obsidian. She built it stone by stone until it stood between her and the enemy chasing them. Behind the wall was all cool, clear blue. Water to float in, to sink in. And high above that pale blue pool the sun was white and warm. She could hear horses whinnying, dogs barking, the bustle of women going about their daily chores, and she heard...crying.

The sound was pitiful and weak. She saw a woman leaning over a willow-thin child whose hair was the color of corn silk. *You must drink this potion, White Frog, or you will die.*

Leave me alone. My name is Rachel, and I want my daddy. The child's cough rattled in Sheen's ears. Between coughs, the child said, *I want to go home.*

A warrior, broad of chest, and tall, entered through the slit in the teepee. He drew a knife from the sheath at his side. Light glinted against the blade. *The wailing of this white-eyed child hurts my ears.* He squatted and grabbed a handful of the white hair, forcing the little girl to rise from the pallet. He placed the knife to her throat.

The woman grabbed his arm. *No, Otaktay. I have medicine from the shaman. It will make her better. Please. You brought me this child because I am...* The woman hung her head in shame. *Because I am barren. She is mine. I beg you.*

The warrior landed a hard kick to the woman's side. He laughed when she toppled over. *Beg all you want, woman. The girl is worthless.* He pointed the knife toward the frail lump lying on the pallet.

The woman grabbed his arm. *If you do this horrible thing, I will ask the shaman to mix a potion to take away your other eye.*

Bah! You white-eyes are all alike. Weak. Again, he pointed the knife blade at the child. *If the shaman's medicine does not work in four days—the girl dies, and you with her.*

And then the water darkened, began to stir. The graceful reeds snapped up like whips. And the water was cold, suddenly so cold Sheen began to shiver. The water covered her mouth, her nose; she struggled to keep from being pulled under, felt herself drowning with Rachel's voice inside her head.

You have to come. You have to hurry.

Without the heart or the energy to build the wall again, she sensed herself growing faint and swaying in the saddle.

And then she felt the strength of his hand gripping her arm, holding her upright to keep her from sliding between the running feet of the horse beneath her.

Guthrie's voice rasped as he called out, "Sheen...Sheen, open your eyes. I know you're exhausted, but now's not the time for falling asleep."

She forced her eyes to open, her mouth full of the taste of putrid water. Eyes shadowed and still glazed from the vision, she pointed to a rocky path that twisted up a tree-covered hill to their right. "To the bluff. There's a hidden pass between the rocks."

The wind snatched at Guthrie's words. "Put the spurs to Jughead. Don't let him start flagging. Push him 'til he drops."

Riding close to Guthrie, Sheen followed him across the grassy hills. She shouted as she pointed. "There. We'll have to go the rest of the way on foot. And don't talk."

Dismounting, Sheen and Guthrie picked their way around the boulders. The lathered horses slipped and scrambled as they climbed. Guthrie looked back. Sheen nodded that she was okay.

They watched the six Pawnee warriors haul up on the reins, riding back and forth, searching, speaking their guttural language.

Sheen whispered, "Behind the trees. The opening is there."

"What the devil?"

"This way." Sheen led the sorrel around jutting rocks, stopping at the opening of a cave. "'Tis not wide enough to ride through. We'll have to lead the horses."

She led them through a rock-walled passageway so tight the horse's hips scraped against the sides. Sheen coaxed Jughead onward and Guthrie followed, urging the stallion forward when he balked.

"Sheen, even Indians with any sense at all wouldn't bring a horse in here," he said as he pressed his shoulder into the stallion's rump and slapped him on the hip.

"Exactly. 'Tis a passage long forgotten and used by no one. But it will lead us to Rachel."

She craned her neck to see ahead. "There. 'Tis the light!"

Emerging from the passage, Guthrie squinted at the harsh sun lighting up the sky and the valley just below the bluff.

Sheen dusted cobwebs off her limp gown. "I think Otaktay's camp is but a day's ride from here, depending on how fast we travel. I cannot tell you more."

"Well, I'll be damned. You didn't go to sleep in the saddle, did you? You had a vision."

"Aye, that I did."

"Rachel?"

"Aye, Guthrie...Rachel." She did not tell him his daughter was very ill or about the white woman, or that Otaktay had threatened to kill the little girl.

Expressing concern, Guthrie asked, "Can you ride, or do we need to rest?"

Though her bones felt as if they were melting from exhaustion, she lifted her boot to the stirrup. "I don't think the Pawnee will find the passageway, but we should not take the risk. I can rest later."

Guthrie leaped onto the stallion's back. "Wherever this path takes us, I hope it's straight to Otaktay."

The sound of angry warriors faded in the distance as Guthrie and Sheen spurred their horses down the hill.

****

For two days, Guthrie and Sheen were well into the mountains, threading a bewildering maze of canyons, ravines, and gorges. Small wonder, Guthrie thought, that he found it impossible to locate Otaktay. After every raid, he and his warriors faded without trace into the remote hideaways inside the Anaconda Mountains, to one of the secret strongholds the cavalry had yet to find despite the help of Indian scouts.

The Santee chief had picked well. The valley was a virtual paradise. A gurgling stream lay about a hundred yards from the village. Jays and sparrows frolicked in the trees. Butterflies fluttered among brilliant flowers. Two squirrels leaped from branch to branch in energetic abandon.

A loud cry shattered Guthrie's reverie. Drawing rein, he rose in the stirrups and spotted warriors entering the narrow mouth of a high-walled canyon. Realizing there might be lookouts posted on the rocky heights, he slid from the stallion's back and motioned for Sheen to do the same.

"Stay alert, Sheen. From this point on we'll need eyes in the backs of our heads."

Dropping to his belly, he commanded her to stay with the horses.

"Nay, I'm coming with you."

It riled him that she was unperturbed by the warning in his voice. He exhaled his frustration. "Then keep up, because I won't wait for you."

Together they wormed their way through the undergrowth. Lying prone on a rocky bench on a facing slope, they looked down on the village known only to Otaktay and his band of renegades. Forty wickiups were spread out over the verdant valley floor. Women were busy weaving baskets, mending clothes, and cooking. Children scampered about as children everywhere do, laughing while they played.

Sheen scooted forward for a closer look. Keeping her voice low, she whispered, "It's just as I saw it in my vision."

"Do you know which one Rachel is in?"

Shaking her head to indicate she did not, she pointed. "My guess is she's in that one."

"What makes you think so?"

Sheen indicated the woman stepping through the opening of a wickiup. A leather strap held the woman's brown hair in place, and she wore a tattered calico dress, her skin paler than that of any Sioux.

A wizened old man followed the woman from the dwelling. The two had barely spoken when a warrior, taller and more powerfully built than most, also came out. He was dressed as a warrior should be, but there was something about him that suggested he was somehow different. The man gestured angrily at the white woman, who defiantly stood her ground.

The old man held his hands skyward, mumbled an incantation, and then walked away.

The warrior slapped the woman, causing her head

to jerk sideways. She lifted her skirt and ran toward the trees.

None of the Sioux attempted to stop their captive from going into the brush. It troubled Guthrie a little that she was allowed to traipse off as she pleased. He assumed that the Sioux had impressed on her how hopeless it would be for her to try to escape. Captives who did so were either killed or harshly punished.

He motioned for Sheen to slide back from the rim. They retraced their steps to the summit of the ridge. Sheen asked if he had a plan.

"The woman puts a wrinkle in whatever plans I had. Don't know who she is or how loyal she is to the Sioux."

"She's been a captive for a long time, but she has no loyalty to them. She is the woman in my vision. We must save her, too, Guthrie."

He nodded. "We'll wait until dark, when everyone is asleep, slip in, get Rachel and the woman, then get the hell out as fast as we can. Hopefully the woman knows where the main entrance is through the mountain. It'll buy us some time."

Remembering the vision and the way the warrior chief had abused and threatened the white captive, curiosity caused Sheen to ask, "What will Otaktay do when he finds the woman and Rachel gone?"

"He'll come after us. Not so much because he values them but because we took something that belonged to him. It's a matter of pride."

Sheen seemed to consider Guthrie's words. "We must let her know we are here to save Rachel."

"If you've got a plan, I'm all ears."

"She ran into the woods. What if I talk to her?"

"Are you loco, Sheen? No, it's too dangerous."

Something smacked Guthrie's hip. He looked down. It was a small stone, lobbed at him by the captive woman. She was pointing to the right.

Pivoting, he stared, seeing nothing suspicious. Then a dark outline took shape, the silhouette of the head and shoulders of a warrior on his belly no more than fifteen feet away. Without hesitation, Guthrie pulled the Arkansas toothpick from the sheath at his waist. As much as he wanted to use his revolver, he couldn't risk the sound.

He gestured at Sheen and she understood—get the horses.

The warrior stood and drew back on the bow. The string twanged. Guthrie shifted, and felt rather than saw the arrow's shaft go by. He threw the knife. The warrior was punched in the chest as if by an invisible fist.

Guthrie raced over and jerked the blade from the man's chest. He glanced at Sheen to tell her to get down and found that she already had and was holding the horses' reins. The captive squatted beside her. He wondered if he could count on the woman to help them when the warriors closed in. She might change her mind about wanting to leave and turn against them to save her own hide.

The golden furnace in the sky was straight overhead. Other than the screech of a hawk to the east, the valley was quiet. No camp dogs barked.

Bent low, he rushed to where Sheen and the wild-eyed woman held the horses.

A lizard scuttled across a rock, stopping to survey its surroundings. In the background bubbled the stream. It was hard to believe the tranquil scenery harbored a swarm of renegades, that violence could erupt at any second.

The brunette whispered, "I thought we were goners for sure."

Guthrie's voice was quick and to the point. "You going to help us or betray us?"

"Mister, if I was of a mind to let these savages know you was here, I could've done it sooner. My name is Sara Beth McDonald."

Guthrie clasped the hand she offered. "Guthrie Tanner, ma'am. This is Sheen O'Reilly. How long have you been here?"

She scrubbed a dirty hand over her face. "I was took by the Pawnee, then the Sioux stole me from them. It's been a long, living hell."

She touched her hair. "I must look a sight. I can't remember the last time I had a brush and a mirror."

Ignoring the woman's sudden concern over her appearance, Guthrie cast a worried glance over his shoulder. "Is this Otaktay's camp?"

Sara Beth clenched her hands into fists. "That damned brutal savage? Yes, it is. How did you find this place? Did my folks send you?"

"No one sent me, ma'am." Guthrie was anxious to have the talk over. "Is there a little girl in the camp? She'd be about seven. Her hair is the color of corn silk, and her name is Rachel."

Sara Beth clasped her hands to her cheeks. "They call her White Frog, 'cause of her hair and fair skin. I fear she's going to die."

Guthrie turned to Sheen, his voice gruff. "Did you know this?"

Sheen tried to keep the sadness from her voice.

"Aye, I saw her in my vision. I didn't want to add another burden to your shoulders."

Clenching his fist, his throat bobbled as he spoke. "You keep telling me you're a fairy doctor. I've seen you do things beyond any man's understanding." His eyes pleaded with her. "Can't you conjure up a magic spell that will save my little girl?"

Sheen squatted across from him, folding her arms in front of her, which made her breast swell against the front of her dress. Her annoyance was evident. "Nay, Guthrie, I do not cast spells or carry magic potions in my pocket." She looked at Sara Beth. "Do you know what is wrong with the child?"

The woman shrugged her shoulders. "Can't say that I do. The med'cine man made a foul-smelling concoction. I been giving it to her by the spoonful every hour or so, but it don't seem to be helping. Poor little White Frog—oh, sorry, I mean Rachel—is burning up with the fever. She keeps crying for her daddy."

Guthrie thought Sheen's features were impossible to read when she said, "Once we are safely away from this place, I will examine Rachel to determine the cause of her sickness. This will let me know which herbs I need to collect. Hopefully, we aren't too late to save her."

He agreed without hesitation. At the moment, his main concern was getting them safely away. He knew a sick child would slow them down.

"Once we get Rachel, we'll have to ride like the hounds of hell are after us. That means not leaving the same way we came." He shifted his glance toward Sara Beth. "Miss MacDonald, do you know a fast way out of here?"

Kneading her fingers as if she were working with bread dough, she reflected for a moment. "Does this mean you're taking me with you? Please?"

He saw Sheen give him a sharp glance, and squared his shoulders. "Leaving you behind was never an option, Miss MacDonald."

"Sara Beth. Call me Sara Beth. It sounds so much better than 'Hotah.' "

"Hotah?" Guthrie and Sheen spoke the word simultaneously.

"It simply means—white. But it's spoken more like an insult." Her shoulders sagged as if the weight of being a captive had finally caught up with her.

A stern look came over Guthrie's face. Every minute they delayed was an extra minute that they might be discovered. "We'll need an extra horse. Carrying double will only slow us down."

"Getting a horse won't be a problem, Mr. Tanner." Sara Beth lowered her eyes, red spots mottled her cheeks. Embarrassment leeched into her voice. "You see, I'm one of Otaktay's squaws."

In a moment of rare compassion, Guthrie touched the brunette's arm. "That's in the past now. All that matters is you showing us the fastest way out of here, so we can get you to your folks."

"I'm not sure they'll want me. Not after... Well, you know."

Guthrie could only imagine the inner turmoil the woman was going through. No woman should have to experience such a living hell.

"Although I have as much freedom as the other women, I'd better get back before someone gets curious and comes looking. Besides, Rachel needs me."

Sara Beth lifted the tattered hem of her dress and turned to leave. "Otaktay and his men have returned from another raid. They brought lots of whiskey. There will be much celebration tonight."

"Good. When they're all drunk, we'll come to your teepee."

Her voice was emphatic. "No. Please. I wouldn't want you to see me...indecent. You'll be safe here. Stay out of sight. When the time is right, I'll bring Rachel. I know Otaktay's secret passage in and out of here."

Chapter Twenty-Seven

A full moon lit the forest in hues of dusky blue and green shadows by the time Sheen opened her heavy-lidded eyes. She couldn't believe she'd slept. She lifted her hand to feel the stallion's velvet muzzle nuzzling her cheek. The great horse sniffed her hair and nudged her on the shoulder. She sat up and stroked the animal's cheek.

She scanned the woods, bleary-eyed, searching frantically for any sign of Guthrie.

Then she saw him. His body rigid, alert, searching, he was a shadow in a halo of light.

She whispered to the stallion and the gelding, admonishing them to be swift, and reminding the gelding that she'd turn him into a rabbit if he didn't behave. "We have a wee sick child to save, and 'tis no time for living up to your name, Jughead."

She placed her fingers on his soft muzzle and shushed the animal before he could nicker a response.

Leaves rustled and Sheen sensed more than saw Sara Beth approaching.

She held her finger to her lips as if cueing the horses to silence. She whispered, "Guthrie?"

"I see her. Get ready to ride."

A hushed voiced sounded in the dark. "Mr. Tanner, I'm here."

"Rachel?"

"Her, too."

Anguish tugged at Sheen's heart as he lifted the blanketed lump from Sara Beth's arms. He folded the flap away from the child's face. Moonlight revealed colorless cheeks and closed eyes. The child was more dead than alive.

"We have to go, Mr. Tanner. It doesn't matter how many miles we put between us and this place, Otaktay is an expert tracker. What he can't see, he can smell."

Sheen lifted the child from Guthrie's arms as he mounted the stallion. "I don't understand. Why would he care about a dying child and a woman he doesn't respect?"

"Because, Miss O'Reilly, we are his property. And though he is a murdering thief, a savage with no compassion for anyone, Rachel and I are his property. He cares not two whits about us, except that you stole what is his, and we will all pay dearly if he catches us."

Sheen relinquished her hold on the child to Guthrie's waiting arms. "Aye. To be sure, Otaktay is a spawn of Satan. Guthrie, we must hurry from this place."

****

Guthrie gathered the reins in his left hand and secured his right arm around the frail body, holding her against his chest. He swallowed the angry roar building in his throat. The child whimpered. "Hush, baby girl. Daddy's got you, and I won't rest until you're safely home."

He cast a glance toward the brunette. "Lead the way, Sara Beth."

She pointed to the east. "We'll skirt around the camp so as not to set off the dogs. Once we're a mile or so away, we can put the spurs to the horses. It's easy riding until we get to Devil's Gap."

"How far?"

"My best estimation is four, maybe five miles. Pray for moonlight. Otherwise we'll have to dismount and lead the horses through the gap."

"Why's that?"

"Because once out of the gap, we'll be on a narrow, winding shelf. It's treacherous, even in the daylight, and a long ways down if you fall over the edge."

"There's no other way out of here?"

"None, except for how you came in. It's closer, but even more dangerous. 'Specially in the dark."

The stallion pawed the ground. Guthrie was as impatient as the stallion to be away from this place. The weight of misery rested on his shoulders.

"Sheen?"

"Don't worry about me. Jughead and I will keep up."

"Then let's get the hell out here. Sara Beth, lead the way."

Following the captive woman's lead, the trio skirted a wide berth around the encampment to avoid arousing the dogs. As soon as Guthrie and the women reached the meadow, they spurred the horses and raced toward the eastern side of the canyon until they reached a collection of boulders, each the size of a small cabin.

Sara Beth signaled with her hand to stop. Guthrie fought to bring the excited stallion under control. He twisted about, looking. "What is it? Why are we stopping?"

She pointed. "There. Look closely. It's difficult to

see in the dark, but there's a slit barely wide enough for a horse and rider to pass through. Once outside the gap, we'll need to go single file."

"Where does it lead?" Guthrie wanted to know.

"It winds down and around the mountain and away from Otaktay. I warn you, it's steep and the going is slow."

Guthrie stiffened, then composed himself. "Sheen, you think Jughead will get skittish?"

The moonlight revealed her smile. Guthrie liked her smile. In fact, everything about her soothed him. Even when he tested her temper. "Nay. He has heeded my warning."

"And the stallion, have you bewitched him too?"

He watched her brow furrow as she cast an irritated frown toward him. "You have the sense of humor of a dried bone, Guthrie Tanner."

The night mountain air was cold. Guthrie feared for Rachel's health as he gathered the blanket closer around her. "I won't risk our safety. We'll lead the horses through. Except for you, Sheen, I'll need you to hold Rachel. Can you manage?"

"Aye."

"Good, you'll follow behind Sara Beth. I'll bring up the rear."

"'Tis not a good plan, Guthrie. Jughead doesn't know Sara Beth's horse. He trusts the stallion. We'll follow you."

The look on his face told her an argument was about to take place. "'Tis no time for arguing the matter, Guthrie. I don't know how long it will take for Otaktay and his men to sleep off the whiskey, but I do know we must be long gone from this place when they discover Sara Beth and Rachel missing."

"Damn, woman. Do you always have to be right?" Guthrie continued to grumble his irritation as he tied the sorrel's reins to the stallion's tail. "Just making sure the damned nag doesn't take it in his head to skirt ahead of us and plunge over the edge."

Sheen smiled.

Guthrie kissed his daughter's fevered brow and spoke a few endearing words, then for a few seconds gripped Sheen's hand.

"At least we're safe until morning." He quietly moved to the stallion's head, grasped the reins, and clucked the horse forward. He tried not to think of the tremendous risk they were taking.

****

Sheen rode in silence, her arms holding the lethargic child close to her chest.

The bright moon lit up the night sky like a beacon, and the cold air caused Sheen to shudder. All was quiet except for the sound of hoof beats. To keep from falling asleep, she concentrated on counting the number of times the sorrel's head bobbled in sync with each step it took.

The going was slow. No one spoke. Not even when rocks thrown from the horses' hooves cascaded off the narrow shelf and tumbled over the mountain's side.

Her arms ached from holding the child. Her back and legs ached for fear that if she shifted in the saddle she might somehow throw the horse off balance and cause them to all tumble to their deaths.

By the time Guthrie and the women led the horses off the mountain shelf and onto solid ground, the sun's orange crown was peeking through morning clouds.

Sheen drew a deep breath, thankful when the horses began their final descent and made their way through a cleft in the side of the Anaconda Mountains and onto a wide road that was smooth and free of shadows.

Guthrie's deep voice said, "We'll stop here long enough to give the horses a short rest."

Rest was a luxury they could ill afford until they reached Fort Smith. He figured a fort filled with soldiers was the one place Otaktay would avoid. "One hour is all we can spare. Then we have to push on."

He reached up and relieved Sheen of the child.

"Carry Rachel to the shade of those rocks. I'll examine her while you tend to the horses." And then to the brunette woman, she said, "Sara Beth, we could all use a cup of coffee. Would you mind?"

While Sara Beth built a low fire and prepared the pot for brewing, Sheen removed the blanket from the child. Without the bulk of the heavy cloth, Sheen was taken aback by the little girl's emaciation.

She observed the bruising under the eyes and the sunken features. Sheen used her thumb to open the child's mouth. There were no white spots on the tongue to indicate scarlet fever or cholera. Yet her body was hot to the touch.

Gently lifting the remnants of the yellow skirt, Sheen carefully examined every inch of Rachel's body. She checked under her arms, behind the crook of her knees. She felt along the length of her neck.

Sara Beth approached with a cup. "I thought maybe you could get some cool water down her throat."

"That's very kind of you. The condition she's in, she cannot swallow. Fetch me a spoon from the sack with the pots and pans. Perhaps I can spoon some into her mouth."

Sheen puzzled over what was causing the child's illness. When Sara Beth returned with the cup of water, Sheen braced the child's head. Her finger touched a round knot beneath the damp hair.

"Sara Beth, I feel something behind Rachel's ear. Hold on to her while I lean her forward."

The child whimpered and Sheen cooed soothing words.

Guthrie returned and squatted on his haunches. Sheen noted the worry in his eyes. "Is it cholera?"

"She has nothing to indicate scarlet fever or cholera." Sheen pushed the damp, lanky lengths of blonde hair forward to reveal the underside of Rachel's neck. Sheen ran her finger over a series of tiny knots hidden behind Rachel's ears. She used her fingers to separate stands of hair for more knots.

"What is it, Sheen? What have you found?" Guthrie made no secret of his concern as he leaned forward to look at the red and inflamed areas.

Sheen said, "Ticks. Rachel is infested with spotted mountain ticks and they are sucking the life out of her."

Sara Beth sobbed. "It's my fault. I never thought to check for ticks. If she dies, I'll never forgive myself."

Sheen counted aloud. "I count five, but I'll need to strip her completely to see if others have bedded in the private parts of her body."

Guthrie's voice shook when he spoke. "Damn. Dammit all to hell."

"Cursing won't help. They are embedded too deeply to pull them out. If I pull too hard and leave the head in, it's the same as leaving the entire tick in her wee body."

"Then how do you propose to remove them?"

"I'm going to make them drunk."

Sheen almost laughed at the bewildered look exchanged between Guthrie and Sara Beth.

The two watched as Sheen placed her finger on a bloated gray body. Careful not to squash the tick, she rolled it round and round in a circle until the parasite released its hold and Sheen lifted it from the skin and handed it to Guthrie, who placed it under the toe of his boot.

Sheen repeated the action until she had removed all five of the bloodsuckers. "Guthrie, I'll need the whiskey from your saddlebag to cleanse the poison from the bites."

While he ran to where he'd tethered the horses, Sheen removed the dress and bloomers from Rachel and handed them to Sara Beth. "Turn these inside out and give them a good shaking. Then check to make certain no more of these nasty creatures are hidden inside the pleats, especially at the waistline or in the hem."

The brunette did as she was instructed while Sheen carefully examined every inch of Rachel's body. Speaking to no one in particular, Sheen said, "Did the child not get enough to eat? She is so thin that her ribs feel like washboards."

"When Otaktay brought her to me, Rachel was so upset and scared she didn't eat for days. It was a long time later that she told me about seeing what he'd done to her mother. I don't believe I've ever once seen Rachel smile. Not once."

Sheen accepted the tattered dress from Sara Beth.

The garment was threadbare and almost falling apart. Through blurry eyes, she said, "I've experienced the same sadness as Rachel, for I too watched my mother murdered." And a sob broke from Sheen's throat at the memory.

Guthrie returned with the bottle of whiskey and handed it to Sheen. "Will she recover?"

Sheen poured the amber liquid over the bite areas. Rachel cried out. "Oh, I know it burns, little lass. I don't mean to hurt you." And to Guthrie, "Aye, she will recover...from the tick bites. From what she's endured these long months, I cannot say."

"What can I do to help her, Sheen?"

She reached out and touched his cheek, and longed to do more. "Love, patience, understanding, and making her feel safe is what you can give her. In time, the memories of what she has endured will fade, and Rachel will smile again. In the meantime, she needs nourishment."

She looked into the blue of his eyes. He was so solid, so smart, handsome, and behind all his gruff and huff, he had a kind heart. And he loved her. No one had loved her for a long time. Sheen ordered her thoughts to stop.

"There's honey in the food sack. Mix one teaspoon with one teaspoon of whiskey and a half cup of water. Then heat it just until the honey thins. Not too hot. We don't want to burn Rachel's mouth. Poor wee lass, she's suffered much for one so young."

Guthrie brushed a strand of Rachel's hair. "I understand the honey, Sheen, though I admit the whiskey has me puzzled."

She offered him a chastising smile. "Aw, 'tis not

magic, as you be thinking, Guthrie Tanner. True, the honey is for energy, but the ticks near sucked the life out of her. The whiskey is to shock the blood into flowing again. And look at the child's lips, parched from the fever. She needs water, too."

Sheen shaded her eyes from the sun. "I'll finish examining Rachel while you mix the potion."

When he returned, Sheen said, "Hold Rachel while I spoon the liquid between her lips."

"Let me do it, Sheen."

"Nay, Guthrie. Feeling the strength of your arms around her is important. She will be frightened when she opens her eyes. It should be her daddy's face she looks into, not the face of another stranger."

"It's times like this that I feel I've known you forever, and yet you still remain a mystery to me."

Sheen didn't answer as she forfeited Rachel to the arms of her father. Dipping a spoonful of the honeyed whiskey, she tested the temperature before lifting it to Rachel's lips.

"What if she refuses it?"

"She won't. I've never known a child, sleeping or not, to refuse anything sweet."

As if Sheen had ordained it, Rachel sipped the warm nectar. "Aye, 'tis a good girl you are. Have another." Sheen wiped the child's mouth when a bit of liquid dribbled down her chin.

When she'd drained the cup, Rachel heaved a sigh and her head lolled against Guthrie's arm. Sheen saw the panic in his eyes. She reassured him with a smile.

"Why isn't she waking up, Sheen?"

"Rachel is in a dark place, but see how her eyes are moving against the eyelids? She is struggling to return to us. Speak to her, Guthrie."

He kept his voice low and gentle. "I've missed you, Punkie Pie. You're safe now, and I'm never going to let anything else hurt you again."

He was answered by a mewing sound. He shrugged his shoulders as if not understanding.

"Rachel has found a safe place in her cocoon of darkness. She's afraid to come out. We mustn't allow her to stay in the dark. 'Tis time she rejoins the living."

Sheen feared what she had to do to save the child, knowing it would affirm Guthrie's beliefs that she was a witch. She heaved a sorrowful sigh.

"Guthrie, do you remember why I have the rope burns around my neck?"

He nodded. "Because in their ignorance, people believed you were evil."

"Aye. I must ask you to believe that I am truly not evil, and that I am no witch. If Rachel is to live, you must trust what I am about to say and do."

It seemed forever before he spoke. She watched the war of emotions playing over his face. "In these many weeks I've known you, I've seen you do some pretty amazing things. The way you birthed Dyani's baby, the way your mare attacked the Pawnee brave who would have killed me. I'm trusting you, Sheen. Do what you have to do to save my Rachel."

"Whatever I do, whatever I say, 'tis very important that you do not interrupt. Do you understand?"

Guthrie leaned forward and pressed his lips to the Sheen's brow. "Understood."

Sheen said to Sara Beth, "The horses need tending, and so does the coffee."

"I don't rightly know what's going on, but I've

seen things the med'cine men do that's beyond reasoning. I'll leave you to do whatever it is that's between you and healing this little girl." The brunette gathered her skirts and walked toward the trees where the horses cropped grass.

Sheen drew in a breath like a sob, but what came out was an incantation of words that Guthrie didn't understand. And then popping her hands together, Sheen rubbed them vigorously until the hot friction burned her palms. Placing her hands on either side of Rachel's cheeks, she leaned forward, placed her mouth over Rachel's, and blew until Sheen felt her own lungs were depleted.

She drew back and sucked in to replenish her oxygen. "Rachel... Time to wake up. Open your eyes."

****

In a secondary way, Rachel was aware of her father's voice. She thought it was a dream, like the many dreams she'd had since the Santee had kidnapped her. She listened to the woman's voice, kind and gentle and soothing, but didn't understand the words.

After a while there was something hot and burning on her face. It hurt, and she wanted to be away from it, and then there was a wind that tasted like honey and smelled like wildflowers. And she heard her name.

Rachel opened her eyes and looked into Guthrie's. Her voice rasped from the many days of not speaking. "Daddy?"

Tears spilled from Guthrie's eyes and pooled in the deep crevices of his bronzed cheeks as he choked back a sob.

Rachel sat up and put her arms around him. "I've missed you, Daddy."

"I've missed you, too, Punkie Pie."

"Can we go home now?"

"You betcha."

The child released her hold on Guthrie to look at Sheen. "It was you, wasn't it?"

"Aye, 'twas me calling you."

"I mean, I prayed for my Daddy to come get me. Are you an angel?"

"Nay, I am not, but I did hear you calling for your daddy."

Rachel snuffled as she placed a tiny hand inside Sheen's. "They killed my mommy."

The expression on Guthrie's face pierced Sheen's heart. She thought he begged her for a way to answer his daughter. Sheen caressed Rachel's cheek. "When you are safe in your bed, I'll tell you a story that will help you forget the bad things you saw. I'll try to give you good thoughts."

Rachel snuggled against her father's chest. "I'd like that."

Sara Beth appeared with cups of coffee in her hands. "You both must be awfully tired."

"Not really," Guthrie quipped. "Twenty or thirty hours of sleep and we'll be good as new." He thanked her and took a grateful sip.

****

For a few moments, Guthrie could afford to forget about Otaktay and his renegades, forget the lives he was risking.

And then there was Sheen. At the moment, she sat sipping her own coffee. How could he ever repay her for all he'd put her through, including saving Rachel's life.

"It's occurred to me, Sheen, that I'll never be able to properly thank you for what you're doing."

"There's no need," she said.

She crossed her legs, her dress rising as high as her knees. She had sleek, silken limbs, the kind any man would drool over.

"How many days do you think it will take to reach the fort?" Sheen asked as she reached forward to slide the skirt of her dress toward her ankles.

"Five, if we don't lose any of our horses, and if we don't run into Pawnee...and if Otaktay doesn't catch us." He didn't add that their prospects were as slim as a toothpick.

Sheen snapped erect, her body tense. "We have to go. He's coming."

"Otaktay? No, it's too soon." Sara Beth protested.

Motioning for the woman to be quiet, Guthrie dashed up a series of boulders. He returned moments later. "Heard the clomp of hooves coming down the same trail we used. We'd better get a move on."

Guthrie lifted Rachel into his arms. He and the women raced to the horses. He handed the little girl to Sheen, while he swung into the saddle, then reached down to collect his daughter. He traded looks with Sheen. "If we get out of this alive, there are things I need to tell you."

Sheen blinked away tears. Whatever she had thought to say was interrupted when Sara Beth called out, "If we need to make a stand, Mr. Tanner, I can shoot."

"Good to know, Sara Beth. Hope it doesn't come to a standoff."

Chapter Twenty-Eight

Guthrie wanted to curse like mad. It had never occurred to him that Otaktay might not drink as heavily as his warriors. He'd hoped to put at least two, maybe three days between him and his enemy. In the grand scheme of things, Guthrie had planned that once they were a day's ride from Fort Smith, he'd send the women and Rachel on ahead to the safety behind the fort's barred walls while he laid an ambush for Otaktay. Wishful thinking is all it was.

As if sensing the urgency of his rider, the tobiano squealed and reared, pawing the air. Guthrie brought the stallion under control.

"Sheen, you and Sara Beth ride due east. Keep to the track. It'll lead you straight to Fort Smith. The stallion can outrun your horses. I'll lag behind. Don't worry, I'll keep you in sight. Whatever happens, don't stop. Do you understand?"

"Yes, but Guthrie..."

"There are no buts, Sheen. I want all of you safe. We'll run 'em hard for ten miles, then slow to a canter. Once the horses have had a good breather, we'll move to a fast gallop. Keep to this pattern and maybe the horses will last the next five days. If I have to drop back and take a few pot shots at Otaktay, do as I've told you, and don't look back."

He nudged the quivering stallion closer to the

sorrel gelding. He leaned forward and kissed his daughter on the cheek. "I love you, Punkie Pie."

"Daddy, I'm scared. I don't want to go back to the Indians. They're bad."

"You'll never have to go back. Not ever." His eyes implored Sheen to help him reassure his little girl.

Sheen held the child tight. Through blurry eyes, she offered him a nod of understanding. "Be a brave girl for your daddy."

"Are you brave, Sheen?"

She considered the question. "So as not to worry your daddy, you and I will help each other be courageous."

Sheen felt a bit of the rigidity leave Rachel's emaciated body. "You won't let me fall off?"

"Never, my wee lassie. Never."

Guthrie offered a last reassuring nod. "All right, let me see you kickin' up dust." He removed his hat and fanned it against the sorrel's flanks. "Hiyah. Get on outta here."

****

Three days from the fort, the sun blazed high and warm in the midday sky, its reflections glittering on the prairie that was still dotted with patches of snow. A flock of crows circled against the turquoise sky, their cries carrying far on the still spring air.

Guthrie kept his eyes peeled and his rifle ready. Except for an occasional caw from the crows, the only other sounds were the clopping of their horses' hooves and the squeak of saddle leather.

The long sleepless hours were beginning to tell on Guthrie. His thoughts wandered, drifting again and again to the memory of Sheen in the pool of water at the cave. And though she had not shared her most precious gift with him, she had warmed the coldest, loneliest parts of him, reawakening his spirit to life and love. Yet he could find no words to tell this woman what was in his heart.

Glancing at her now, he could see her straining forward in the saddle. He imagined her expression taut and apprehensive. For the space of a heartbeat he thought she was only staring at the mountains. Then, following her gaze, his pulse leaped as he saw riders, dark dots against prairie green, shortening the distance between them and the fort.

His arms and shoulders ached from the constant restraining of the tobiano stallion that fought the bit keeping him from running ahead of the horses in front of him. Without hesitating, Guthrie kneed the animal and galloped toward the women.

He hauled up on the reins, causing the spirited stallion to prance and snort as if annoyed at having to slow down.

Sara Beth cried out, "It's him, Mr. Tanner—Otaktay."

"Are you certain?"

"Sure as I am that if he catches up what he'll do to us won't be pretty."

Ahead Guthrie could see the hump of rocks where the rough trail joined the arrow-straight road to the fort.

"We're three days out. I'll draw fire and hope they light out after me. If you have to run your ponies into the ground, don't stop until you get to the fort."

Sheen's faced turned ashen. "I'm going with you. Sara Beth can take Rachel to the fort."

Guthrie's eyes narrowed into slits. "Now's not the

time to argue, Sheen. Ask for Sergeant Paddy O'Hanlon. Tell him where I am. Otaktay's an enemy of the army, too. O'Hanlon will see that troops are dispatched."

"Daddy...Daddy?" Rachel struggled in Sheen's arms. "Please come with us."

His daughter's pleas tore at his heart. "Be a brave girl. Do as Sheen says. I'll be along before you know it."

"Guthrie..." She let the words trail off, her meaning clear.

The sound of his name, spoken softly, sent a quiver through his body. He wanted to linger, to take her into his arms. Keeping his expression stern, he barked, "Go. Get outta here."

Without further words, the women took flight, urging their mounts toward the hump of rocks and safety.

Knowing the necessity of diverting Otaktay and his band of renegades away from the women, Guthrie planted his boots tight in the stirrups and squeezed his legs against the stallion's sides. Then lifting the Hawkens to his shoulder, he sighted down the barrel, picked his target, and fired.

The repercussion echoed across the plains. Seconds seemed to tick by slowly before he knew his aim was true. A rider toppled from a running horse. "Well, that's one red bastard who won't kill again." Guthrie spoke only to himself and the crows circling overhead.

****

Sheen stiffened reflexively at the echoing blast from Guthrie's rifle. For the umpteenth time, she checked the road behind her, her spirits unexpectedly

274

sinking when she failed to see Guthrie.

"It's been an hour, Sheen. Can't we slow a little and give the horses a breather?"

"Nay, not until we've made the ten miles."

"I hope Mr. Tanner plugged one of them murdering scoundrels right 'tween the eyes."

"Aye."

"What'll we do when it gets dark?"

"Guthrie said the road was straight. We'll slow the horses to a walk, but we'll keep going."

"Well, I know it ain't opportune, but I've really gotta pee. And Rachel could use a swig or two of that honey mixture you fixed up."

In her heart, Sheen agreed with the woman. "Aye, ten minutes."

Using caution, they swung the horses behind the shadows of a large boulder. Stiff and with sore muscles screaming, Sheen saw to Rachel's comfort while Sara Beth relieved herself.

High above, against the turquoise sky, two great dark birds circled on the rising air. Sheen's spirit brightened as she watched them, thinking they might be a mating pair of golden eagles. But when they turned, showing the high angle of their wings, she realized they were vultures, circling and watching for signs of death.

Too drained for tears, she closed her eyes. Her lips moved in the broken fragments of a prayer, ending with, "Sweet mother, guide me."

The air went thick and heavy. A rabbit darted from its hiding place between two rocks. A panicked brown streak. And Sheen knew what she had to do.

What was taking the woman so long? Sheen thought. "Sara Beth, hurry. Time's wasting."

The brunette emerged from the shadows, adjusting her skirt. "My bladder was about to bust. Sorry."

"Never mind that. I want you to listen, and no arguments, do you hear me?"

"By the look on your face, my gut tells me I ain't gonna like what you're about to say, but go ahead. I'm listening."

"Guthrie needs me. Take Rachel and ride to the fort. Don't dawdle. Do like Guthrie said and ask for Sergeant O'Hanlon."

"But...but..."

"You have to trust that I know what I'm doing, Sara Beth. If I don't go—" Sheen cut her eyes toward where Rachel rested in the shade.

The brunette crossed her arms over her ample breasts. She squinted hard at Sheen. "I've seen my share of spirit women in the camps I've been in. They're different from us ordinary womenfolk. My guess is you're one of them."

Green eyes went wide, then narrowed speculatively. "I'm Irish, not a Sioux spirit woman. Guthrie is one man with one rifle and a hand gun. I have a rifle. Three weapons against Otaktay and his men are better than two."

Sara Beth's eyes glinted as her smile widened. "Well, you've got more gumption than most, I reckon."

"Then we're agreed. You'll take Rachel and go on without me?"

Sara Beth gathered the reins of her horse and swung into the saddle. "I'll take good care of Rachel."

The child whimpered and snuffled as Sheen lifted her into the woman's waiting arms. "Come with us, Sheen. I'm scared."

"I'm going to help your daddy. You mustn't be frightened, my sweet lass. We'll be along as soon as we can." Kissing the child's pale cheek, Sheen implored Sara Beth, "Look after her." Then, as an afterthought, she added, "I have a small cabin about a hundred miles from the fort. Mr. Tatum, the peddler, knows of it. Should it become necessary, he'll show you the way. Do you understand my meaning, Sara Beth?"

The woman choked on her answer. "I do; and may God protect you both."

****

Sheen urged the sorrel into a gallop. She'd passed the last two hours thinking about Guthrie, replaying their time at the cave together, and the exchange between them after they'd stopped to tend to Rachel.

Vultures circling overhead darkened the sky. Heartbreak and fear threatened to undo her. She needed to stay strong, needed to remind herself of her commitment to her purpose—to save Guthrie.

The sound of men yelling and the thunder of horses' hooves jerked her from her thoughts.

As much as she wanted to wheel the sorrel and make a run for it, she knew it was too late even before the band of Sioux warriors surrounded her. She was outnumbered six to one and had no weapon except the rifle. In seconds she was a prisoner.

"This is an outrage," Sheen stormed at the man who grabbed the sorrel's reins.

A warrior with eyes that reminded her of a rattler leered at her. Sheen's faced turned ashen as she frantically searched the ground littered with bodies. Guthrie's wasn't among them. "Where is Guthrie Tanner? I command you take me to him."

The stench of death was in the air, the smell of blood and sweat assailed Sheen's senses.

The warrior's beady eyes narrowed to mean slits as he answered her in broken English. "You wish to die with the white man?"

Hearing his words, Sheen began to struggle, but two husky warriors had a firm grip on her arms and were already forcing the sorrel forward.

She kneed the gelding in a frantic effort to break loose, but her captures were ready for her. They closed in, tightening the circle.

"I will make you sorry. All of you."

The man who had spoken in English met her threat with a triumphant snort of laughter. He reached forward and grabbed her braid, giving it a hard yank. "Woman with hair of fire...I make you mine."

After miles of travel, her mount was beginning to weaken, stumbling repeatedly and breathing hard.

"My horse is tired. You must stop and let him rest."

"Hope he doesn't die, woman, or you will walk the rest of the way."

"Where are you taking me?"

"To watch your white man die."

"Plà ar do theach."

"I do not understand your gibberish, woman." her captor said.

She met his reptilian stare with one of her own. "A plague on your house."

"Are you a witch who casts spells?"

"I am no witch, but I am your enemy."

He regarded her sternly before laughing...a harsh, sinister sound.

Sheen's inner thighs were rubbed raw from hours of scrubbing against saddle leather. She was lightheaded from not eating and feared she'd fall out of the saddle, and the inside of her throat burned from lack of water. Her discomfort was growing by the minute. And, for the first time, she valued her gift and prayed that when she needed to call upon it, her talents wouldn't abandon her.

Silently she spoke to the sorrel, encouraging him to be strong, not to give up. She promised that when this ordeal was over, he would have green pastures to romp in. She reached forward and laid a series of loving pats against the sweaty neck. *"Tis a good and loyal laddie you've been. Even when I threatened to turn you into a rabbit."*

The gelding bobbed its head and snorted. It heaved a deep sigh, and Sheen felt a bit of strength surge through the sorrel's body.

The day was still young when they arrived at the base of the secret passageway to Otaktay's stronghold; where she and Guthrie had stopped long enough to examine Rachel.

The snake-eyed man ordered Sheen to dismount. She slid from the saddle. Her legs trembled. Bone-aching fatigue and an overwhelming sense of loss made her weary. Her voice almost cracked when she spoke. "Take me to Guthrie Tanner. The one you call—white man."

A tall, stoutly built man walked forward. His face and body bore the scars of many battles. The most distinguishing and frightful feature was his face. Lips thick, square jaw, and the eye—a sightless gray marble.

"Who are you to make demands, woman?"

Swallowing hard, she forced herself to meet his cold gaze. "You speak—English."

"You are no different from the other white-eyes who think all red men are incapable of intelligence."

"I do not think ill of any person until I am proven wrong."

"Very passionately spoken." Otaktay glanced at the circle of listeners, playing them with the skill of a politician. "Have I proven you wrong?"

His contemptuous gaze measured her, testing her mettle.

"You have. Many times over." She placed her hands on her hips. "I will ask again. Where is Guthrie Tanner?"

The silence that followed was only broken by the raucous call of a passing crow.

All eyes were suddenly on Sheen.

"I demand an answer, Otaktay. Or shall I call you by your true name—*Many Kills?*"

She could sense the warrior chief's anger welling. It took no special powers to see it in the bristling eyebrows and in the clenched fist at his side. She could feel her own tension building as she waited for the explosion.

Otaktay's eyes were coldly challenging, his face flushed like an overheated stove, and his lips pressed tightly together as if to hold back an outburst of rage. And then he threw back his head and laughed. The warriors who had gathered around joined in.

The reprieve lasted a moment before his hand snaked out and twisted the long braid of her hair around his hand, pulling it tight enough that her scalp felt as if it were being ripped from her head. She refused to cry out.

"It is a shame to contain such fiery beauty in a braid." With a swift upward movement, his knife sliced through the cord holding the plaited hair. He sheathed the knife and with deft fingers loosened the red strands until the hair floated around her shoulders.

He jerked her around so that she landed hard against his chest. She felt him against her skin, and channeled a protective moat of energy between him and herself.

He was dirty. Evil. A soul, or what remained of one, darker and more chaotic than a stormy night. His thoughts felt eaten away from the inside out. She doubted the strongest fairy doctor could mend such vast, self-inflicted damage—even if the fairy doctor wanted to try.

Meeting his gaze, she forced herself to swallow. His one good eye held hers so intently that she could see her own reflection in the depths of his jet-black pupil. She understood now why he was hated and feared by all who knew his name. Otaktay was a man without a soul. A man who thrived on cruelty.

He puffed up his chest. "I like a woman with fire. You will be my woman until I say you are not."

She raised her eyes and glowered at the man. "I would rather die than become your squaw."

Otaktay raised his hand and lashed it across her face. "A taste of what is to come if you resist." And then, as if to drive home his point, he added, "You will feel the bite of my whip until you beg to share my blanket."

He reached for her, and laughed. Loudly.

Sheen's palms suddenly turned damp. "No," she

cried. "You will not force me to lie with you!"

He roared. "No woman denies me." The sound of his voice was deafening, and loud enough to stir the entire camp.

Her cheeks burned. The very thought of what Otaktay threatened to do to her sent her pulses racing.

"A stallion breeds when he feels the need, and his mares are always willing."

Sheen shrieked, "They are animals. How dare you compare me to the beasts!" Her hand shaped as a talon, she raked the warrior-chief's face with fingernails. "You do not have breeding rights. The devil take you, *Many Kills.*"

He held out his hand, and a black whip was placed in it.

Instinctively, Sheen raised an arm to shield her face. She locked her eyes on the eyes of her gelding. A blur of the whip shot through the air. In that instant Jughead stepped forward, bumping Otaktay's shoulder. The whip fell just short of its mark. A gush of warm blood rolled down the corner of Sheen's eye.

Otaktay bellowed. "What magic do you use to command the horse to protect you?"

"I have no magic. He is merely a loyal friend."

"Then control your loyal friend, or I will make you watch while I beat him to death."

The warrior chief's threat was simple, but effective. He gestured to the two men holding Sheen. "Bind her hands. Put her with the white man."

She clamped the inside of her mouth to keep from crying out as strips of rawhide bit into the tender flesh of her wrists. As she was being led away, she shrugged from the short stout brave's grip, and turned to face

Otaktay. Her voice dripped ice. "*Hotah!*"

Sheen had struck a nerve. She knew she had wounded him as she meant to wound him, and could see his thoughts were raw and scattered.

A muscle twitched in his cheek. "You dare insult me?"

"Which parent was white, Otaktay? I'm guessing it was your mother. She was a captive, and ill-used. You were the product of her attacker's seed. Seed that she didn't want in her body.

"I'm guessing she hated you every day of her life and never let you forget it. And every time you murder and rape and scalp a white person, you're killing the *white* part of yourself, over and over again."

She watched the hot flush of outrage swell his face and knew she'd overstepped boundaries and perhaps sealed her own death warrant.

He hissed the words, spraying her cheek with drops of spittle. "I should cut out your tongue and feed it to the crows. Instead, you will watch the one you call Guthrie Tanner die, slowly and quite painfully."

The insane look in his eye frightened Sheen. His one-eyed gaze lanced her like a shaft of ice. The blow came before she could avoid it. Her mouth filled with blood, and bells of pain rang inside her head.

She spat the gore from her mouth. She did not back down from his stare. "'Tis the night of the witching moon, Otaktay."

"Bah! I know nothing of this moon you speak of." He flung his arm wide. "Take this crazy woman, who talks nonsense, away."

The short stout warrior shoved Sheen, causing her to stumble and lose her balance. Her mouth filled with dirt and leaves when she fell. Her anger turned to rage as Otaktay and his warriors laughed.

Offering a silent prayer to the All Mothers for guidance, she pushed to a standing position and thrust out her chin, her temper seething.

The gibberish her enemy spoke meant nothing. The leer in his eyes implied everything, causing her to recoil at his touch.

He chortled as he placed his broad hands against her back and shoved. She landed next to where Guthrie lay on the ground.

Looking at Guthrie with tears in her eyes, she shuddered. The back of his shirt was cut to ribbons and deep bloody welts crisscrossed his back. His arms and legs were bruised, and his face was a mass of purple swollen flesh.

"Guthrie, it's me, Sheen. Can you hear me?"

He moaned, but opened his eyes. The concern in his voice was evident. "They caught you? Rachel?"

"Nay. I sent Sara Beth and Rachel on ahead to the fort."

"Why did you come back?"

"For you, Guthrie. I came for you."

"He'll kill us both. You know that."

She wanted to touch him. To soothe his wounded body. "They didn't tie your hands."

"Reckon they figured I was in too bad a shape to run off."

"Do you have enough strength to untie mine?"

Pain caused his hands to tremble. Nonetheless, Guthrie worked the knots on the rawhide until the strands fell from Sheen's wrists.

The sun was setting when she reached out her

hands. Fingers as gentle as falling snowflakes touched him. She was a healer, and she needed to heal him. There was not enough time.

"Oh..." She felt his face, the blackened, swollen eyes, the puffed lower lip. "Sweet mother, what have they done to you?" she whispered.

"Probably looks worse than it is. Nothing that won't heal," he muttered. "What about you? They didn't...hurt you, did they?"

"There is no need for worry, Guthrie. I am all in one piece."

He touched the bruise on her cheek. "We get out of this alive, that son of a dog-eater will pay for hurting you."

Sheen fumbled for one of his hands, lifting it to her lips to kiss the bruised knuckles.

He stroked her hair, his fingers tangling in the silken copper stands. "You shouldn't have come back, Sheen."

"I had to. I had to make sure you were alive." She lay beside him and slipped her arms around him, then drew back as he flinched from the pain in his ribs.

Guthrie gazed at her, searing her with his love. "You look like an intensely wild and beautiful moon goddess."

She sat up and the night wind caught her hair, unfurling it like a banner as she faced him. "We must get to the horses. If I help, can you walk?"

He groaned as he heaved himself to a sitting position, then with Sheen's assistance used the strength of his legs to push himself fully erect. He wobbled.

"Take my shoulder," she said, turning to one side so he could reach her.

Guthrie's bruised and battered body had stiffened in the hours of lying down. He clasped her shoulder, leaning on her as he had never leaned on anyone in his proud and defiant life. He owed her more than she would ever know; this small, brave fairy doctor, his *witch*, who had worked her magic and reawakened his body and spirit.

Step-by-teeth-clenching step, they made their way through the dim shadows to where the horses were tethered.

Chapter Twenty-Nine

The warmth of the sun had faded by the time Sheen and Guthrie reached the horses. A fevered chill wracked Guthrie's tortured body.

He moaned and rested his aching head against a tree. Keeping his voice low, he spoke through clenched teeth. "Damn, they've unsaddled the horses. Can you ride bareback?"

"I can manage."

Guthrie's face twisted with pain, but his eyes shone with approval. Fatigue consumed him, overwhelmed the strength that kept his bones and muscles working. His entire body ached, his legs and arms heavy as lead weights. It took every ounce of strength he had to keep breathing.

Leaning against the tree, his knees buckled from his own weight. "Take the stallion and get the hell out of here. I'll fight until the last breath before I let them catch you."

He lifted Sheen's fingers to his lips and kissed them. "There's so much I regret not telling you."

She quieted him. "You've already apologized more times than is necessary."

"But I've never said...'I love you.' "

She laid her palm against his flushed cheek, hot with fever. "'Tis these sweetest words I've longed to hear."

She cupped his cheeks with her hands and, lifting his head, gently kissed his bruised and battered lips.

"It's only a matter of time before one of the guards discovers we're gone," he admonished her. "Go, now. And Sheen, take care of Rachel. Tell her how much I love her."

Sheen's voice broke. "I'll never let her forget you. I promise."

****

Sheen closed her eyes, her gut churning, knowing full well Guthrie might not survive the day. If a bullet or an arrow didn't kill him, then his injuries from the brutal beating would.

His life meant more to her than she'd ever dreamed. If she left now, she might live to reach the fort. If she stayed here with him, she prayed for a quick death, for death was surely far better than what Otaktay had in store for her.

She tried to steady her thoughts. Sweet mother! She was a healer, and a fairy doctor. She would not ride away and leave Guthrie here. Nor could she bear the thought of never seeing him again.

Seeking a solution to their escape, she was struck with a revelation. "Guthrie, 'tis my birthday. 'Tis Friday, and the day of thirteen."

She didn't know if he lacked understanding of the date's significance, or if delirium was slowly overtaking his mind, or perhaps it was both that caused the puzzled expression to crease his brows.

"I will command the stallion to lie down so you can get on him. He is strong enough to bear both of us. We will ride double, and I can keep you from falling."

Guthrie rasped. "Embrace your gift, Sheen. It's

what makes you special. They broke something inside me. I can feel it." He smiled, his grin weak and pale. "Now do as I say and go."

Sheen squinted. A trickle of fresh blood oozed from the corner of his mouth. She feared the kicks and fierce blows to the stomach had caused him to bleed from the inside, and she knew he might not survive the bone-jarring ride to the fort.

The sound of men yelling jerked her from her thoughts. The forested area where the horses were tethered welled with warriors. Her arms were yanked and tied behind her back.

A fierce-looking guard wrapped his hands in Sheen's hair and forced her to where Otaktay stood, tall, dark, and imposing.

Two more brown-faced men hooked their arms under Guthrie's and rudely dragged him across the leaf-strewn earth.

The hem of her tattered and dirty dress dragged along the ground like a broom, dragging leaves and dirt with her. The point of a spear jabbed her in the back, forcing her to stand straight and rigid. Otaktay said, "Foolish woman. You have sealed the white man's death warrant. For your punishment, you will watch while I teach him a lesson."

At his signal, Sheen's mouth was stuffed with a dirty rag and a bandanna was tied securely over her lips. Her chest heaved furiously as she struggled against her restraints.

Holding him under his arms, two guards dragged Guthrie forward and forced him onto his knees.

"Hold this white dog," Otaktay commanded. "Tie his hands behind his back."

Sheen watched in horror as long agonizing minutes passed. Otaktay stepped up to Guthrie, who went white-faced but said, "Only a coward rapes and tortures women, and steals innocent children."

Otaktay stepped closer. He leered at Guthrie. "The child with the curly hair, the one called White Frog. She is yours?"

Guthrie refused to speak.

The Santee chief balled his fist and rapped the side of Guthrie's head. Sheen gasped as Guthrie retched from the pain. Yet he stoically faced his enemy.

"You cowardly sonafabitch. You murdered my wife."

A lurid grin twisted the chief's face. "And now I get to take another woman from you. Maybe you would like to watch while I take her, or maybe I will give her to my men."

"Let her go. She has nothing to do with this. A little kindness must lie somewhere in that black heathen heart of yours."

Otaktay laughed manically, then leaned forward and whispered hotly in Sheen's ear. "You should not have tried to escape. But let me tell you this, squaw, there is only one way for you to get away from me—through the door of death."

He raised the level of his voice so all could hear. "I am going to slit your white man's throat. But I will give you a few minutes to pray for him. How about that, white man? Is that enough compassion from me?"

The air seemed to crackle with energy. An owl swooped low in front of Sheen.

An omen.

The knife in his hand, Otaktay displayed it proudly,

holding it for a long moment directly in front of Sheen's eyes to prolong the torture.

A sneering grin on his face, he grabbed a handful of Guthrie's blond hair, forcing his head back so that the large blue veins on either side of his neck bulged visibly.

Otaktay crowed, "I am going to slit your miserable throat just enough so that it will take until morning for you to bleed to death."

A whimper built in the back of Sheen's throat, but she closed it off. She pressed her lips together to keep them from trembling. She looked at Guthrie. Grief swam in his eyes, swirled there, then cleared. He mouthed, *Be brave.*

The vision she'd had in Dyani's kitchen rose up inside her head—with the sickening realization that she'd already dreamed and forgotten this very scene. She was glad Guthrie didn't know the full extent of torture that Otaktay had in store for him. It was strange to realize that she was about to relive another nightmare.

Sweet Mother! Help me. I must save Guthrie.

Sheen sat unmoving, her hands tied behind her back. She let herself feel nothing, not the throbbing in her head or the rawhide strips that cut into her wrists. She should have been terrified. Instead she squeezed her eyes shut to close off the anger and channel all her efforts into keeping her thoughts from being scattered.

From nowhere a bumblebee flitted close enough for Sheen to feel the soft fan of its wings against her cheek. *Mother!*

The tiny wings whirred and Sheen thought she heard music. This puzzled her. What message was her mother trying to send to her? And then the chant built inside Sheen's mind. An old chant, one that was familiar, and yet Sheen knew she'd never before heard it. It billowed and flowed, the words needing to escape the dirty rag binding her mouth.

A voice that only she could hear said, *You have been tested, my child. It is the thirteenth hour of the thirteenth day of your twenty-third year and time to come into the fullness of your powers. Beware, for you will find that supremacy can be intoxicating, inciting greed and meanness.*

Sheen responded, *Are my powers strong enough to save the man whom I cherish with all my heart?*

A blue halo circled the full moon. A cold wind rippled a chill up Sheen's spine.

And the All Mothers keened their answer in a song, forlorn and foreboding, the words audible to only Sheen.

> *Hush, child. The darkness will rise from a deep sleep to carry your enemy down...down to the bowels of the earth.*

> *Your spirit is our spirit. Our vengeance will unfold for the child of our bodies as your birthright is foretold.*

Every sound, every smell, and every color Sheen could sense bespoke the violence of death—screaming, and splashes of scarlet against the green earth and dark sky.

Bursts of lightning streaked across the ether, while a simultaneous thunderclap shook the earth.

The cicadas and woodhouse toads lent their voices to the song, adding to the eerily keening wind.

Otaktay's warriors clustered around him, and the

warrior chief cried out, "What evil is this you perform, woman?"

Another boom of thunder struck the air in a flash.

The warriors huddled together. Their voices cried out, rising through the crackling air. "Our chief, save us from the *bruha*."

Otaktay lashed the men with his whip. He cursed. "You dare cower like yellow dogs?"

As if drunk with fear, the men stumbled over each other, trying to make their escape.

Turning his diabolical eye toward Sheen, he challenged. "I am Many Kills. My men call you *bruha*—witch. Let us see if you have strong magic, because I am going to torture you, and you are going to beg—scream!—to die. But you will not die until I am good and ready to see you draw your last breath."

Anger surged through her veins and blackness, powerful and intense, filled her heart. She would not allow this devil of a man to continue to maim the innocent. She stared back. *You are a murderer of the innocent—men, women, children, and even the poor beasts. Be careful what you ask for.*

Sheen spread her hands beyond the ties at her wrists, concentrated on the song of her All Mothers, and embraced the magic. It hovered over her like a silver fog. It saturated the night air. It fluttered through her like an improbable breeze, pulsing with wonder and possibility, and she thought that if she reached out, she could grab a handful of it and hold it close. And then a huge jolt of it exploded through every channel of her, leaving her hands free and her eyes wide, her muscles tight, and her mind as disoriented as if the world were spinning out of control.

All of nature exuded power, but not all of that power was as soft as the still night air. Some of it, like lightning, was downright dangerous in its strength—her strength.

A cold shock of sweat broke over Sheen. She looked at the warrior chief to see him enraged and fearless, his skin as pale as death. He was reaching for her, a war club in one hand, his broad-bladed knife in the other. The war club swished at her face, its stone head heavy enough to pulp flesh and bone in a searing instant…and left her untouched except for the removal of the torturous gag.

What caught her vision was beyond him—figures at the edge of the forest. The All Mothers gowned in the gossamer rays of translucent moonbeams, blue-green lights menacing in their unearthly dance.

A jolt of white-hot energy tracked through Sheen. She spun around and lifted her freed arms higher and the surge of power that passed over her made her feel almost weightless. Forces joined with her own, streaming from her mother, her grandmother, and the All Mothers from centuries long before as she called forth the spirits of all who had suffered from the hands of Many Kills.

****

The specters of death hovered over Otaktay's shoulder. A fog swirled toward him, a fog of forms and faces. Palpable misery brushed the edges of his bewildered brain.

Moans and shrieks.

Were the cries his? No. They could not be. He was a mighty warrior, and today was not his day to die.

Yet diaphanous arms caught him around the

mouth, muffling his scream as they dragged him from Sheen and Guthrie's view and into a swirling darkness.

The howling wind hurt the warrior chief's ears as squares of blue-green light danced around him in the darkness.

He struggled as the specters wrenched his arms with formidable strength, and the warrior cried out in pain.

A white gauzy figure floated toward him, her finger stiff and pointed to strike him in the chest. "Meet those who will judge you and then determine your death."

Angrily, he spat, only to watch the spittle pass through the woman's face and out the other side. "Who are you?"

Lightning lanced the sky, all corners and forks, and then vanished into the darkness.

"I am Keelin, Queen of the All Mothers. The Fates have decided your punishment." Again, she pointed her finger.

Another roll of thunder struck, echoed. The rush of wind sounded even louder.

Otaktay raised his hands over his head to fend off the blue-green luminous lights that bobbed toward him.

The once mighty Santee chief screamed as his bones cracked with loud snaps. He screamed again, falling to the ground, while the luminous figures floated around him. He wiped drool from his lips. He shivered against an incredible chill, and he groaned deep in his chest. His heart beat wildly as he screamed with pain and rage.

His legs quivered as he forced himself to stand. Everything fell into slow motion around him like a nightmare in which he struggled, only to be pulled downward. His breath tore from his chest as the ground beneath him opened its massive jaws.

"No...nooo!" He clawed and scratched the air.

Rotting, putrid odors of decay assailed his nostrils. Realization struck him—today was his day to die.

His only regret was that he had not been able to taste of the woman with hair the color of fire while making the white man watch.

The last thing Otaktay knew were the blood-curdling cries of voices calling for his soul.

His lips trembled as he sang the words of his death song.

And then the moon turned out its light and the world was dark.

Chapter Thirty

Guthrie had never seen the moon so round, so brilliantly lit, nor ringed with a radiating blue halo. Disbelief shook him as he watched the scene unfolding in front of him.

Sheen glistened in the light, trimmed with silver. A strange mixture of the girl he'd come to love and a woman he wasn't sure he had it in him to know. She was so...unreal. Everything about this night seemed unreal.

He glanced around the camp. Broken and twisted bodies of dead warriors littered the ground. The wind kicked up again, became the tormented moans of lost souls. Then they, too, vanished.

Residual blurs of blue-green light danced across the blackness, fading into nothingness.

It was over.

Only silence echoed the madness of what had happened. Guthrie needed words. He needed normalcy. What the hell had just happened?

****

Bursts of luminescent images lingered, even as darkness swept over them again. Sheen was tired, more than horse-riding-tired. She was soul-tired.

As the energies spread back into the night, the wind, the prairie, and the earth returned to their normal pace. Fighting a flood of emotions, she sank against

Guthrie's side.

She hid her face in her knees, but not before her tears spilled over. Guthrie pulled her against his chest and tried not to moan as he hugged her hard. She cried in earnest. He stroked her hair and told her it would be okay.

He lay back, still holding her, not fighting his own emotions. He just held her, let her cry until she couldn't seem to cry any longer and she lay limp, exhausted, in the crook of his arm. Finally she blinked up at him, her eyes swollen, nose red.

"What just happened, Sheen?"

"I couldn't stand losing you, so I called on the All Mothers for help. They evoked the wrath of all the souls of the innocents Otaktay and his warriors have murdered."

Guthrie used a thumb to wipe a tear from her cheek. "Then this is who you really are?"

"Some will call me a witch. But, truly, I am a fairy doctor." She hesitated. "Except now I have come into the fullness of my powers."

"What happens next?"

The air around them hushed, as if all the night creatures were waiting for her answer, too.

She closed her eyes, drained of energy, lost between two worlds. The touch on her shoulder was soft and gentle. Familiar. She opened her eyes and looked around, to fully regain her bearings—and to do something other than stare into Guthrie's blue eyes.

This wasn't the time or place to go into a detailed explanation of her abilities.

She dragged her attention back to his question. "Guthrie, I didn't ask for this...curse. I don't like hearing the voices of ghosts, or delving into the minds of the living, and not being able to shut out the visions. Seeing the past is bad enough, but I've never wanted to see the future. Not mine, yours, or any living being's." She spread her hands wide, and shrugged her shoulders. "I don't know what is going to happen next, not until it is time for it to happen."

He tried to smile. "I didn't mean about the future. I meant about us."

Perspiration dotted his forehead. He eased out a ragged breath. He coughed. Fresh blood splattered the palm of his hand. He groaned softly as fiery daggers of pain stabbed through his body.

He was growing lightheaded and his vision was beginning to blur. He seemed to see little black spots floating in front of his eyes.

And there he lay. Tired and beaten. Still willing to accept her, even after what he'd witnessed.

Her hands hungered to touch him—if not in passion, then healing.

"Take your pants off," she said as she reached for a blanket that lay nearby on the ground

His eyes widened, fully alert. "What?"

"I have healing powers. You need healing," she said with a wobbling smile. "Take your pants off, or I can't do your legs."

He stared at her, then flashed a weak grin. "I appreciate the offer, but the pain, I don't think I—"

"If not for yourself, then do it for Rachel."

He hesitated, glanced away from Sheen, while his fingers fumbled with opening his trousers.

Sheen lifted her skirt and raced to where the horses were tethered. She found her saddle and undid the clasp on her saddlebag. She rummaged until her fingers found two vials, one of cedar wood oil and the other of yarrow. On second thought, she decided a few drops of lavender oil would also be soothing.

Returning to where he lay, she said, "Can you turn on your stomach?"

"Just...lie on my stomach?" His voice was thick with uncertainty.

"Mm-hmm...and relax."

By the grimace on his face, Sheen knew the effort had cost him. "Okay. Now what?"

After a deep, strengthening breath, she turned back to him. His six-foot-plus length was as bare as the day he was born, stretched across a blanket. She tried to relax the knots in her stomach.

"You will need to let your arms rest at your sides," she prompted, rubbing her hands together to warm them. "Close your eyes and let your mind drift. Think happy thoughts. If I need you to move, I'll let you know."

He answered her with a muffled moan.

She poured a few drops of cedar wood oil into her warmed palms. On her knees, she leaned over his broad back and laid her hands on him. The warm, tingling sensation as the aura of their energies met felt very strong, increasing as she skimmed her palms up the dip of his spine, over the rise of his shoulder blades. The smell of cedar wafted up at her as it met his warm skin.

She whispered, "I'll try not to hurt you. Relax."

She concentrated on Guthrie's healing, brushing aside any uncertainties about her newest powers that threatened to undo her.

Mindful of the deep and already festering welts,

she gently massaged his strong back, down his sides and over his ribs. She worked her way up to his shoulders, then, more gently onto his neck. She noticed that his eyes had drifted shut.

Good.

At the base of his skull she traced tiny, firm circles with her fingers, working them into the thick, dark blond hair. As she worked down the full of his body, she used her weight, not just her hands, to apply pressure. She tried to feel him, tried to listen to the body beneath her touch.

She perceived the slim, pale scar along his shoulder where he'd broken his collarbone when the horse had fallen on him. She knew, as she worked her way down his left arm, that she would feel a faint ridge along his elbow, where he'd broken it falling out of a tree. She sensed his childhood ailments, and knew he'd suffered from pneumonia. But this was no child's body.

Once she started, she never removed both her hands at once; she wouldn't willingly break the ebb and flow of their energy. And she hummed, an ancient tune filled with words known only to fairy doctors.

When she needed more oil, she turned one hand over on him, and used her free hand to fill her palm with more cedar-scented lubricant. She kneaded the muscles in his arms. She used her thumbs to work his palm, then paid attention to his other arm and hand.

She moved one hand to his thigh, then the other, before starting work on his legs—calf muscles, ankles, and the soles of his feet.

After thoroughly kneading the muscles of each leg and foot, she returned again to his back, using the balls of her fingers to ease away the last of his pain.

She paused to catch her breath, her hands spread across the pliant firmness of his shoulders. She bent close and whispered, "Guthrie, I need you to roll over."

His eyes didn't open. She looked more closely, then let her shoulders relax. He'd fallen asleep. She could wake him as gently as possible and continue. But he needed the sleep more, to let the healing continue.

She told herself it was time to stop touching him. She cocked her head, noticing how the gleam of oil, in the faint illumination of moonlight, highlighted the contours of his muscled body.

Right hand on his back, she slid her left hand lightly to his neck. She turned her wrist so the back of her fingers skimmed his jaw, then played with the hair that curled at the nape of his neck.

Her pulse sped. A sweet warmth completely different from the scent of cedar oil filled the deep recesses of her womanly core. She considered waking him.

It sapped her strength, this healing thing she did.

Frustratingly, achingly so, she remembered when they were at the cave. She remembered what his hands felt like, and the unspoken promise of his lovemaking that she had adamantly rejected.

The night creatures serenaded her with song. She listened for a moment, knowing the All Mothers were still with her, watching, protecting, before turning her attention back to Guthrie. She mumbled a few words and, without effort, gently rolled him to his side. She braced him while shifting her position to roll him onto his back.

Once again, she vigorously rubbed her hands to generate heat and, when they were warm, dripped oil of lavender in the palms and patted them together. She'd felt his response to the cedar oil, and knew his healing was taking place. She also knew the magic of lavender oil.

****

The pain started to fade beneath her fingers. One minute Guthrie was clenching his teeth against the throbbing, certain the ache would only increase as his surprise at Sheen's forwardness wore off. She was, after all, a...what? Fairy doctor? Witch?

He inhaled the richness of the cedar wood oil's scent. Then, beneath the magic of her fingers, the jolts of each painful throb calmed to small waves, then to a faint pulse of sensation. The pain that had indicated broken ribs and internal bleeding grew immensely hot until he almost cried out, before the agony cooled as Sheen's fingers drew across his body.

The rest of him got warm and stayed that way.

As the aching throbs faded, he grew aware of her touch elsewhere and sensed her as she leaned into him to reach his face.

He didn't remember turning over, yet he rested on his back.

She'd lowered her hands from his face, bracing them against his chest, still leaning against him.

Happy thoughts. The words echoed inside his head. His mind drifted...drifted...to a happier time.

He found himself spreading his hands wide until he caressed her back, and his thumbs slipped beneath her arms toward the softness of her breast. He didn't want to lose the feel of her against him like this.

He wanted to kiss her. Oh, God, he wanted to kiss her. He slipped his hand upward and found her head already tipped toward him. Cradling her, he rose closer, blindly seeking her mouth with his own. He couldn't believe he had the strength for sex—his need for her was too great.

His eyes closed, he sighed. Her lips tasted of tears, salty and fresh, and pure. He drank her in, the familiarity and the newness of her. She caught him behind the neck with one hand, tasting him back, curious and passionate. He drew his hand, the one under her arm, forward to capture her breast in his palm.

He felt like he'd come home.

He relaxed and relished those happy thoughts... remembering...remembering.

In a breathy sigh, he whispered her name. "Abigail..."

Sheen shrieked into his mouth and pushed away from him.

The screech jarred him awake. Guthrie's eyes opened wide. He was disoriented and off balance. For a moment he didn't recognize the woman bending over him. "Sheen?"

The expression on her face caused him to groan inwardly, recalling the name he had spoken wasn't hers.

Hellfire and damnation, why did she have to look at him that way?

Dropping the vials of oil into a skirt pocket, Sheen stood abruptly. "It's almost daybreak. If you're up to the ride, you'll be wanting to get to the fort—to Rachel."

His palms still tingled for want of touching her. His blood pounded through him; his legs felt weak. All from the way she'd soothed her hands across his body.

Abashed, he reached down to cover his throbbing manhood with both hands.

"My pants, Sheen. I need my pants."

Handing him the garment, she extended her palm. "Here, let me help you stand."

Clutching the trousers to conceal himself, he accepted her offer.

Sheen caught Guthrie's hand in her own. It didn't feel the way her touch had moments before. It was neither passionate nor curious. When he stood, her hand slipped away from his, and he instinctively recognized the official end of their brief intimacy.

Chapter Thirty-One

The second day of riding, and the air was clear and quiet, the sky void of clouds. A pair of eagles dipped and soared in a graceful dance on a gentle breeze.

No sound disturbed the fading morning, no sound except the creak of saddle leather and the melodic sweetness of Sheen's humming.

With Otaktay dead and Rachel safe at the fort, Guthrie had satisfied his need for vengeance.

He and Sheen rode in silence. Searing pain ripped through every inch of his battered body. He would heal, this he knew, and yet he still bore the raw scars of his own emotional deprecation. Since the day of finding his wife's mutilated body, his ranch burned, and his little girl kidnapped, he'd neither trusted nor needed anyone, preferring the company of his horse. Nearly two years of riding lonesome.

Staring into the sun, he watched Sheen and listened. Her voice soft and soothing, she hummed to no one in particular.

With every surging stride, Sheen's supple spine rolled in rhythm with her horse, in perfect unity. Her hands were still, her shoulders square and facing straight ahead as her legs hugged the horse's sides. Not a hint of light shone between her buttocks and her mount. She was remarkable to watch.

He imagined her in his warm bed, her long fingers

sliding lightly down his back, her silky legs wrapped around his own. The muscles beneath the jagged wounds along his back relaxed and softened as the tension drained away.

Then the bulge between his legs grew and throbbed.

Hellfire and damnation.

He needed a strong drink to put the woman who had bewitched him from his mind.

Then, carefully thinking of the future, he wondered where he fit in Sheen's life. Better, how did she fit into his?

Sheen's voice interrupted his thoughts as a cry escaped her lips. "Oh, sweet mother. Guthrie, the soldiers are coming. I knew Sara Beth and Rachel would reach the fort safely."

Uncertain of the emotions churning his gut, Guthrie stretched his full height in the saddle. "I see 'em."

The moving column wound like a gray-blue snake across the green grass. The faces of the troopers were streaked with sweat from the hard riding.

Saddles creaked, sabers clattered, and the soldiers watched the hills for unseen enemies. Guthrie lifted his hand to signal that he'd spotted them.

And then there was only the settling of dust as Sergeant Paddy O'Hanlon signaled the column to a halt.

"Well, me laddie, 'tis good to see you alive and still wearin' yer scalp. See ye escaped them pesky Santee."

"Good to see you, too, Sergeant." Guthrie shifted his attention to Sheen. "Sergeant Paddy O'Hanlon, may

I present Miss Sheen O'Reilly."

The red-faced Irishman with a bulbous nose doffed his dusty blue cap. "O'Reilly? Be ye from the motherland, lass?"

"Aye, Sergeant. 'Twas born in County Mayo I was, but I have lived in the Americas since a wee child."

"Aah, 'tis music to me ol' ears to hear you speak, lass. I thought to never hear the Irish brogue again before 'tis time to meet me maker."

Then, as if embarrassed by his intimate chatter, he harrumphed. "Well, now, 'tis saddle weary and hungry I imagine ye are. Ye look fair done in, the both of you."

Sheen offered the man a smile. "Aye, Sergeant. That we are."

The tobiano stallion pawed the ground and champed at the bit. Guthrie knew the animal didn't like standing around. "Sergeant, since you're here, I'm taking it that Miss MacDonald and my little girl, Rachel, made it safely to the fort."

"Aye, that they did."

"My daughter...how is she?"

"Mistress MacDonald told the doctor 'bout the ticks. He checked yer wee one over right smart, he did. Said them nasty varmints near sucked the life out'n her frail self. The lady told doc what Mistress O'Reilly did, and he said she fair saved the child's life. Rachel, she be anxious to see her da, that's for certain." O'Hanlon tsked as he winked at Guthrie.

A wind rolled across the prairie, whipping Sheen's hair. She focused on the column of soldiers, her brain fogged with fatigue. Swaying in the saddle, she could barely acknowledge their presence.

Sergeant O'Hanlon said, "It fair rots me bones to

see ye all done in, lass. 'Tis only an hour's ride. Can ye hang on 'til then?"

Too weary to speak, she answered with a nod.

The sergeant raised his hand and gave the order to about face and forward ho.

And then there was movement, the sound of horses' hooves. A long time later, when the column rolled over the long hill and headed for the fort's large double gates, Guthrie looked up from the reins he held. He could see the flag fluttering in the wind, the troops marching onto the field for retreat, and westward the land was bright with a setting sun. From the parade ground he heard a bugle, the notes bright and clear.

He heard Sergeant O'Hanlon's command, saw the troopers form up, and saw them riding proudly to the parade ground. But he was remembering a long meadow, fresh with new hay, cattle carrying his brand, a house where smoke would rise from the chimney and where shadows would gather in the darkness under the trees, quiet shadows. And beside him a woman held in her arms a sleeping child...a woman who would never be there again with him, in that house, before that hearth. It was all gone, now. The house, the hay, the cattle...Abigail.

****

Sheen tasted salt in her mouth, tears. She drew the back of her hand across her eyes. Their ordeal was over. They had survived. She had survived.

She blinked. Through sticky lashes, her gaze found Guthrie. She sensed his despair. Try as she might, she could not shut out his thoughts of home, of his wife. She drew in a deep breath, then another. As soon as Rachel was well enough to travel, he would leave the fort...would leave without saying good-bye.

By the time their military escort had reached the parade ground, she was too exhausted to think anymore.

As they passed the outbuildings, every pair of eyes turned to stare, taking in her disheveled hair, her torn, dusty clothes. Sheen kept her gaze fixed straight ahead. There were those, the wives of the fort, who would try to shame her. The All Mothers would want her to remain proud.

A willowy figure in a dark blue dress emerged from the mess hall. Sara Beth's brown braids bobbed about her shoulders as she hurried across the parade ground. By the time she reached Sheen and the soldiers, she was flushed and out of breath.

"Praise be to God, you made it. Both of you," she gasped, clutching a white hankie to her bosom. "My goodness, but you look all done in."

Without waiting for an answer, she glared up at the sergeant. "What do you think you're doing? Miss O'Reilly doesn't need your protection inside the fort! Let the poor girl off her horse before she faints!"

Throwing a sideways glance at the woman, Sergeant O'Hanlon bellowed, "Diiis-mount."

A soldier kept a firm grip on the sorrel's bridle as Guthrie reached up and Sheen slid wearily into his arms. Her knees wobbled, refusing to hold her. She stumbled and might have fallen if Guthrie hadn't caught her.

Sara Beth, acting like a mother hen, said, "Don't tremble so, child. After a bath and a good hot meal, you'll be as good as new."

Sheen heard what Sara Beth was saying, but the woman's voice seemed to be coming from far away.

"Miss O'Reilly, you *are* all right, aren't you?" Sara Beth's eyes narrowed sharply. "Did anyone hurt you out there—any of those filthy savages—?"

With effort, Sheen pulled away and forced herself to speak. "I'm fine," she said. "All I need is a hot meal, a bath, and several hours' rest."

Sara Beth smiled. "Don't worry. Everyone's been real accomodatin'. They've fixed up a bunk for you in my quarters, and one for Mr. Tanner in the barracks."

Then shifting her attention to Guthrie, she said, "If you can muster the energy, Rachel is at the infirmary. Doc thought it best she stay where he could keep an eye on her, what with her nearly dyin' and all."

Guthrie offered an exhausted smile.

Sara Beth took Sheen by the arm. "Well, don't just stand there. Let's get you fixed up."

"Thank you," Sheen said, meaning it. She willed herself to walk without reeling as she followed Sara Beth across the parade ground to her new quarters. It helped having the woman by her side, even though Sara Beth had suffered her own ordeal at the hands of savages.

High on its iron pole, the Stars and Stripes flapped smartly in the evening breeze. Seeing the flag seemed strangely alien, as if Sheen were seeing it for the first time through her father's eyes.

She looked over her shoulder to watch Guthrie striding down the boardwalk toward a building bearing the insignia of a red cross on a banner of white. It was only right that his first desire was to hold his child in his arms before tending to his own needs.

Once inside the sparsely furnished room and with the door bolted for privacy, Sheen wearily gave over her personal ministrations to Sara Beth.

"I've been keeping a lookout, hoping and praying for you and Mr. Tanner to arrive safely. Soon as I spotted the dust, I hollered up to the sentry asking if you and him was with the troopers. Once the guard nodded, I started ordering kettles of hot water for you. A full all-over bath is a pure luxury."

The woman's hands fluttered to her cheeks. Her voice softened. "Forgive me, Miss O'Reilly. You must think I'm in love with the sound of my own voice."

Sheen sank into the galvanized tub, allowing the warm water to cover her entire body. "'Tis heavenly," she sighed as she closed her eyes.

Forcing herself not to fall asleep, Sheen looked at the woman pouring hot water into a cup. "Sara Beth, I have a favor to ask."

"Anything. I owe you and Mr. Tanner my life."

"Then I would very much like it if you would call me Sheen. And Mr. Tanner prefers—Guthrie."

Sara Beth's hand trembled, a bit, as she offered the cup of tea. "It's a very pretty name...Sheen. Do you think you can manage a slice of buttered bread while you soak—just to take the edge off your hunger?"

Sheen nodded as she sipped the hot liquid. "What will you do, Sara Beth? Where will you go?"

The words squeaked out in a desolate whisper. "I didn't know until a few days ago about the wagon train..." She pulled the white hankie from the sleeve of her dress and dabbed her eyes. "My husband...no survivors."

"You survived."

"If you can call living in hell all these years to be surviving, I guess so."

"What are your intentions?"

Sara Beth lifted her own cup and sipped. "We were heading to California from Pennsylvania when the wagon train was attacked. I want to go home, where no one will know I lived with the Indians... You know. About things that was done to me."

"You are still you, Sara Beth. You did what was necessary to survive. What will you do in Pennsylvania?"

"I've always wanted to open a sweet shop. That's what I'd planned to do in California. Sara Beth's Sweet Shop. Oh, I know it's a pipe dream. But it's what kept me going. Like if I had something to look forward to, I'd..."

Sheen reached out and clasped the woman's hand. She allowed her energies to meld with Sara Beth's. "The sweet shop will be a success, and while you may not believe it now, you will find happiness."

"What about you, Sheen?"

"I have my small farm on the prairie."

The surprise in the woman's voice was evident. "You live all alone?"

"Not exactly. My animals keep me company, and Mr. Tatum, the peddler, comes around every few months to trade and bring me news."

Sara Beth pshawed. "We all have our secrets, Sheen, that I can understand, 'cause once I return to Pennsylvania, this whole ordeal will be my secret. Why you choose to shut yourself away from folks is none of my business, just like it's not my business how you came to be with Guthrie, but I'd say that man is head over heels in love with you. My guess, by the way you look at him, is your feelings run mighty deep, too."

"Sometimes things aren't meant to be, Sara Beth."

The brown-haired woman expelled a frustrated sigh. "As much as I hated living with savages, I learned you can't count on the long term, only the here and now. If you're as smart as I think you are, you'll grab hold of that man and never let go. If you don't, you'll regret it the rest of your life."

Before Sheen could respond, a sharp knock sounded at the door. Sara Beth huffed out, "Go away. She ain't decent."

A male voice said, "Food tray, ma'am. For Miss O'Reilly. Compliments of Mrs. Wheeler and the post ladies."

"Leave it by the door. Oh, and tell Mrs. Wheeler after Miss O'Reilly has rested we'll come by and thank her in person."

Sheen toweled off. "Who is Mrs. Wheeler?"

"The post commander's wife. She and the other wives call themselves the Fort Smith Ladies Society."

Sheen donned a nightgown donated by one of the post wives. She struggled to keep her eyes open while savoring a rich stew and crusty bread, washed down with more hot tea.

Though she'd not met any of the women, Sheen sensed a biased nature and knew if she closed her eyes and opened her mind she would hear the ugliness whispered behind Sara Beth's back. "Have they been kind to you, Sara Beth?"

Now the tears surged. It was Sheen's turn to give comfort as she wrapped her arms around Sara Beth. "You've earned the right to cry. You've been through an ordeal that most of these women wouldn't have survived. They only judge you because of their own ignorance. You've done nothing wrong."

Sara Beth pulled away. She wiped her eyes and blew her nose. "Thank you, Sheen. Your words are more comforting than you'll ever know."

Sheen yawned, allowing Sara Beth to fuss over her. Settling in the cot, she didn't hear the door open and close, or Sara Beth's whispered, "Rest well, my friend."

****

A pale hand reached up to him. Guthrie caught and grabbed it to his lips. The blue eyes that gazed at him glittered with tears. Through a jagged haze of emotions, he looked at his daughter. Rachel was a miniature of her mother. He kissed the tiny knuckles and offered a quick prayer of thanks heavenward. He felt God had pardoned him for leaving South Carolina and bringing his reluctant wife to Montana.

"How's my girl?"

The child snuffled. "They killed Mommy."

His eyes drifted upward to the white-haired doctor who'd patched him up so many months ago—a lifetime, it seemed.

"A little on the thin side, but surprisingly healthy for what she's been through."

"I'd like to take her home when's she's well enough to travel."

"A couple more days of rest and a few more teaspoons of cod liver oil should do it." The doctor furrowed his brow into a serious frown. "Rachel will need extra understanding and patience. I'm sure you appreciate my meaning."

A bitter smile twisted Guthrie's lips. He answered with a nod.

Rachel tugged on his sleeve. "Daddy?"

"Yes, Punkie Pie?"

"How can we go home? The bad Indians burned down our house."

It was a fair question. He'd been so hell-bent on finding Rachel that he hadn't given much thought to the smoldering remains that had greeted him when he rode into the ranch yard that awful day.

Keeping his voice light and—he hoped—cheerful, he said, "I have some very nice friends, Otto and Dyani Werner. Dyani has a new baby boy. How would you like to stay with them while I rebuild the house?"

The panicked look in Rachel's eyes startled Guthrie. Flinging herself against his chest, her puny arms clutched as if her very life depended on never letting go. Shudder after shudder rolled through her body. "Nooo."

He glanced at the doctor, a silent plea for help. "The child's body will heal. How her mind heals is up to you. Leaving her, even with trustworthy folks, might not be the best option right now."

He was her father. He was supposed to be her hero, and he hadn't been there to protect her. Guthrie smoothed the silken blonde curls. He placed his lips atop her head and whispered, "It's okay. We'll figure it out as we go, but I promise to never leave you again."

The doctor poured a teaspoon of liquid and offered it to Rachel. "Open wide."

When she wrinkled her nose and shook her head, he reached into his white coat pocket and produced a peppermint stick. Without hesitation, Rachel opened her mouth.

As if needing to explain, he said, "A diluted mixture of laudanum. Right now, rest is the best medicine."

Guthrie pulled the dark green blanket up to his daughter's chin. He winced as he stood.

"From the looks of you, it was no tea party you attended. Better remove your shirt and let me have a look."

Guthrie trusted Sheen's curative powers. "I'll mend, Doc. Thanks all the same."

The old man opened a cabinet and withdrew a pint. He lifted out two glasses and filled both with a shot of amber liquid. "Well, a dram of whiskey, then."

Guthrie accepted the glass, returned the doctor's salute. He sucked in a deep breath as the alcohol burned down his throat and deep into his belly.

"Go get yourself a bath, some chow, and good sleep, son. I'm here if you decide to let me look you over."

Bone-weary, Guthrie gave one last look at his sleeping child, then eased from the room.

Chapter Thirty-Two

Sheen shifted on the narrow bed. Forcing her eyes open, she yawned and stretched, not believing she'd slept, and barely remembering Sara Beth rousing her long enough to spoon-feed rich strong broth.

A ray of sun filtered between the window's wooden shutters. She smiled at the dust motes dancing like tiny fairies in the shimmering light. Swinging her legs over the side of the cot, she padded across the room to where a green gingham dress draped over a chair. A note on the table stated the gown was a gift from the fort's ladies' society.

After attending her morning toilette, she stood at the window, where she spotted Guthrie striding across the parade ground. Her gaze followed him as he approached. For a brief unreasonable minute, she resented him for spoiling the pleasures in her life's little routines. She longed to return to her cabin on the prairie, in the middle of nowhere. Just she and her animals. Where life would be bright again.

He was dressed in his usual trousers, dusty boot tips poking from beneath, long-sleeved blue shirt, hat pulled forward to shade his eyes from the morning sun. But the main reason he looked so good was that she knew she'd never see him again.

She was leaving, but not with him. She tried to stir up some enthusiasm as she stepped from her room.

He tipped his hat. "Morning, Sheen. You're looking fit. I checked in on you a couple of times."

"It seems like I've slept for ages."

He squinted up at her. "I guess two days seems like a long time, especially when you're exhausted."

She shrugged one shoulder. "You are looking well, yourself. Rachel?"

Guthrie stepped up on the porch. "Doc says she should be healthy enough to travel tomorrow."

Sheen leaned forward and kissed him.

He would have kissed her back if she hadn't been so quick. One minute her lips had skimmed his, the next minute she had backed away, looking embarrassed. "What was that for?"

A mule's bray and the rattling of pots and pans caused both Sheen and Guthrie to turn. A sudden tension filled Sheen, and she knew what she had to do. It was the only sensible decision. For a moment she felt as if she were teetering on the edge of a dark abyss.

Strong hands gripped her arms. "Sheen, what happened? Are you having one of your visions?"

Her gaze slid from his face to the peddler's wagon, and then back to Guthrie's.

"Mr. Tatum is here. After he's done with his trading, I'm certain he will agree to give me a ride to my cabin."

Guthrie searched her face as if looking for something he couldn't find. "I thought—" He spread his hands—"that maybe you could, that is, that we could—"

She refused to meet his questioning gaze, choosing instead to stare into nothingness. "You've called me 'witch' one time too often. You've witnessed me coming into my powers. It can never work between us, Guthrie. As much as I love you, I fear the time may come when you will grow to resent me. I couldn't bear your hating me."

He raised his hands to her face, his palms cool against her cheeks. He leaned closer. She tried to turn her head. He leaned even closer. Her breath stalled in her lungs. If he kissed her, she feared it would undo her resolve to leave.

She placed fingers against his lips, agony knifing through her heart. "You'd better go. Rachel is asking for you."

Confusion played across his face. "How do you—" He shrugged as if he'd figured it out. She was a witch, after all. "I guess you're right. I'd never be able to keep a secret from you or win an argument. You'd always know, wouldn't you?"

She knew he wanted to tell her something more but didn't know exactly what to say. She didn't know whether to hope or fear that he might come after her once he'd rebuilt his ranch. Sighing deeply, she said, "'Tis for the best."

The rattle of trace chains and the crunch of wheels on dirt drew their attention toward the peddler's wagon. Old Mr. Tatum angled the wagon close to the board walk. "Howdy, Miss Sheen. You're lookin' mighty fit."

She gave Guthrie a quick glance, his eyes slightly narrowed, a frown tugging the corner of his lips. "Mr. Tatum, how long before you finish your business here?"

The old man seemed to squirm under her scrutiny. "Well, I'd planned to wet my whistle after doing a little tradin'."

"If you can see your way clear to leave before noon, I'd be beholding to you. I've been away, and it's time I get home."

Tatum stepped from the wagon. He hitched up his britches. "Oh, yes, ma'am. News travels like wildfire. I done heared all 'bout it. But, like I said—"

"Mr. Tatum, I believe you owe me a favor for talking out of turn about me."

She almost laughed at the way the little man squirmed. "Can you be ready 'round noon?"

"Aye, that I can, Mr. Tatum."

She offered him a small smile as he climbed back up on the wagon seat and slapped the leather reins across the mule's dusty back.

"Why, Sheen?"

An uncomfortable silence ensued. She would walk over hot coals for Guthrie Tanner. She loved him that much. She laid a palm on his chest. "It doesn't bear explaining, because you already know the answer."

He closed his eyes for a brief moment. Finally, he looked at her. "You're sure this is what you want?"

She sniffled. It took a while to find her voice. "Sometimes, we're not meant to have what we want."

He kissed her forehead, then drew back.

She nodded. Tears threatened to spill over as she watched him turn and walk away.

****

Just as the noon sun was sitting high in the cloudless sky, Mr. Tatum pulled the wagon alongside the boardwalk where Sheen stood. Her eyes began to smart again, and she wondered if anyone ever died of an overdose of sadness.

A little crowd gathered. Sheen hugged Sara Beth,

inviting the woman to come visit and knowing it would never happen. She thanked Mrs. Wheeler and the ladies society. She'd already said her private good-byes to Rachel and now that emotional farewell flashed through her mind.

Why can't you go home with us, Sheen?

I have my own home, and my animals are lonesome without me.

But I like you, and so does my daddy. He told me so. And then the child had brightened. *You could bring your animals to live with us. Do you have a puppy?*

Sheen had yearned to tell Rachel about the three-legged fox, the doe and fawn. But it was better this way. Fairy doctors were meant to live alone—weren't they? And then she remembered her own mother and father, and how they'd loved each other. Her father had embraced his wife's gifts, had never feared them.

Until Guthrie could come to terms with what she was and accept her unconditionally, there was no future with him.

Shaking herself back to reality, she climbed into the wagon, using the wheel as a step. She felt Guthrie's large calloused hands around her waist as he gave her a boost to the wooden seat. Desiring to lean into his scent, she let his embrace swallow her. She wouldn't cry. Not again. Not for him.

He stood there, a confused frown crimping his brow. "Take care of yourself, Sheen."

I guess I'll have to, won't I? She kept the thought to herself. "Aye. You do the same, Guthrie."

She refused to look back over her shoulder as the sentries opened the fort's massive gates, and Mr. Tatum drove the wagon through.

Chapter Thirty-Three

Four months passed, and the days on the prairie were measured in loneliness and quiet, vast empty spaces, in hills choked with jack pines rising in emerald contrast to the buffalo grass growing gold in the valleys; measured too in scudding clouds and the touch of autumn in the air, fresh as a first kiss, inebriating as wine.

At last the spool of time unwound. The final thread fluttered free on the morning of September third.

Sheen smoothed the fresh dough into four separate pans and set them in the oven to bake. It was hard to imagine life as it had been a few months ago.

A lowing from the barn served as a reminder that the cow needed milking. Sheen grabbed an apron from a wall hook. After tying a neat bow at her waist and gathering the woolen cape around her shoulders, she lifted the lid of a wooden keg and filled a tin cup with chicken scratch.

Stepping down the porch steps, she called, "A good morning to you, Agata and Penny, and to you, Mr. Cluck." Sheen spoke to the chickens, and the geese, to a doe and fawn, a three-legged fox, and to the crows lining the fence, while she scattered feed over the ground.

As she made her way to the barn, a moment of *déjá vu* washed over her.

Strong and disturbing.

Dismissing it as another one of her feelings, she trudged to the barn, grabbed the pitchfork, and filled the cattle crib with fresh hay. Then, having lifted the milking stool from a nail, Sheen settled next to the cow. "Well now, Colleen, 'tis a fine morning for milking." Sheen laughed as the heifer answered with a swish of its tail.

The hairs on her arms prickled. The words she'd spoken sounded familiar, as if she'd spoken them before.

Déjá vu.

This time the feeling was stronger, more powerful. She was reliving her first moment of sensing Guthrie, as it had happened months ago.

She stopped and listened and, through the open barn door, scanned the horizon.

Nothing.

Her second sight wasn't cooperating.

Expelling a frustrated sigh, she leaned her forehead against the Jersey's warm, tawny haunch and concentrated on the sound of milk pinging against the bottom of the empty bucket. She closed her eyes, her hands working with a memory of their own.

He's coming.

The image grew behind her eyelids. He was coming... He was here, but where?

Forgetting the milk pail and the cow, Sheen raced from the barn. Like a mirage the tobiano stallion galloped down the hill and into the yard, his rider sitting tall in the saddle.

Sweet mother. It was a remarkable sight.

Her breath caught in her throat.

Thunder rumbled across the hills. Or was it the beating of her heart? She couldn't be sure.

Long jagged arcs of lighting streaked across the sky, and rain began to spit. Water soaked her. Not exactly the romantic scene she'd pictured time and again in her mind.

Racing toward the porch, she waved Guthrie to the barn, knowing he'd take care of his horse before coming into the house.

She had time.

With trembling hands, she toweled her hair dry, giving it a quick combing with her fingers. She changed into her newest dress, a peach-colored frock that complimented her hair and complexion.

And then the door opened and there he stood with his saddlebags slung over one shoulder, rain from the sopping garments puddling at his feet.

But it wasn't the saddlebag that made her heart go still, or the way his wet shirt clung to his well-formed chest that made her breath refuse to leave her lungs. No, it was something else entirely. It was that hint of vulnerability that made her want to trace the long column of his neck and run her fingers through his thick blond hair. A nameless pull that made her want to fill the space between them, though he stood barely a hand's breath away. She wanted to breathe the same air he breathed. She wanted his warmth and his masculine scent wrapped around her and to feel the strength of his powerful arms.

Sheen searched for something to say. "You are drenched through and through. Let's get you out of those wet clothes before you catch your death." She groaned inwardly, chastising herself for acting like a nervous ninny.

He grinned. "Hello, Sheen." His fingers touched her cheek.

"Go change into dry clothes. I'll make a pot of coffee."

She bustled about the kitchen, slicing fresh-baked bread, slathering it with freshly churned butter, pouring scalding coffee into two cups. Anything to keep her hands busy and her emotions calm.

The bedroom door opened and there he stood.

He waited for her, restless, but with a good-natured, patient smile, blue eyes warming her despite the chilling rain outside.

She whispered, "Hold me."

A moment of confusion flickered across his face, but that didn't stop him. He gathered her smoothly into his arms and drew her against his gray woolen shirt. Her own arms wrapping instinctively around his waist. She laid her cheek against his heartbeat; felt his suddenly strained breath on her hair.

She pushed back to look into his face. "Why are you here?"

He didn't answer. He just looked very, very sad.

"Guthrie?"

His gaze stilled on her face. "After Abigail, I never thought I could love again. Never thought I'd want to love again. The hurt ran too deep."

He leaned nearer and lightly brushed her lips with his. "Watching you ride away in that peddler's wagon was like losing a part of myself. Knowing what we'd shared together, all we'd suffered through, and then the realization that I'd lost you... I need you, Sheen. In the worst way."

In all these months away from him, she couldn't imagine herself with anyone other than Guthrie. The wait had been difficult, but she had to know for sure that their souls were intertwined.

"Guthrie, I could never give myself to a man who isn't my husband."

He backed away, his tanned face burning with discomfiture. "You're a respectable woman. I would expect nothing less. If you're willing, we'll leave in the morning. It's a week's ride to Billings. I'm sure there's a preacher or a judge who'll marry us."

She wanted him. Wanted to be with him, as fully and completely as possible. Wanted to consummate their life, their friendship, their love together for as long as possible.

"Guthrie, in Ireland when there is no priest or minister to read the marriage banns, we have a custom called *handfasting*. It is the same as a real marriage as long as we speak our own vows and hold them holy."

"Whatever you desire, Sheen. I'm willing to walk through fire to make you happy."

She worried her bottom lip. "What about my being a fairy doctor?"

"When a man loves a woman as deeply as I love you, it doesn't matter who you are or what gifts you have. I told you once to embrace your gifts. Remember?"

"Aye. I do."

He gathered both of her hands in his. Dainty compared to his large calloused paws. "Would you like to ride to Otto's and Dyani's so that we can have proper witnesses?"

She shuddered as he feathered kisses down her

neck. "The All Mothers are here. They will be our witnesses."

He drew back, glancing around the room.

Sheen laughed as she pulled him to the window. Gossamer globes of blue-green floated at the window.

He scratched his head, looking confused. "How...I mean—"

"They know everything." Sheen's eyes grew serious. "But, Guthrie, you must promise to never swat at or kill a bumblebee or any other wee creature."

"I...umm...why?"

"Because the All Mothers take different shapes and forms. Some are tree frogs, others are owls or ravens. The bumblebee is my mother. Her name is Keelin."

She laughed again. "Stop staring at me, Guthrie."

"They won't watch while we're on our... honeymoon, will they?"

The sky closed over, turning from gray to black as thunder rumbled. Rain beat down on the cabin's tin roof.

"Nay, Guthrie. Such times are sacred, and with the storm outside, the All Mothers are assuring we'll have total privacy on our wedding night."

A seriousness spread over Guthrie's face. He held Sheen's hands next to his heart. "Then I, Guthrie Tanner, give heart and soul to you, Sheen O'Reilly. To hold you dear with a promise of faithfulness, to treasure and protect, through sickness and sorrow, through glad times and sad times. Until death parts us."

Sheen's eyes fell closed at the brush of his lips on hers. Yes. He felt the bond, too.

"I, Sheen O'Reilly, take thee, Guthrie Tanner, as my soul-partner, to hold you dear with a promise of love and devotion to you and to my new daughter, Rachel, through sickness and sorrow, through good times and sad times. Until death parts us."

Rachel! She had not thought of the child until now.

"Guthrie, where is Rachel? Why isn't she here with you?"

He hugged his new wife close, lifting her feet off the floor. "There was nothing to go back to. The house was completely destroyed in the fire. After we left the fort, I took Rachel to Otto and Dyani's. I figured after what my little girl had been through, she needed to know that all Indians aren't bad. I also knew Dyani had enough love in her to help heal Rachel. We spent two months together before I felt Rachel was comfortable enough for me to leave her.

"Otto gave me the loan of Bert. We rode to the ranch and started rounding up as many cows wearing my brand as we could find."

"Did you rebuild the house?"

His face was close to Sheen's, his face grim. "We drove the cattle to Billings. After giving Bert his share of the pay, I started to buy lumber. Somehow, rebuilding the house just wasn't important anymore. I went to a land broker and put the ranch up for sale. Got a fair price for it."

Sheen's lips moved, forming words, but no sounds came out. Had she made a mistake, speaking that vow? Why hadn't she opened her mind and listened? Was she so daft with love that she'd become addled?

The room glowed gold and pulsated. Sheen almost laughed out loud. The All Mothers were scolding her. To Guthrie it was a flash of lightning filling the room.

She had to ask the question. Had to know. "What

329

are your plans, Guthrie? Are you going back to South Carolina?"

"This will always be your home, Sheen. I'm hoping it will be mine and Rachel's, too."

She felt the nervous lump in her stomach dissolve and float away. It was time to meld their lives into— forever.

Taking his hand, she led him to the bedroom. "Guthrie, I've never been with a man. Will you teach me?"

He lowered his mouth to hers. "You have on too many clothes. I'll step out while you change."

"Nay, Guthrie. Stay."

She turned her back as she shed the dress, her petticoat, the chemise, and then bloomers. She heard the bedsprings squeak and knew Guthrie was waiting for her.

He opened the blankets and she slid in next to him and lay perfectly still. He rolled to his side. He pulled her face to his. Stopped, staring into her eyes, giving her the opportunity to push him away.

She whispered, "I want to know you."

He closed the distance between them, her softness warm and inviting. He explored her mouth with his tongue and let his hands roam, moving down to her breast. "I want to feel you, Sheen. Will you let me?"

She shuddered. "Aye."

He feathered kisses down her neck and brushed the tips of her breasts with his lips. Arching her back, she pressed herself against him, wanting more.

She was fumbling with his hard arousal, managing to make him gasp through their kisses. He brushed a lock of hair from her cheek.

He eased his big hand between her legs, stroking the delicate skin of her inner thighs, and she moaned with pleasure. His fingers explored her as she explored him, light touches sending ripples of pleasure through her.

Leaning over her, he did intimate things with his hand, much more thoroughly than her explorations. He watched her face the whole time, held her gaze even as he brushed his thumb against her inner core, its rhythm somehow matching the instinctive swivel of her hips. She felt something pressing at her, then felt him—his finger—slide inside her, and she gasped.

He paused, his eyes showing his concern.

She clutched his shoulders. "Don't stop."

The sensations were new and wonderful because he was giving them to her. She felt as if she were drowning in the most wonderful way.

When he moved his hand, she was lost and cried out. His kisses and soft murmurings assured her he was still there. She wrapped her arms around his waist to hold on to him, even so.

"I don't want to hurt you," his voice rasped with desire, his eyes full of sincerity and desperation.

"You can't hurt me," she insisted, trying to touch him with all of herself, her legs and her belly and her breasts and her arms. She took her hand and slowly slid it down the length of his swollen man root.

"You keep doing that and I won't last much longer."

Her eyes filled with uncertainty. "Am I doing it wrong?"

He groaned. "No. That's the problem. You're doing it just right."

Regaining strength to lever himself beside her again, his fingers played at her breasts, swirled around her belly button, then drifted between her legs to work more of their magic.

Then he kissed her. His chest to her breasts. Mouth hot against her ear. His knees nudged hers farther apart; she felt his hardness against her thigh. *Please. Soon—*

He slid into her.

Sweet mother.

Her eyes widened in awe at the sensation. Pushing, stretching. She moaned.

He stopped. "Are you all right?" His question tickled her hair away from her ear. She realized she'd squeezed her eyes shut, and she opened them. She loved opening her eyes to his concerned face. The look in his said their souls had married long ago.

She nodded, not trusting herself to speak. He held her gaze a moment longer, making sure she wasn't pretending to be okay. And then he kissed her...and began to move.

Inside her.

She held tighter, not exactly uncomfortable, but still very relieved when little waves of desire began to lap through her once again. She relaxed, let herself float on the sensations, moving her hips languidly with the rhythm he'd set. She liked this. She definitely liked this. She'd like it even more if they went faster.

They did.

She laughed, then feared she'd hurt Guthrie's feelings, but he grinned back, brighter than the sun, not trying to hide his own pleasure.

He kissed her again, longer, harder, and began to move even more desperately against her and in her.

When his thrusts got intense, she wrapped her legs around him, held on to him, and trusted. The sensation was of lapping waves crashing over her, drawing back, coming even closer only to pull back again. Teasing, taunting. It followed the same rhythm as his thrusts, a slightly different excitement from what he'd given with his hand.

Better.

This was all of him, every inch of him, skin and bone and muscle and heart and mind.

When the wave finally did break over her again, she let herself gasp and cry out, not afraid of drowning, because Guthrie wouldn't allow that to happen. He'd said so in his vow to her.

And then their bodies launched together in the swirling, explosive sensations they shared.

They lay together, almost still. But even as she caught her breath, even as her vision cleared and the rushing sound faded, she moved slowly against him. Remembering this.

He slid out of her too soon for her liking. She didn't mind so much, since he gathered her against him, and she curled into his embrace. They cuddled together, warm and wet and sated, drifting with the buzz of insects outside, the songs of toads, and cicadas.

Supporting himself on an elbow, he traced a finger between her breasts and up to roll the nipples between his thumb and forefinger. "The All Mothers?"

Even in the dark, she flushed. "Yes, but they're not watching us, just over us. They're happy, and so am I."

Sheen lifted her lips and kissed Guthrie, hard and with complete abandon, devouring the sweet taste of his mouth, her need urgent and unfettered.

Her boldness touched his heart, and her brazenness made his loins ache, again. He could feel his own heart beating, and hear it thudding in the silence as she looked at him, hopeful and with emerald eyes that shimmered with desire.

She had never looked so beautiful as she did at this moment. Long legs. Slim hips and round, smooth buttocks. Firm breasts. Her nakedness washed in moonlight, she looked vulnerable and utterly enticing.

Her scent filled his nostrils and he shuddered with desire. Sheen pressed her body full against him, breasts, belly, and thighs. There was no hesitation. Her tongue darted past his lips.

His senses came crashing down.

He wrapped Sheen in his arms, his mouth covering hers, his hunger insatiable and growing. At the touch of her fingertips against his back, a shiver rippled through his body. He slid between her legs and into the softness of her folds. A little cry slipped past her lips. She clutched him tighter.

Arching beneath him, she met his pace. The bedposts banged against the wall and the ropes beneath the mattress strained as he drove deep inside her, harder and harder, with an aching need blind and wild.

A guttural sound, a low moan of complete satisfaction, rumbled from his throat as he came to rest inside her. Damp with sweat, he kissed her lightly on the lips, and then he whispered, "Do you know how much I love you?"

Her cheeks radiant with a rosy flush, she said softly, "I think you just showed me."

He laughed a low, throaty laugh and kissed her cheek, his long legs still between hers, his upper body resting on her breasts.

He closed his eyes. With her body and her heart, Sheen had won his soul. She was not like Abigail—stiff and inhibited. He winced, the agony of his past still painful as a fresh wound.

Her slender hand skimmed down his back and came to rest on his shoulder. "Do you regret what we've done, Guthrie?"

He looked into her eyes. They were deep and dark green and filled with the afterglow of their lovemaking. They were innocent and naïve. She looked at him with love and hope.

"No, my sweet girl. I don't regret it." He searched her face, tired but glowing. He wrapped his arm around her, pulling her close. "You read my thoughts, didn't you?"

"I didn't mean to. It just happened. Are you angry?"

"Never. You deserve a better man than me."

She gulped back a sob.

"Nay, Guthrie. There is no better man than you, and I'll have none other."

She had tears in her yet, but they were quiet, and they were healing. They glimmered on her cheeks as she held his hand against her heart.

She drew closer and spoke against his lips. "When the weather clears, we should pay Otto and Dyani a visit. It's time to bring Rachel home so we can build our lives together."

Outside, blue-green illuminations flitted back and forth in a dizzy dance, and the cicadas and woodhouse toads serenaded the night.

A word about the author...

Loretta C. Rogers resides in Florida. Once an avid horsewoman, she is happiest when traveling with her husband on their motorcycle.

The Witching Moon is Loretta's fifth novel published by The Wild Rose Press, Inc.

She enjoys hearing from readers and invites all to visit her website:

www.lorettacrogersbooks.com

Thank you for purchasing
this publication of The Wild Rose Press, Inc.
For other wonderful stories of romance,
please visit our on-line bookstore at
www.thewildrosepress.com.

For questions or more information
contact us at
info@thewildrosepress.com.

The Wild Rose Press, Inc.
www.thewildrosepress.com

To visit with authors of
The Wild Rose Press, Inc.
join our yahoo loop at
http://groups.yahoo.com/group/thewildrosepress/